ESCAPE TO THE COUNTRY KITCHEN

HANNAH LANGDON

Storm
PUBLISHING

Ebook ISBN: 978-1-80508-357-3
Paperback ISBN: 978-1-80508-359-7

Cover design: Rose Cooper
Cover images: Shutterstock

Published by Storm Publishing.
For further information, visit:
www.stormpublishing.co

For Mum
who keeps looking forward and is an inspiration

ONE

Juliet raised her head an inch from the brocade sofa cushion and instantly regretted it. It was throbbing with pain and the room spun sickeningly. She dropped it again, feeling the raised pattern settle back into the grooves it had left on her cheek. Maybe she could just stay here for – oh, about a hundred years, until she felt better? But she could *feel* someone looking at her, and she opened her right eye a fraction to see who it could be. Her eye met two dark brown ones, staring at her keenly.

'Oh, it's you, Moriarty,' she croaked, lifting a feeble hand to pat his head. He was a small, hairy black dog of indeterminate breed. 'Morning. Ugh, I suppose I'd better get up...'

Hauling herself to a sitting position, she wiped away a little trickle of dribble from the side of her mouth and made sure to open both eyes. Then, under Moriarty's confused gaze, she picked up a discarded circular silver tray from a large, buttoned leather pouffe, rubbed it with a corner of the cushion to wipe away the drinks rings and contemplated her smeary reflection. Good grief. Last night she had aimed for a Louise Brooks/vintage Hollywood sort of look, with her severe dark bob and pale skin, but today she looked more like a vampire in need of some blood. She tugged fruitlessly at her hair, which was either sticking out at strange angles or stuck to her cushion-imprinted cheek, and peered at her blotchy skin. Lifting a tentative hand to her mouth, she huffed experimentally and recoiled at her own foul breath. No wonder poor Moriarty looked concerned. She groaned as the door opened. Who was it now?

'Morning, Juliet.'

'Oh, *God*, do you *have* to speak so loudly?'

It was her sisters, Martha and Frankie, both looking as appalling as she did, in their own way. Frankie probably pulled it off the best, as she usually rocked a sort of dishevelled chic anyway, with her short dyed blonde crop and uniform of torn jeans and band T-shirts. The shadows under her eyes were darker than usual, and her skin a sickly shade of greenish white, but her mischievous grin was undiminished. Martha was usually the freshest-looking of the three, with her innocent, rounded face and long chestnut hair with its fringe that she was permanently pushing away from her eyes, as she never got around to having it cut. Neither was dressed, but at least they had managed to crawl into pyjamas and not just pass out on the sofa fully clothed. Mind you, Juliet had done it in the most spectacular beaded and sequinned dress, hired for the occasion, which had helped to make her the undisputed belle of her Bright Young Things-themed party. Despite how she looked now, last night she had oozed chic.

'Morning, girls.' She winced as pain shot through her head. 'Do you feel as bloody awful as I do?'

'Worse,' declared Frankie, producing a strip of tablets from her breast pocket – where, Juliet suspected, there was always useful medication of some sort or another – and popping two out into Juliet's hand. 'What *was* in those cocktails? Happy birthday, by the way.'

'Thanks. And God knows. Dad was pouring them, so it could have been almost anything.'

Martha lowered herself gingerly into a fraying tapestried armchair.

'Happy birthday, Jools. Those cocktails were delicious but lethal. Oh, hello, Moriarty, come on up.'

He immediately sprang onto Martha's lap and snuggled down with a sigh of pleasure. Juliet managed to raise a small smile at the sight of him so content there with her sister.

'At least he's happy, but I suppose he didn't touch those poisonous cocktails.'

'Sensible creature,' said Frankie. 'I wonder how many more of these I can take in one go?' She inspected the strip of pills, then swallowed one. 'I feel like I've been put through a giant mangle.'

Juliet was just about to lie down again to rest her still-aching head, when a pile of faux fur blankets in the corner suddenly moved and a man appeared, stared wildly around at them all, and then dashed from the room.

'Who on earth was he?' asked Frankie.

'No idea.' Juliet shrugged.

'Well,' said Frankie, going to the window. 'Whoever he is, he's off down the drive.'

The heavy oak door opened again, but this time a most welcome sight appeared.

'Good morning, girls, and happy birthday, Juliet! You're all looking radiant, I must say.'

Their aunt entered, carrying an enormous tray laden with breakfast, and grinning at the sorry state of her nieces. She was a slight woman, in her sixties, with elegant silver bobbed hair and kind eyes.

'Morning, Aunt Sylvia.' Juliet got up to help her with the tray, swiftly scooping the debris of glasses, napkins, a single pink satin glove and a man's dress shirt collar off the pouffe so she could set it down.

'Ooh, Aunt Sylvia, you knew just what we needed: carbs,

carbs, fat and more carbs,' said Frankie, eyeing up the tray greedily.

Looks like the pills have kicked in, thought Juliet, although she had to admit that whatever they were, they were starting to perk her up too. Even Martha, who had probably been suffering more than any of them as she almost never drank, was looking more cheerful at the sight of the heaving plates of buttered toast, hash browns, beans and clouds of scrambled eggs. A cafetière steamed gently and just the smell of the hot, fresh brew settled Juliet's rolling tummy.

'Come on then, girls, tuck in before it gets cold.'

Sylvia unstacked plates and cups as the three sisters gathered round to partake of the feast. Juliet would never normally eat so much – especially all those greasy, delicious carbs – but this hangover, and the fact that today was her actual birthday, demanded it. For a moment or two, they ate in silence, then Frankie let out a happy groan.

'Aunt Sylvia, I don't know how you do it. These scrambled eggs are delicious. Mine always go grey and rubbery.'

'Thank you, dear. Is the food all right for you, Juliet?' asked Sylvia, concerned. 'You do look a bit green around the gills. You don't feel sick, do you?'

Bless Aunt Sylvia, always so kind and observant, quite the opposite of how Juliet's mother had been.

'I'm okay, thank you, and I'll be better once I've eaten this. Thanks for bringing it.'

'My pleasure. Now, tell me what happened at the party after I gave up far too early and went to bed,' said Sylvia. 'It looked as though you were all having a wonderful time, although I did have to extract our neighbours' sons from the rose bushes. Our lovely estate manager, Will, would have been furious if they'd squashed his Gertrude Jekylls.'

'Will is a bore,' said Frankie, pouring herself a second cup of coffee and looking at her now-empty tablet strip with disappointment.

'He's not! He's kind and very conscientious,' said Martha. 'And he does love those roses. The party was really fun, Aunt Sylvia – it was a shame you left so early.'

Juliet smiled, looking down at her dress and remembering how she and her sisters had gone completely over the top with their outfits so that they looked like film stars – she dark and severe, Frankie sexy and dissipated as Jean Harlow and Martha all soft waves and melting eyes like Olivia de Havilland. The invitation had stated 'fancy dress if you want', but most of the guests had turned up in jeans, like they would to any local party, making the three of them stand out even more.

'Well, you've certainly made a mess of the place. How are we going to get it all cleaned up? You haven't forgotten that Rousseau has called a family meeting, have you?'

'No, I haven't, and don't worry about the clear-up.' A smile spread across Juliet's face. 'I knew I wouldn't be in any fit state this morning to deal with it, so I've organised for Agnes and her crack team of cleaners to come and sort it out. They may have an average age of ninety-five, but they've got more energy than I had when I was four.' The doorbell rang. 'Oh, maybe that's them now.'

Sylvia went into the hall to answer it. She returned swiftly, not with a gaggle of lively nonagenarians clutching dusters, but a vast bouquet of flowers.

Martha jumped up to burrow around in the acres of tissue paper for a card.

'Ooh, birthday flowers! I wonder who they're from? Look, here it is.'

She handed the tiny envelope to Juliet, who was trying to stay cool but was excited to find out who had sent her such an extravagant present. She flipped open the flap and pulled out

the card, the message written centrally, the edges decorated
with an ornate but tasteful pressed pattern.

'Read it out,' said Martha.

Juliet's smile at her sister's unquenchable romanticism
quickly changed to a frown as she saw who had sent the gift.
Why couldn't he just leave her alone, today of all days? She
stuffed the card back into the envelope and tossed it onto the
tray full of dirty plates.

'They're from Toby.'

She glanced again at the bouquet. She should have realised.
Beautiful though it was, it was laden with creamy oriental lilies,
which she hated, finding them cloying and sickly. Her horrible,
controlling ex-boyfriend Toby had always thought they were
elegant and – she nearly gagged – *ladylike*, and that she *should*
like them, so he always forced them on her, another small step
to make her into a different – better – person. The smell was
drifting over to her now, and she felt her breakfast rising in her
throat.

'I'm sorry, Aunt Sylvia, can you take them away? Please.
Put them somewhere I can't see – or smell – them.'

She let her eyes slide away, rather than meet her aunt's
concerned gaze.

'Of course, darling. I'll find somewhere for them. Forget
they ever arrived.'

When she had left the room, the sisters sat in silence for a
moment. It was Frankie who spoke first.

'Bastard. I'm so *glad* you finally broke up with him.'

'So am I,' said Martha. 'Even though you both know how
much I love a happy ending. Although I really do think that *not*
being with him is the happiest thing.'

Juliet sat in silence, pressing down the surge of unwelcome
feelings as shame battled fear and sadness and rage.

Martha continued.

'Are you *sure* he won't worm his way back in? I worry –

shared friends, working at the same paper, attending the same parties... It can't be good for you.'

Juliet sighed. She just wanted this to stop now. She was suddenly desperate to get back to London, to be away from the sympathy, the kind looks, the expectations. To be somewhere she could be herself. Couldn't she? Well, anyway, somewhere she could be the sharp, witty, hard-shelled version of herself that worked perfectly well. *It did. Really it did*, she told herself firmly.

'All right, thanks, I'm fine. Perfectly fine. Hadn't we better think about getting ready for this meeting? You'll have to tip that dopey dog off your lap first, Martha. Look at him, he's set in for the day.'

Subject cunningly changed. All three sisters were always happy to be distracted by animal talk, particularly if it was about their precious dogs.

'I wish I was too. Look at him, he's so cosy.' Martha smiled down fondly at the scruffy dog.

Frankie sighed.

'I still miss Gulliver, though; he was such a... *presence*.'

Juliet certainly couldn't argue with that. Gulliver had been a Flemish Giant Rabbit, about the size of a spaniel, and had lolloped around the house charming and confusing visitors in equal measure. He had been docile and biddable, even house-trained, but had got on the wrong side of their father by taking a liking to the Tudor wooden panelling, which he had gnawed almost back to the brick in some places. But now Gulliver had gone to the great rabbit hutch in the sky, and Frankie often mused about what to replace him with. Recently, she had been threatening to investigate micropigs, which were at least, thought Juliet, unlikely to chew the fixtures and fittings. Her sister was just drawing breath to start discussing her next poten-tial pet, when the door opened again. Not Sylvia this time, but Rousseau, their father. How on earth was *he* so fresh and well-turned-out? He drank more than the rest of them put together last night, and was last seen at three o'clock in the morning charming the woman who ran the Post Office with promises of a portrait and fulminations over the angle of her cheekbones. He may be nudging seventy, but, Juliet had to admit, he had lost none of his magnetism. She supposed that charisma never aged and felt that familiar tug of inadequacy that she didn't have much natural charm – as Toby had never hesitated to drive home to her. Who she really was had been hidden so successfully behind the haircut and all-black wardrobe as well as satirical cartoons she drew for a living that even she wasn't sure any more who she really was, or even wanted to be. Oh well, it wasn't like fast-paced London life left much time for personal reflection. It was being here, back at her family home of Feywood, that made her more contemplative, and that meant it was time to leave.

Rousseau came over and kissed her.

'Happy birthday, darling. But why are you all still lolling around here in your pyjamas – and you still in your glad rags, Juliet? Fabulous dress, by the way, my dear. Anyway, I want you all in this family meeting in an hour, dressed, if possible.'

Grumbling, the sisters made feeble moves towards getting up, pushing aside dogs, plates and cushions. As Rousseau opened the door to leave, Frankie lurched forward, pushed him to one side and dashed out, her hand clamped to her mouth.

Juliet grinned after her, then turned to her father.

'Why do we have to have a meeting so urgently, Dad? It's my birthday, don't I get a free pass?'

'I'm afraid not.' Her usually cheerful father's mouth was set in a grim line. 'We all need to be there. I'll see you in an hour.'

TWO

Finishing off a piece of golden, crunchy hash brown, Juliet turned to Martha.

'Do you know what this meeting's about? It's not like Dad to be all serious and secretive. He's not ill or something, is he?'

It had only been a year since their mother had died, and Juliet, who had always had a difficult relationship with her when alive, had not yet fully found her peace. She found her father easier company, and the sudden idea that he might be unwell clutched at her heart.

'I don't think so,' said Martha in soothing tones. 'If anything, I think it's going to be about Feywood.'

'Feywood? Why?'

'Look around you, Juliet. We all love this house, but it's falling down around our ears. I wouldn't be surprised if Dad wants to sell it.'

'Sell it! He can't do that – this is our home.'

Her sweet sister looked down at the floor, the familiar blush rising in her cheeks that gave away even the smallest discomfort. Juliet took a breath, not wanting to upset her, but wishing she would say what was on her mind.

'What is it, Martha? Please tell me.'

'Well, it's just that... Do you actually still think of Feywood as your home? You've been living in London for so long, I kind of thought you'd forgotten about us all. I was so happy when you wanted to have your thirtieth here, I wondered...'

She paused and bit her lip. Juliet took up the sentence:

'You wondered if I was going to come back for good... now Mum's gone.'

Martha nodded, and her eyes shone with tears.

'I hoped...'

Juliet put an arm around her shoulder and pulled her in for a hug.

'Oh, Martha. I'm so sorry. I don't want to come back and live here, but I *do* still see it as my home. I... I'm doing all right in London. Plenty of people I meet there find me familiar because of Mum being such a famous artist, but they don't know me at all, and I'm happy with that. They know a version of me, a new version, and that feels...'

'Safe?' supplied her sister.

'Oh, stop being so wise,' said Juliet, grinning. 'Yes, safe, I suppose. I can get on with work and have a good time without constantly being reminded of who I used to be, who Mum wanted me to be, how disappointed in me she was.'

'She wasn't disappointed, not really,' said Martha, her face crumpling with concern. 'She loved you, Juliet, she did.'

'Only when I was little,' said Juliet. 'When she thought I was her mini me. When I grew up and started having my own opinions about things, then didn't show any artistic promise – or not the promise she wanted me to have anyway – she just... dropped me.'

'But you're a wonderful artist!' protested her sister. 'Your pictures are in the paper every day; you're probably the most successful of all of us.'

'At the moment, maybe,' said Juliet. 'But it's *commercial*

success, those cartoons, they don't have lasting artistic merit. You're already commissioned all the time for your portraits, and they're starting to find their way into galleries and auctions. And Frankie will have her breakthrough any moment. The two of you have the real talent. Mum knew that... I don't understand why that wasn't enough for her.'

'I think she was just trying to push you; she wanted you to fulfil your potential.'

'She hated my cartoons. Don't you remember when she came to that exhibition at sixth form college?'

Martha nodded miserably.

'She swept in, making sure everyone saw the great Lilith Carlisle deigning to attend, then she took one look at my display that I'd spent so many hours on and said, "Rather *derivative*, darling, but I suppose the family talent had to skip someone." Then she wandered over to someone else's display and spent fifteen minutes raving about his use of light.'

'Which wasn't even that good!' said Martha with uncharacteristic cattiness. 'If it's any consolation, he's working as an estate agent now, after art school threw him out.'

Juliet gave a small smile.

'Poor guy. At least I've always known I didn't have what it takes for fine art.'

'Well, I think you're amazing,' said Martha stubbornly. 'And Mum's gone now.' She swallowed hard, and Juliet reached out a hand to touch her cheek. 'She's gone,' she repeated. 'So... what's stopping you coming home?'

'Oh, Martha, being here, just sitting here talking to you... it's making me feel so—'

'Vulnerable?'

'I was going to say 'uncomfortable', but yeah, I suppose 'vulnerable' is fair, and I really *hate* that feeling. Five years ago, I had only just managed to move away from here, from Mum, from everyone who had known me my entire life and started to build something new, a different *me* in London and then I *stupidly* got involved with Toby.'

'You *weren't* stupid,' said Martha fiercely. 'He was an arch manipulator; we all fell for it.'

'Maybe, but I *feel* stupid,' said Juliet. 'And he kept dragging me back to Feywood because he was so starstruck by Mum and Dad, so everything got enmeshed, especially as Mum loved him so much and made it clear that I should count myself lucky he was interested in me. And, of course,' she added wryly, 'he never failed to tell me the same thing. If I ever complained about Mum to him, he would remind me how everyone said we were so alike, then shake his head sorrowfully and ask me to reflect on what he had to put up with, being with me. I fell for it for such a long time.'

'But you got away from him.' Martha suddenly looked worried. 'You *have*, haven't you?'

Juliet nodded.

'Yes, even if he does still contact me – sending those awful flowers this morning. I don't know why he doesn't leave me alone; he was always telling me how difficult I was to be with, how he was doing me a *favour* by staying with me and trying to fix the worst bits of me.'

Martha's eyes filled with tears.

'Juliet, it was all untrue, you *know* that, don't you? Vile man. It was all to try to keep you to himself, make you feel you weren't good enough for anyone else. And he kept you from us too.'

'I know, and I'm sorry.' She stood up and walked over to the window, staring out at the patchy gravel drive and willing herself not to cry. After a couple of deep breaths, she turned back to Martha. 'But now I'm free of *both* of them... I finally feel safe. I don't want to be that vulnerable child again, even if it means not letting people get so close to me.'

'But *I* want to be close to you, and Dad and Sylvia and even

Frankie,' said Martha, brushing away the tears that had now fallen.

'I know,' replied Juliet, biting her lip. 'But coming back here would be too much of a risk to everything I've built up. Sure, I could still work from here... but everyone here knows me, knows how humiliated I've been by Mum and Toby.'

'People are sympathetic – they don't pity you or laugh at you.'

Juliet came away from the window and sat down heavily on the sofa again, pushing her hands through her hair in anguish.

'You don't *know* that. I can't bear it. I don't want their sympathy. I just want to forget all that and get on with my life.'

'And you think you can do that without going back and untangling all that other stuff, realising that the shame is theirs, not yours?'

Juliet's lips tightened.

'I don't know. Maybe.'

'Oh, Juliet, you're so sensitive and caring. I can't *bear* to think of you hiding away behind some scary persona in London that just isn't you.'

Juliet took her sister's hand.

'Hey, it's not all bad. Look at the fun we had last night. I go out all the time in London.'

'With people you barely know. You can fool them, Jools, but you can't fool me. I *do* know you, whether you like it or not. I know you're clever, and witty, and fun, but I also know that you're sweet.'

Juliet scoffed, but Martha continued, 'Yes, you are. You've been badly hurt, but you mustn't scar over too much. Tough isn't you.'

'Maybe, maybe not, but it's working for me now. Please, Martha, just let it go. I'm doing okay, big sister.'

Martha shook her head.

'If you say so. Now come on, we've got to get to this meeting soon, and I'd rather not turn up in pyjamas, although you could pull it off in that gorgeous dress.'

Juliet stood up.

'I think I'd look better for a shower and change of clothes. See you just before half past?'

As they left the room, Juliet decided not to go upstairs immediately. Instead, she pulled on a light jacket and stepped out of the front door into the sweet May morning air. Turning left, she walked through an untended yew arch into what had once been the formal gardens, but now carried the same air of general dilapidation as, she had to admit, did the rest of the house. She stepped carefully in her black velvet shoes over the cracked paving stones that led through two small circular areas, enclosed with more overgrown hedges, until she arrived at a place she had loved since she was small. It was a hexagonal space, with yew on one side while the rest was walled. Espaliered apple trees roamed across all these walls and had just come into blossom. A small fountain should have bubbled in the middle, but now the pool lay damp and mossy. A stone bench stood at one end and Juliet sat down, closed her eyes and took a deep breath, glad of the peace after last night's party and before the meeting that was due to take place.

A moment later, inevitably, the phone she had pushed into her jacket pocket chimed. Almost reluctantly, but unable to resist attending to it, she flicked the screen into life, where she found nothing more exciting than an email from her local health food shop, offering fifteen per cent off nuts and seeds until Monday. She had no idea how she had come to be on their mailing list, but they were one of her most faithful correspondents. Maybe she should start visiting; a healthy lifestyle felt appealing given her sorry state that morning. Nevertheless, she hit 'delete' and then started flicking through her photos from the night before.

'Ha!' she said out loud, as she looked at the first one. 'You didn't see that coming.' She continued scrolling. 'Oh, I didn't realise Soph had come! Oh, Dad, those cocktails looked good, but they really were dangerous.'

She would have continued dissecting the photos if a movement by the archway entrance hadn't caught her eye.

'Hello!' she said. 'Is someone there?'

A man appeared in the doorway, a slight smile on his face.

She jumped slightly and lost her grip on her phone, which slipped out of her hand. She grabbed for it a couple of times, but it bounced further out of her grasp and slithered away down her skirt to the floor. As she leant forward to retrieve the damn thing, her head spun, and she clutched it and her treacherous phone at the same time.

Praying she wasn't going to be sick, she slowly straightened up and forced her eyes to focus on the man, whose eyebrows had shot upwards at her antics.

'Are you all right?' he said, in an accented voice, tinged with humour. 'I'm sorry, I did not mean to disturb you.'

The man was a complete stranger, but undeniably handsome in a rather lived-in way, with his shaggy hair and humorous face with its wide mouth and brown eyes. Juliet knew that she must look completely mad, sitting on a bench, alone, wearing last night's dress with dishevelled hair and a face most likely smeared with mascara, whilst babbling away to herself. She was, unusually for her, thrown, and this made her speak more sharply than she had meant to.

'Who are you? This is private property.'

The man came a few steps closer, his smile broadening, and Juliet started to panic, wondering if he was going to hurt her. God knows, since the time Toby had lost his temper and grabbed her, his hand raised as if he was going to hit her, she was wary of it ever happening again. The man seemed to sense her fear and stopped, holding up both his hands.

'I'm sorry,' he repeated. 'Please, let me explain. My name is Léo Brodeur.' He pronounced it *Lay-o*, in the French manner, which explained the accent. 'I am staying here, working with Sylvia to open a cookery school. I had come out on this lovely morning to collect some apple blossom for a recipe we are developing.'

Relief washed over Juliet.

'Oh, of course, yes, Aunt Sylvia did tell me. I'm Juliet.'

He beamed now.

'Ah, the sister who lives in London and draws such witty cartoons for the newspapers. *Enchanté*.'

Juliet gave a small smile, and he continued.

'Some birthday flowers arrived at the house for you this morning – is today the actual day?'

She stiffened. Did he know that she had asked Sylvia to throw them away? Was she going to have to explain that they were from her horrible ex-boyfriend, and even the thought of them made her feel sick? Her eyes darted around the garden as she tried to think what she should say next, without telling this stranger her private business. But then she looked back at Léo and saw no malice or nosiness. *Breathe*, she told herself. *It's an innocent comment, he's not trying to trip you up, and he'll think you're mad if you start rambling on about a bunch of flowers. Forget the flowers.* She forced a smile and spoke casually.

'Mmm, yes, it's my birthday today, but we thought Saturday was a better day for the party.'

He nodded.

'*Oui*, it was quite the party last night, was it not? I helped Sylvia with some of the food, but I do not think you remember seeing me.'

His eyes were amused, and Juliet tried to draw herself up, fighting a fresh wave of nausea that came with the movement.

'No, I don't. Sorry.'

He raised one eyebrow.

'No matter. I myself am sorry to see that you still suffer after the excesses of the party. I have an excellent drink I would be happy to make you; it will make you feel better.'

Was he laughing at her? Juliet could feel the irritation rise in her tired body. Who did he think he was, interrupting her peaceful reverie to make fun of her hangover?

'I'm perfectly fine, thank you,' she said stiffly. 'I just need to have a shower and get changed; I have a meeting to get to, so if you'll excuse me.'

She stood up too quickly, causing the blood to rush to her head, and felt herself swaying. Clutching at thin air, she thought she was going to fall over and complete her humiliation, when she felt a hand grasp her arm and another wrap firmly around her shoulder. The brown eyes were now so close to her that she could see the warmth in them, tinged with concern, but also unmistakably amused. Because of her.

'Are you all right, Juliet?' asked Léo. 'Maybe you should sit down again?'

She pulled away from him and tightened her jacket around her slender body. To her horror, she felt tears pricking at the backs of her eyes, a culmination of her hangover, her confusion at being back at Feywood and her humiliation in front of this handsome French chef.

'I'm fine,' she said shortly. 'Thanks.'

And she stomped off in as haughty a manner as she could summon up, given her weakened condition. Léo's voice floated after her across the garden:

'I hope to see you later, Juliet, and that you will be feeling better.'

She didn't turn, or answer. She hated being seen like this, unkempt and unwell, and his obvious amusement at her sorry state had compounded things. She very much hoped she would *not* see Léo later, or ever again, preferably.

THREE

Juliet rushed back to the house before she could bump into any more handsome strangers. It wasn't unusual to meet people you didn't know at Feywood: her father, Rousseau, never seemed to mind who stayed, or for how long, just as long as they were entertaining, intelligent company at mealtimes and didn't ask too much in between. But this particular visitor had got under her skin, with his amused eyes and solicitous attitude. Well... maybe it was that after Toby and his controlling ways she didn't need or want any man trying to take care of her. She would look after herself. She ran up the stairs to her room, turning her face from the enormous self-portrait of her mother that hung on the landing, overlooking the hall. When she had lived at Feywood, she had developed the habit of looking away from it, and the movement had become automatic.

Once in her room, she shut the door thankfully and stepped into the shower, letting the hot needles of water rain down on her head and body, driving away the remains of the hangover. She wondered again what the meeting her father had called could be about, and why he hadn't already just told them whatever it was. Any issues, even quite personal ones, were usually brought up at the supper table and vigorously dissected by whoever was there that evening, not guarded and saved for a formal family meeting. She cast her mind back to one particularly memorable time about three years ago, when she had been visiting Feywood. Everyone knew that Martha had a whopping crush on the man who was sitting for her, a particularly nasty specimen who ran some boring but successful business in Oxford, maintaining and hiring out dress clothes and robes to students and staff at the university. He had seen enough of the oil paintings in the different colleges that he fancied one of himself to put in his shop and make him feel like he belonged and had contacted Martha to commission her. For some reason, she had fallen for him, hard, while he behaved like Lord Bountiful because he had the money and she merely had a dazzling, God-given talent. Martha hadn't shared her feelings with her family and her sisters had been unusually tactful, although they had kept a close eye on the situation just in case they needed to step in and prevent anything more than the regular hurt brought by unrequited love. But their father had, one day, simply announced at supper:

'So, is there anything actually going on with you and that Ralph?'

Their mother who, Juliet remembered, had been feeling particularly unkind that day, had chimed in:

'He can't have failed to notice your cow eyes around him, darling. I think he would have reciprocated by now if he was going to. It's probably time to move on.'

As poor Martha had got redder and redder, her parents had continued, her father oblivious to his daughter's discomfort as he merrily recalled stories of friends who had been similarly spurned, doubtless thinking he was somehow being supportive, her mother enjoying watching Martha squirm. It had been Juliet who had stepped in and stopped the conversation.

'Mum, Dad, I don't think Martha wants to talk about it. Leave her alone.'

But she had not been in time to stop her sister's hot tears of humiliation, which sent her rushing from the table before pudding was eaten.

'Look what you've done now,' her mother had said, managing to deflect attention from her own contribution and make it look like Juliet's fault that Martha had fled.

As Juliet turned off the water and grabbed a towel, the familiar feelings of impotence in the face of her mother's brazenness, fury at her own weakness in feeling too afraid to defend herself and guilt at the relief that her mother was dead battled for precedence.

'Oh, shut up,' she said aloud, picking up her toothbrush and feeling glad that no one was there to hear her talking to herself again. 'Don't let her get to you.'

Used to pushing away uncomfortable feelings, she soon managed to change the subject in her head, instead thinking about the week in London that awaited her once she could get away from Feywood. Two industry parties, a dinner and a gallery opening, all of which would be full of familiar faces, hopefully none of them Toby's. He worked in the advertising department of the newspaper she drew cartoons for, so their paths crossed more often than she would have liked. Even without him there, none of the events was something to look forward to, in her opinion, but they would keep her busy and distracted when she wasn't working, and she could keep being the Juliet Carlisle that her London friends seemed to want. It had served her well enough up till now and would be particularly useful this week, to stop her thinking any more profoundly about what she *actually* wanted to do – and be – now she had turned thirty.

Pulling on her smart black trousers and a soft black cashmere jumper she had picked up for a few pounds in a charity shop, she surveyed herself in the mirror. Not even the people she knew in London would be able to guess how often she bought clothes second-hand, and she thanked her artist's eye for her ability to spot a quality bargain. The androgynous clothes, sharp haircut and lack of make-up that had become her signature look was easy to hide behind, but, not for the first time, the thought crept in that some comfortable joggers and a cosy fleece would be good to crawl into, especially on this hangover. But it would arouse comment, and Juliet couldn't bear that, even – or maybe especially – from her own family.

She left the room and closed the door softly behind her, walked along the threadbare deep green carpet towards the stairs and rested her hand lightly on the banister, its wood glowing with centuries of hands slipping along its polished smoothness.

'Are y'all ready for this?' came a voice behind her, and she turned to see Frankie grinning, looking almost as dishevelled as she had earlier, but at least dressed. In that instant, Martha also appeared, face scrubbed and her hair pulled back, wearing one of her denim smocks that left no clue as to her figure underneath.

'It can't be *that* bad, can it?'

Martha nudged Frankie and the three sisters began to go downstairs. Juliet said nothing. She had a lurking feeling in the pit of her stomach that it could be very bad indeed.

'Ah, there you all are, my dear girls, come in and sit down.'

Rousseau beamed at them and ushered them into his study. Sylvia was already there, perched on the edge of a chair that had been brought in from the dining room, looking worried. Will, the estate manager, was also present, standing awkwardly beside her father's revolving leather desk chair. Juliet took a seat in her favourite elderly bucket chair, which had collapsed springs and cocooned you gently in its worn velvet arms. It faced both the studio section of the room and the windows, so she could see straight down the sweeping lawns to the wood at the bottom that gave the house its name. Frankie and Martha took each end of the faded Chesterfield, both tucking their feet up underneath them. The study was a wonderful room which ran along half of the back of the large house and, despite its name, was actually part-office and part-library, with a full half of it used as Rousseau's studio. A renowned sculptor, it was here that he created his pieces which ended up in museums, galleries and private collections around the world. Juliet saw now that he was working on a female figure, rising fluidly from a block of marble and miraculously taking on soft curves from the hard material.

'Ah, Léo, there you are, good, now we can get started.'

Juliet reluctantly drew her eyes from the sculpture towards the door. What was *he* doing here? If it were possible, she thought, he looked even more pleased with himself than he had done earlier. He glanced over at her and gave her a smile and a small wave, but she slid her eyes away and over to her father, who was ready to speak.

'Right, I'm sorry to bring everyone together in this Agatha Christie-like gathering, but this is an important matter which involves us all. Luckily, there is no murderer to unmask.' He beamed round in what Juliet thought was an unusually unsure way, receiving some watery smiles in return. He continued hastily, 'Although you have all already met him, I would like to formally introduce you to Léo Brodeur, who has come to run the cookery school with Sylvia. I hope you will make him welcome, especially as he has rooms here in the house, in the new wing.'

There was a murmur of greeting and Léo nodded around vaguely at everybody. Juliet averted her eyes and thought, not for the first time, how very British it was to name that part of the house 'new' when it was a good two hundred years old. New at some point, she supposed, and the name had stuck. Rousseau went on:

'Well, it seems that, unfortunately, Feywood finds herself in some financial difficulty.'

Juliet heard Martha's sharp intake of breath and realised that her sister had been right. Were things really so bad? Her eyes travelled up to the flaking, yellowing paint above the window, which had been used to cover the effects of a water leak about ten years ago, then to the crumbling wooden window frames. Maybe they were.

'I am very thankful for Will here, who has been doing some clever number crunching. It has revealed that although the situation is not yet desperate, it may well be soon.'

Frankie interrupted.

'But Dad, how can there be money problems? I mean, Feywood isn't mortgaged, you're still working, Martha and I both give you rent, and the cookery school will help, once it gets going, surely?'

There was a silence as their father stared miserably at the edge of his desk. Juliet wished he would just get on and tell them what was happening, but knew he loathed this kind of conversation. He would much prefer everything always just to be... pleasant. Will spoke up.

'Rousseau, would it help if I explained?'

Their father nodded gratefully and relaxed fractionally into his chair.

'Right. Well, Frankie, you're correct that Feywood isn't mortgaged, but I'm afraid that your mother took out rather a large loan – to the tune of one hundred and fifty thousand pounds – when she was very unwell, partly for medical bills and partly for...'

He paused, uncomfortable. Juliet could feel the distress rising inside her. She knew she was about to say something she'd regret, but she couldn't stop herself.

'Partly to buy a load of expensive stuff to make herself feel better about dying, and to hell with us having to deal with the fallout once she had gone?'

There was a shocked silence, and Léo's hand flew to his chest.

'Don't look at me as if I'm some kind of monster, *you* didn't know her,' said Juliet, glaring darkly at him. 'Shopping was always her favourite medicine, even for a slight sniffle.'

He held his hands up in surrender.

'I beg your pardon, Juliet, I did not mean to offend you.'

She put her face in her hands and groaned.

'So, is that it then, the loan, or is there more?'

'More, I'm afraid, and it gets more serious. The roof, as you may already know, has been patched up repeatedly over the past thirty years, and it has now reached the stage where it desperately needs to be replaced. On a house of this size and age, with its listed status and the requirement for specialist materials, we are looking at costs of around one hundred thousand pounds. Many of the window frames also need to be replaced and most of the electrics haven't been updated since the 1930s.'

Juliet's older sister was the first to speak.

'How are you going to find that sort of money? Can we help?'

'Bless you, Martha.' Their father was ready to take the reins again, noticed Juliet, now that the really bad news had been delivered. 'Yes, you girls will all have to help, we will all need to. The cookery school is very close to opening, and that should bring in good revenue, especially now that Léo is on board. We have already arranged that with Sylvia, thank you.'

'Of course, Rousseau. I grew up here too; I couldn't bear to see it sold.'

She reached over to squeeze her brother's hand, and he continued.

'Martha, Frankie, you are already living here and paying rent and other costs. If you can make any other small contributions, it would help us chip away at the problem and show the bank that we are doing our best. Any help you can give with the cookery school guests would also be greatly appreciated.'

'Yes,' said Sylvia. 'The four rooms on the east side that overlook the gardens are nearly ready for guests; well... they're not quite five-star luxury, but they're clean and we've moved out all the clutter and put in some decent furniture from other rooms. We can sleep a maximum of eight, although we don't yet have any parties that big on the books. It would make a huge difference if you could help look after the housekeeping, rather than us having to pay Agnes or anyone else. They won't need more than some dusting, the bathrooms kept clean and sheets and towels changing.'

Both girls nodded sombrely, their faces creased with concern and tears welling in Martha's eyes.

'But what can *I* do?' asked Juliet. 'I don't want to lose Feywood, but I have no money. Nothing really.' She looked around at the strained faces, all now turned towards her. 'I don't see how I can help,' she added in a small voice, already knowing the answer. Nobody spoke. To her dismay, she felt a lump forming in her throat and tears in her eyes. 'I'll have to come back, won't I?' she whispered. 'Work from here and give you rent, help with the guests.'

She tensed every muscle in her body, pressed her tongue to the roof of her mouth and summoned up all her willpower to stop the hateful tears from falling. She never, never cried in front of anyone else, not anymore, and had no intention of starting now. It was Martha who spoke next, her voice gentle.

'That's not so bad, is it, Jools? You always say you have nothing left over at the end of the month with the rent you pay in London, and you could work from home. We're not so far from the city if you need to go back for meetings.'

'Yes, join us here in the sticks,' interrupted Frankie. 'We can all huddle over a single candle together at night – very Dickensian.'

Léo laughed and Juliet glared at him, then turned to her sister, half-furious, half-despairing.

'Oh, hilarious – I suppose this is funny for you, but it's my entire life you're talking about upending.'

Her voice cracked and she clamped her mouth shut. What more was there to say anyway?

Kind Will stepped in again, giving her a chance to compose herself.

'Juliet, we're so sorry that it has come to this. We do have a suggestion for returning to Feywood that might make things easier.'

Not trusting herself to speak, Juliet nodded. *Return to Feywood*, she thought, panic rising hotly through her body. She couldn't bear it. To be sequestered here again, to lose what she had made of herself, what she had become, for better or worse. Wouldn't it mean being a child again, losing her prized freedom? Maybe not, with her mother dead...

A voice cut into her thoughts, her Aunt Sylvia's kind voice.

'Juliet, dear, Rousseau has already discussed this with me, and I suggested that you might like to look at the space above the cookery school, the old haylofts from when it was a stable? There are roof windows so it's bright and it's warm and clean with running water, so with a few alterations you could use it to live and work in, if you liked.'

The softness and concern in her aunt's voice threatened to tip Juliet over the edge, and she couldn't, just couldn't, cry in front of all these people. She had no idea how she felt, and she certainly didn't want them to start filling in the blanks before she'd had a chance to *think*. She stood up abruptly, preferring to look rude over seeming vulnerable or, God forbid, pitiable.

'It's fine. I understand. I'll think about it.'

She turned and left the room, then fled up the stairs, taking them two at a time, to her childhood room, where she made straight for the bathroom – the only room where she was confident of a secure lock and relative privacy – and finally released the sobs of fear and helplessness and, yes, of relief.

* * *

After Juliet had left the room, it was Rousseau who broke the ensuing silence, his voice full of sadness.

'Poor Juliet, so miserable at the thought of coming back to Feywood, but I don't understand *why*.'

His face fleetingly looked like that of a child, crumpled in confusion.

'I think it's such a *lovely* place to live – you do too, don't you, girls? You seem happy here.'

Léo watched as Martha and Frankie exchanged glances. *Clearly more to know here than Rousseau realises*, he thought. It was Martha who spoke.

'Yes, Dad, of course we are, but it's... very different for Juliet.'

'Different? But why? Haven't you all always been welcome?'

'Yes, but... you know that she and Mum struggled to get on, and I think that moving to London was her way of—'

'Of having some sort of teenage rebellion, a bit late, I should say,' her father interrupted. 'Well, that's out of the way now, and with Lilith gone, I don't know what she's making such a fuss about.'

He clicked his tongue impatiently and cast a glance towards his sculpture. Léo realised that the man had had enough of the discussion and needed to work; he recognised the urge himself. He turned to cooking for all sorts of reasons, not all of them for professional progress: it could be soothing, to dissolve anger, to clear the mind and help him find fresh perspective. He sympa-thised with this great sculptor, who needed to work more than to deal with his petulant middle daughter, who was doubtless still working off that hangover which had made her look so ravaged this morning in the garden. He shook off the creeping memory of how attractive she had looked, regardless, and of how intrigued he was by her complicated reactions to her family home. Complex women had always been a weakness of his, however bad they were for him.

'Mr Carlisle...'

'Please, Rousseau.'

'*Merci*. Rousseau. I think all will work itself out. We will go now and let you work. Sylvia, I must show you some of my ideas for the vegan entrées we want to teach.'

Sylvia smiled gratefully at him.

'You head back, Léo, and I'll catch you up. You girls go and find your sister, she needs your support.'

The room emptied behind him as Léo strode out and through the house, exiting through the large kitchen to walk across to the old stable block which had been converted into Sylvia's – and now his – cooking school. As he crunched along the gravel path, he shook his head in anger at Juliet's reaction to the news.

Selfish woman. Doesn't she understand that until now she has been given far too much, and that what she is being offered is incredible? Who could resent returning to this wonderful house, being given living quarters, a studio, food? She's happy enough to use it as a party venue, but it's not good enough for her to live in? But what was it her sisters had said about Juliet's relationship with their mother? Not enough to understand, but enough to be an interesting puzzle. And the tears that had sprung to her eyes were intriguing. Maybe there was more to this Juliet than there seemed?

He reached the door of the school and stepped into its

familiar warmth, the centuries-old flagstones burnished and worn beneath his feet, the smell of garlic and fresh basil in the air from the salad he had been developing earlier that day. He had been up since dawn after struggling to sleep, as usual, his mind relentlessly turning over the events of the past six months, digging and worrying away to see if there was anything he could have done differently, anything that could have saved such fallout and protected him from blame and humiliation, that had eventually forced him to flee France for this secluded country house where there was not a *paparazzo* poking his camera through every window. As he removed a smooth ball of pastry from the fridge and began swiftly working to create a crust for his experimental filling – he had raided the kitchen garden and beyond for pansies, phlox and lilac flowers to complement the goat's cheese and rainbow radishes – his anger diminished, as he had known it would. She may well be selfish and spoiled, this Juliet, but she was very pretty indeed with her sharp hair and her sulky face and that mysterious body under the tailored, mannish clothes. Maybe having her living upstairs would not be such a terrible thing.

FOUR

Juliet splashed cool water on her face and surveyed herself in the tarnished mirror. Not too bad. She had always considered herself lucky not to be an ugly crier; it was when her pale skin really came into its own, instantly sucking any redness away and leaving her as porcelain-complexioned as ever. She was patting her face with a towel when she heard knocking at the bedroom door and her sisters' overly cheery voices. Was Frankie singing?

'Juli-eeeettt! Darling Juli-eeettt!'

'Come out, come out, wherever you are.'

They rattled the doorknob as they slowly pushed their way in; bless them, they knew to give her plenty of warning so she could compose herself or hide, whichever was most necessary. In the end, she did neither, instead coming out of the bathroom and sinking onto her bed. She felt wiped out. Frankie restlessly paced by the window as Martha sat down next to her.

'Poor Juliet, are you all right? Oh no, silly question, of course you're not all right. I'm sorry that all this is affecting you so much.'

'Did you know about it?'

'No, not before that meeting. Dad and Will have been whispering in corners a lot though, so, as I said, I did wonder if something might be up.'

'Which, of course, it was,' broke in Frankie. 'They'll have to finally put the village tenants' rent up. Dad's so soft-hearted he hasn't increased it for years. Come on, let's go down to the pub, we could all do with something to eat and the hair of the dog. Or are you dying to get back to London?'

Juliet had thought she was, but now that London was being snatched away from her, she wasn't so sure. That sense of belonging that she had worked so hard to establish had been pulled from under her feet, and the thought of the capital wasn't the welcome escape it had been an hour ago; it seemed more like shifting sands, and she wasn't sure she was ready to step onto them.

'I'll stay one more night – I don't feel up to it right now. I suppose a drink would do us good.'

'That's the spirit.'

Frankie grabbed one of her sisters' hands in each of hers and pulled them to standing.

'At least we can avoid Wet Will and Léo... although I must say that accent is sexy, even if it is clichéd.'

Martha poked her.

'You can hardly accuse him of having a clichéd accent, he can't help it, he is actually French. I think he's nice.'

'I suppose so, but what's he doing here, running a cookery school with Aunt Sylvia in the middle of nowhere? I thought he was a big shot chef.'

Juliet grabbed a black blazer from the back of a chair.

'Come on, we can Google him at the pub. Let's get away from Feywood, at least for a while.'

. . .

The sisters trooped downstairs and scuttled out of the big front door. Juliet was glad not to see anybody else; she didn't feel like being questioned again about what had happened, however gently or sympathetically. And then there was Léo, who had been shooting her daggers and obviously thought she was a precious princess living off Daddy's money. At least a trip to the village pub would stop her having to think about all that for a while.

As the three girls walked down the drive, some figures appeared, walking towards them. Juliet waved.

'Agnes! Thank you so much for coming on a Sunday. I'm afraid it's hellish up there.'

The tiny, aged lady, who was carrying what must have been her own bodyweight in buckets, mops, brushes and colourful spray bottles, just laughed.

'Don't you worry about that, Juliet – keeps us busy, doesn't it, girls?'

The 'girls', not one of them under seventy-five, nodded vigorously.

'Means fewer trips to the gym, keeps us fit.'

They waved their laden arms as they carried on up to the house to blitz the appalling mess left from the party.

'It wouldn't surprise me in the least if they did go to the gym,' said Frankie, tottering across the cattle grid that spanned the end of the drive, the gate wide open, as usual. 'They probably intimidate all the muscle men. I wouldn't want to take any of them on in a fight.'

When Juliet had stepped off the last section of the cattle grid, she paused to look back up at the house. There was no doubt that it was a beautiful building, built of grey stone in a 'L' shape with gabled roofs and a magnificent arched porch above the huge front door. But the spring sunlight was bright and unforgiving, and she couldn't deny that Feywood was looking tatty, especially when thrown into relief by the bubbling fecundity of nature all around: hawthorn bushes foaming with blossom, trees heavy under the weight of their burgeoning buds, the grass green and lush. The roof was indeed patchy and sagging, but it wasn't just that: the stone-mullioned windows had moss growing lavishly on them and ivy was making a determined assault on all the gutters. The sweeping gravel drive was thin and muddy, and all the brickwork needed smartening up.

Frankie wandered on ahead, talking into her mobile phone, but Martha paused next to her and looked at the house.

'The old lady's showing her age, isn't she?'

Juliet nodded and carried on walking along the lane, Martha maintaining an understanding silence by her side. Feywood really looked as if it was in trouble, and it saddened her. Apart from the difficulties with her mother, which had only escalated when Juliet had been a teenager, she had had a wonderfully happy upbringing in the beautiful old house and knew how lucky they all were to live there. With both her parents engrossed in their art, she and her sisters had roamed the estate freely when not at school, or working on their own art projects, and she knew every inch of it: the damp cellars where mice scuttled from your torch beam, the spot on the landing which creaked shrilly and alerted the household to your illicit nocturnal ramblings, the magical woods where, as children, they had seen fairies and elves, they were sure they had.

'I just can't believe that Mum left us in this mess – or maybe I can.'

Martha now linked her arm through Juliet's.

'Juliet, she did have cancer—'

'It's the fact she hid it all from us, though. And now I look like I'm fiddling while Rome burns, gallivanting around London while the rest of you put buckets under the leaks and pray for a miracle. If I'd *known*, of course I would have done something. It's just classic Mum, you always end up feeling so outmanoeuvred, so... impotent.'

Frankie had finished her phone call and turned around, grinning.

'Who's impotent? One of your city lads? Maybe you need a nice strapping country boy to show you a haystack or two.'

Juliet was not in the mood for Frankie's teasing.

'Ha ha. Come on, at least we're here now. Let's go and get a bloody big drink.'

She pushed open the door of the pub and entered its cool, dim interior. It was the pub they had frequented since being teenagers and the beams were soaked with plenty of Carlisle sisters' history and high jinks. They were always given a warm welcome, and today was no different as the proprietor, Renee, spotted them.

'Hello, girls, how fabulous to see all three of you in one go. And I think it's birthday greetings to you, Juliet?'

She nodded reluctantly.

'I'll never forget your eighteenth, I never did get the stain out of the wall – had to move that monk's bench in front of it in the end. Well, what can I get you? Surely not any more snakebite and black?'

'God no, never again. I think we'll just share a bottle of that New Zealand Sauvignon, please.'

'And some chips?' asked Frankie hopefully.

'You're in luck, the kitchen's open. Go and sit down, and I'll bring it over. Inside or out?'

'Oh, inside, please.' Juliet didn't want to see anybody she didn't have to, and people were always wandering past the perfectly situated pub.

The sisters made for their favourite table, tucked away in an alcove by the stairs. Renee brought over the bottle and glasses, and Juliet started sloshing out the wine.

'You see, that's the sort of thing I dread, people knowing everything about me, and never letting me forget. I'll be forced to relive that eighteenth birthday party at least once a week if I move back.'

'She was only being friendly, just teasing, she didn't mean any harm by it.'

'Martha, I know that, but I wish you could understand how I feel. It's so – cloying.'

'That's it, though, I don't understand. I find the familiarity comforting, not suffocating. I like feeling known.'

'But I don't feel known. It's like they know one version of me, one that was always overshadowed by Mum anyway, and coming back here... It would be like I was sentenced to being that person again as if all the work I've done since I've moved away will have been for nothing, just ignored, and I'll be the difficult middle sister who didn't inherit the family talent but tries her best, bless her.'

A silence followed this outburst, and Juliet took a long and welcome drink of wine. When she looked up, she saw her sisters' shocked expressions. It was Frankie who spoke first.

'Juliet, I had no idea that was how you felt. Apart from anything else, you're incredibly talented – just look at how you've broken into that ridiculously male-dominated world of satirical cartoons. You're a trailblazer.'

Juliet shrugged.

'I've done well, I know, I just can't get over the way Mum considered it a poor second to everybody else's fine art, or your installations. But it's not just that. I couldn't get anything right – my hair, my clothes, my friends, the music I liked. It was constant nit-picking and criticism.' She looked unbearably sad for a moment. 'I don't know why she hated me so much.'

'She *didn't* hate you!' burst out Martha, grabbing Juliet's hand. 'She just... I think she felt you were the most like her out of the three of us, and maybe that was hard for her... If anything, she loved you the *most* and wanted the best for you. She just went about it badly...'

She trailed off, and Frankie spoke.

'And with Mum gone, surely you're established enough now to come back on your own terms?'

Juliet fell silent again. This was the problem. She knew what her image was now; heaven knows it had taken her enough time and effort to establish. She came across as tough and sharp, up for an argument, strong-willed and independent, witty, feisty and wild. But, inside, she knew how fragile that image was. How, once she shut her front door at night, she shed it with relief and had started more and more to indulge in pastimes nobody would expect. She bought, then sketched and photographed flowers, one of her greatest pleasures, and had even sold some of her pictures to a country lifestyle magazine – under a pseudonym of course. It was the sort of twee publication that her London friends mocked and would have been horrified to learn of her attachment to. She had started dreaming up some ideas that she thought would make a good children's book, using her signature cartoon style, but in a far softer way than her sly, satirical newspaper drawings. She avoided the news, other than what she needed to know for work, and preferred watching gentle reality shows about sewing or baking to the gritty Scandinavian crime dramas she read synopses of so she could join in the conversations at parties. To be fair, she did still enjoy the occasional party and she liked meeting new people. She knew she was at a crossroads and had to decide, or uncover, or just *realise* who she was, and feared that coming home would force her back into a box that she was unhappy with, whether that was her eighteen-year-old self, desperate to push away from her mother, or the persona she had been projecting more and more convincingly over the past decade. Juliet noticed her two sisters looking at her with concern, and she raised her glass.

'Yeah, I know, I shouldn't still let it hold me back, it's silly. But can't we drop it?'

Martha didn't seem ready for that.

'I have to say, it might be good for you to leave London, at least for a while. You must see Toby all the time, and it can't be nice.'

In Martha's world, things should always be nice.

'No, it is not "nice", but I can handle it.'

'But he was so awful to you—'

'Yes, I know, and I don't want to drag it all out again. So can you drop it?'

Martha looked down at her lap and flushed. Juliet knew she had been overly harsh to her kind and sensitive sister, but they had already talked about Toby once today and that was quite enough. He had been abusive in his levels of coercive control, and although in managing to escape him she knew that she had shown great strength, she still felt the whole episode as an open wound, where any mention of it was like squeezing fresh lemon juice on to sore flesh. She knew, too, that what had happened, the way he had treated her, was not her fault, but that didn't stop her feeling intensely shameful about it. She didn't want pity, or kindness; in a way she would rather have been castigated for her stupidity, that might have been more of a relief. But even Frankie didn't do that, even she treated Juliet sympathetically whenever the subject arose, and it was sometimes more than she could bear. Her mother, naturally, had loved Toby and couldn't understand why, as she put it, Juliet 'didn't just stand up to him as an equal'. If only she had known how hard she had tried, but he had a way of twisting your words so that you were always in the wrong, insisting you had said something you hadn't. She knew the name, now, for what he had done, gaslighting, and she was shocked at how skilfully he had confused and manipulated her.

Juliet suddenly realised that her heart was racing, and that she was staring at the table, while her sisters looked at her in concern. She gave them a shaky smile and upended her empty glass.

Frankie picked up the wine and refilled their glasses, pretending to wring out the bottle once it was empty. This small, rather weak joke broke the ice that was rapidly forming at the table, and Martha and Juliet smiled. Juliet grabbed Martha's hand and squeezed it, and the smiles widened.

'Now, if we are going to talk about men,' said Frankie, 'then I think we need to bring Léo back to the table. I must say, I like his commanding Gallic air, I'd be inclined to honour and obey, if it wasn't for the way he was looking at *you*, Juliet. Scorchio!'

She picked up a stray coaster and fanned herself theatrically. Juliet raised an eyebrow.

'I don't know what you're talking about.'

But Martha grinned and snatched up the baton.

'Yes, I agree with Frankie. He was *definitely* smouldering in your direction. I think you've lit *un petit feu* under that one.'

'Oh, shut up, both of you. He was *glaring* at me, not smouldering. He obviously thinks I'm a spoilt princess, and since he found me in the garden this morning, talking to myself with my hair sticking out at all angles and breath like an ageing Labrador, he also, no doubt, finds me hugely *amusante*.'

'Well, if you move back, you'll be seeing a lot more of him. Maybe he'll grow on you?'

'Frankie, really, stop it. He is not going to grow on me – no man is. Men only ever want you to do what they want, to a greater or lesser degree, to change you and mould you.'

'Not all men are like Toby.'

'No, Martha, I know, but I think it's a rare man who doesn't think he could make just a *slightly* better job of you than you have of yourself. I'm sick of it. Wherever I go, here or somewhere in London, it's not going to be with a man in mind.'

She pushed away the image of the brown eyes and ready smile. Handsome he may be, and even sexy, but that was irrelevant. Attractive men were, in her experience, like cream cakes: tempting and fun in the moment, but something you only lived to regret, whether on your hips or in your heart.

'Yeah, yeah, I give you three months. Anyway, let's Google him, I want to know why he's here and not ripping up Paris like he should be.'

Frankie pulled her phone out of her pocket and started tapping away.

'Are you sure we should? It seems intrusive.'

'Martha, if we find anything, it's public knowledge, so it's not as if we're rifling through his pockets or reading his diary.' She paused as she scrolled down. 'Ooh, and if we did, we'd find it made *very* interesting reading.'

She flashed the phone towards her sisters, who barely had time to make out a blurry picture of Léo kissing a dark-haired woman, before she spun it round again.

'It's all in bloody French, of course; hang on, I'll read it out, and we can have a crack at it: *Le chef de renom, Léo Brodeur, pris dans un accrochage avec la star de télé-réalité mariée Veronique Mercier.*'

'Let me see that.' Juliet snatched the phone from Frankie. 'Well, the first bit must just be "famous chef", renowned maybe, I don't have a clue about the next bit, and then it says something about a reality TV star *mariée* – must be "married".'

Martha took the phone from her and inspected the picture.

'Maybe he is married to her, but this photo looks like it was taken in secret. Maybe she's married, but to someone else?'

'Yes! I bet that's it. He's been involved in some scandal and had to flee to England to escape it. I'm going to see if I can find anything else.'

Frankie took her phone back and tapped away for a few minutes, eventually throwing it down in disgust.

'Everything's in French and way beyond what any of us

remembers from school. I suppose he isn't famous enough here for it to have made the British press.'

'Well, I'm not disappointed,' said Juliet, picking up her coat. '"Love rat" seems to me to fit the bill perfectly; I don't need to know any more. I feel better after this, so I'm heading back to Feywood. Are either of you coming?'

They both declined, so Juliet set off alone, glad of the peace so she could process all the new information of the past few hours and start making some decisions about her future.

FIVE

Léo was removing his floral quiche from the oven when Sylvia came in.

'What have you been making, Léo? It smells – oh, and *looks* – marvellous.'

'*Merci*. And you have arrived in perfect time to try some. Please, sit down.'

'Wonderful, I'm famished. After that uncomfortable meeting, Juliet's birthday lunch has apparently been forgotten. Frankie said it was looking unlikely and then I saw the girls going off down the drive. Heading to the pub is my guess, and Rousseau will survive on black coffee until supper time.'

'Well then, let us enjoy a pleasant lunch *à deux*. This is something of a trial, after we discussed how we could ask our students to identify and use things that we grow here at Feywood. So, to make this, they will need to venture into the kitchen garden and then beyond. The goat's cheese is also local, made at a farm just three miles away in the hamlet of Netherford. The wine I'm going to pair it with is, alas, French. I am beginning to learn about English wines, though, and I aim to use them exclusively, eventually.'

'It's so pretty!' Sylvia cut a piece and tried it. 'Léo, that is delicious. I don't know how you do it. Your flavours... I would never have thought to put these together. Our students will love it – it's a feast for the eyes as well as for the stomach.'

'Wonderful! I will add it to our repertoire.'

They ate in a companionable silence for a few minutes, savouring the quiche and the perfectly matched wine.

'Léo, I'm sorry about that meeting earlier. This family... None of them is bad, but there is such a headstrong streak. Everyone always believes themselves to be right. And I'm afraid we can all be somewhat tunnel-visioned, focused on our own goals without stopping to balance that with others' needs. Juliet is a dear girl but had a difficult relationship with Lilith, my sister-in-law, and then a romantic relationship which... well, I won't share the details with you, but it was a painful time.'

Léo sipped his wine thoughtfully. Sylvia saw the good in everyone, that much he knew, and while he respected her opinion, he wasn't going to believe just yet that Juliet was nothing more than a sheep in wolf's clothing. He had met one too many women who would have you believe that and turned out to be the big bad wolf after all.

'I was... surprised, the way she spoke about her mother. She is very lucky to have grown up here – why doesn't she want to help?'

'It's more complicated than that. Although she won't talk about it, London has been an escape for Juliet, a chance for her to spread her wings. I'm not sure it has always been healthy, but even the bad parts have acted as some kind of purifying fire. I suspect that she is still not wholly at ease, that she is looking for something different. If she *does* come back to Feywood, I would like to ask her for her help promoting the cookery school – with your agreement, of course.'

Léo pushed away his empty plate, took up his glass and nodded. He would do anything for this lovely woman who had

– although he wasn't sure to what extent she realised – provided him with sanctuary and purpose at a critical time in his life, when he thought he would be chased out of France by the vitriol of the judgemental public, people he had never met who still felt it their place to hound and vilify him for what had happened with Veronique, without knowing the full story.

'Of course, Sylvia, I would be glad to work with your niece and get to know her. You are clearly very fond of her.'

'You know, I am. I love all three girls, but despite Frankie's youth and recklessness and Martha's dreamy gentleness, it is Juliet who I feel is the most innocent somehow, the most vulnerable. Despite her prickly exterior, I just want to give her a hug most of the time, although she hardly ever lets me.'

After lunch, Sylvia went to speak to her brother about some of the logistics for opening the school, and Léo tidied up the kitchen. He was pleased with how the quiche had worked out and knew it would be something their students would enjoy cooking as well as eating. His earliest days had been spent working in the kitchens of a bistro local to where he grew up in a small village near Reims, then he moved on to pot washing and watching the chefs at work at a larger brasserie in Paris. Finally, he had worked his way up to running the kitchen of a top Paris restaurant and been so nearly in reach of his first Michelin star. Throughout it all, Léo had loved to explore the ways ingredients came together perfectly in a dish as deceptively simple as a quiche.

Over and over again, he took the basics of pastry, eggs, milk and cheese and trialled different types, quantities and even temperatures of these, before adding fillings and flavours that would work both in taste and texture. Some were successful: the brie, mushroom and thyme, with minced dates sprinkled through, had been divine; the ill-fated attempt at 'freshness' with too many wet ingredients, including cucumber, less so, and he had still to perfect a vegan version. But the calmness and amount of time available to him at Feywood were perfect for working up new recipe ideas, and despite the mess he had left behind him in France, he felt himself soothed by the opportunity to immerse himself in his creations.

As the big sink filled with water and bubbles, he ruminated on what Sylvia had said. He had graciously agreed to her asking Juliet to work with them, although what a cartoonist had to offer, he did not know. But privately he was unhappy about the idea. If she did come back to her childhood home, she would be bound to make life uncomfortable, with her surly face and entitled ways. He already felt so ravaged by the press and the public – not to mention his own guilt – over Veronique, that he had been hoping for a quiet retreat, not a battle every day. God knew he didn't need another heartless woman in his life – however attractive. No, Léo preferred a homebody, someone who would not chew him up and spit him out – again. But as he dried the dishes, he remembered the word Sylvia had used to describe Juliet – *vulnerable*. Although his first thought was that this could not be further from the truth, he recalled the young woman's tired, wary eyes and tightly controlled emotions and wondered briefly – generously, he thought – if there could be something more going on behind that brittle exterior.

SIX

Juliet enjoyed the short walk home from the pub, hazy from the wine and bolstered by this new information about Léo. *Of course* he was a love rat. She might have guessed – all that twinkling and then the judgemental face in the meeting – that he was a hypocrite as well. The first to find her lacking when he was the one with the grubby secret. And what of her other predicament? Although she had been rallied by talking to her sisters, she was no less confused. What would a return to Feywood mean for her? Maybe she could find a way to stay in London while still sending money home, lodge with a friend maybe? But that didn't feel right either. It was as if she had been offered an opportunity for change, something she knew she wanted and needed, but the opportunity came with its own dangers and fears. She sighed deeply as she turned into the drive and picked her way back across the cattle grid. Perhaps more thinking time would help.

Avoiding the house, Juliet skirted around the back and walked across the lawn, pausing briefly to decide which route to take. For a moment, she looked towards the woods, always tempting in their cool, dark greenness, but they were not what she needed today. If she went into the wood, it would confuse her already fuddled senses and beckon her home with the promise of days spent lying on a pillow of moss, gazing into the tangled branches and letting her mind wander for hours, like a teenager. No. It was clarity she needed, and space, and the practicality of the kitchen garden was the place that would offer that. It was worryingly close to the cookery school, but she was prepared to take the risk of bumping into Léo and wouldn't hang around if she did. She walked determinedly over that way, and once through the wrought-iron gate, headed to her favourite spot, a bench in a cool corner next to a small greenhouse. The beds there were growing no-nonsense produce, spinach and radishes, and she found this grounding, rather than being swayed by the woods or the scented rose garden. She pulled out her phone and switched it off, without even looking at the pull-down menu with its array of notifications. *Silence. Peace.*

But fifteen minutes later, Juliet had achieved nothing and was beginning to feel frustrated. As she had sat there on the sun-warmed bench, with no distractions other than the odd blackbird pecking away, she had expected the clouds in her mind to part and some sort of revelation to make itself known, but her brain had, she felt, let her down. All it had done was ponder irrelevant and unhelpful things, such as why *did* the Prime Minister wear that tie last week, what *was* he thinking? And although this, in turn, gave her an idea for a sketch, it got her no closer to making a decision about her future. When she tried to force her mind towards returning to Feywood, she felt suffused with panic and indecision, and switched to comforting thoughts of work. Maybe a list of pros and cons? But even they were slippery and nebulous. There was no particular advantage to being in London for work, not with all the technology available these days. When she thought about her social life, all that came to mind was the sour taste of a hangover, coupled with the gripping fear of having done or said something excruciating after one too many Old Fashioneds. Conversely, the thought of Feywood, with its shabby beauty and cocooning peace made her think of her mother, and old resentments surged to the surface.

'This is hopeless,' she said aloud, standing up and about to march out of the garden, when her aunt walked through the gateway, dressed in loose clothing and carrying several garden implements. She waved when she saw Juliet.

'Hello, darling, I didn't expect to see you in here. How are you feeling?'

Juliet sat down again abruptly on the bench as Sylvia came over. On seeing her niece's demeanour, she let the tools fall to the ground with a clatter, sat down and put her arm around her. Initially, Juliet's body stiffened, as it always did at unexpected human touch, but then she softened and leant against her aunt.

'I'm sorry that meeting was such a shock to you. I'm not sure Rousseau handled it as well as he might have done, but he is terribly worried about Feywood and wanted everyone to understand the gravity of the situation. It ended up looking as if it was all on you, but it's really not like that. We all have to buck our ideas up, him included, and stop hoping that the leaking roof and crumbling bricks will magically disappear while we enjoy cocktails on the terrace.'

'I know, I do understand, and I want to do my bit. I love Feywood as much as everyone else, and I'm happy to help, but I just don't know what to do, where to go...'

She trailed off and stared miserably at the spinach. Sylvia squeezed her shoulders.

'There's a bigger decision here, isn't there, darling? You're on the brink of a change, a deep change, and you don't know whether to step along its path or stay on your own.'

How could her aunt be so wise, see through her like that? She nodded.

'I... I can't see what to do, Aunt Sylvia. I've always been so sure before, but now I feel paralysed. London has given me so much, but I know that it is depleting me, too, and I don't know how long I can keep going there the way I am. I do feel that I would like to take a new direction with my work, but I'm doing so well, and I'm frightened of throwing that away. And coming back here…'

She trailed off into silence.

'Oh, Juliet, the mistake you're making – if you don't mind my saying – is that you are taking all of this far too seriously.'

Juliet looked up sharply.

'Too seriously? But this *is* serious, this is my life – I can't just act on a whim.'

'Dearest Juliet, you are not going to do anything of the sort. I'm not telling you to throw anything away, it's more that – oh, you're so young!'

'I'm thirty. Thirty!'

'Yes, thirty, and that *is* very young. Don't make a decision that cuts off any choices; there's no need for that. Why don't you look at it as trying out a new path, nothing more? You can always retrace your steps if you need to. I know you are talking about serious things – your life, your career – but in a way the decision you make today is no more final than trying out a new hair colour.'

'Mum always said…' she whispered. 'Mum always said that I was flighty, that I couldn't stick to anything. And now you're telling me that doesn't matter?'

'I don't think you're remotely flighty, nor that you have ever been. Your mother was terrified of life, then terrified of death. She loved you deeply, Juliet, and wanted to see you safe and secure. She didn't understand that you needed to find your calling in a different way from your sisters, to whom their life path showed up naturally and easily. You're a more complex character, and I think she mishandled you. Don't shy away from opportunity because you think that otherwise you're fulfilling some declaration about yourself that your mother made.'

Juliet didn't reply. She felt shocked in both senses of the word – deeply surprised, but also energised by Sylvia's words. This wasn't how she had seen her mother at all, but she knew that Sylvia's judgement was sound, and she was worth listening to. She had always felt guilty for loving her more.

'Darling Juliet, come and look at the space above the cookery school, come and see if you could feel yourself living there. It wouldn't have to be forever. Think of it in a temporary way. Come on.'

The two women stood up and walked through the kitchen garden towards the school. It was housed in what had been the stables, and Sylvia had achieved a remarkably sensitive restoration and repurposing of the seventeenth-century building. From the outside, it had barely changed, other than the addition of some period-style windows. Inside, the original herringbone brick floors remained untouched, and the stone walls had merely been whitewashed, which gave freshness but retained the rustic charm. Two of the original five loosebox partitions remained in place: one sectioned off a storeroom-larder and the other housed a scrubbed wooden table, around which the students could sit to share the meals they had created. The rest of the space had a state-of-the-art kitchen with a large island. Pans and large bunches of drying herbs hung from ceiling racks and tack hooks. A door at the side led to the tack room, which had been converted into a loo and cloakroom for bags and coats. It was the first time that Juliet had seen it, and not only was she impressed, she was relieved that Léo was nowhere to be seen.

'Aunt Sylvia, it looks amazing. Better than I could ever have imagined. When do you get your first students?'

'We open for business in a couple of weeks, and we're fully booked until the autumn. I can't believe how many people want to come.'

'I can. Anyone would want to come and enjoy this wonderful place – and your tuition. You've been writing for magazines for years, so everyone knows who you are, and how brilliant your recipes are.'

'And don't forget Léo,' said Sylvia mildly. 'I'm delighted that he took up the partnership with me, and very grateful. It's helped enormously financially, and he is a big draw.'

'I suppose so.'

Sylvia smiled.

'Let me show you the space upstairs, see what you think.' She led the way to a wooden staircase in the corner that wound up to the floor above. 'It's very basic at the moment, but I have some simple ideas that would make it liveable.'

Juliet looked around as she reached the top of the staircase. Basic was an appropriate word, she thought, trying not to show her dismay as she studied the large, bare wooden area. True, large windows had been installed, and it was flooded with light, but that was all there was. Windows and planks. But there was something else, too, something that started to creep up on her as she watched the dust motes dancing in the sun. Up here, under the old beams untouched for over four hundred years, there was history, and peace. No sounds of cars, or sirens, no shouts, just the echo of long-gone hooves, the memory of the swish of hay being forked up, the ghost of an ancient mouse scuttling across the floorboards. No gigantic portrait of Lilith in sight. She turned slowly to her aunt.

'I love it.' The words were almost involuntary, then came spilling out. 'I love it, Aunt Sylvia, I do. I want to live here.'

Suddenly, she could see herself there, her sloping desk under the windows, a bed, an armchair. Maybe she could curtain off a corner to use as a darkroom, when she was experimenting with photography using film. Her painting bench would fit beautifully just there...

'I'm very glad, darling. We'd already factored in putting a small bathroom up here – you can see that the plumbing is there – and we've kept the other loosebox partitions, so we can section it all up very easily. No room for a proper kitchen, I'm afraid, just a sink, kettle and a tiny fridge, but there's downstairs, of course, when it's not in use, and anyway, it would be lovely to see you up at the house for meals with the rest of us.'

Juliet nodded.

'Yes, I'd like that. It sounds like a good balance.'

Balance was something her life had been missing for a long time, and now she wondered if it was this that she had been craving.

'I'll organise the bathroom and arrange a few other bits and pieces. Just tell me when I can do it so that there's minimal disruption to you and Léo. I really do want to do my bit to help save Feywood.'

'I know you do, darling. The cookery school opens in a fortnight, so if you can get it sorted out as quickly as possible, that would be best. I'm so happy you've decided to stay.'

'I will, I'll start making some calls straight away.'

Juliet felt suffused with an enthusiasm she hadn't felt since she was a child. This wasn't the nervous excitement she felt at the prospect of a big night out with lots of braying, competitive city boys, or the fear-fuelled adrenaline of presenting new work to a newspaper editor. This feeling made her tingle with antici-pation as her life seemed to unfold enticingly before her, a land-scape of possibilities. How odd, she reflected, that making her life smaller seemed to be having that effect.

Her aunt cleared her throat and broke through Juliet's thoughts.

'There is one more thing.'

'Of course, Aunt Sylvia.'

'I spoke to Léo earlier and told him that I would like to commission you to do some work for us. He agreed.'

'What sort of work? I can't boil an egg, you know that.'

Her aunt laughed, perhaps a little too readily, and hastily straightened her face to continue.

'Er, no, I definitely didn't mean help in the school. No, the fact is that I would like to carry on working on our website and literature. We're doing well for business so far, but it wouldn't hurt to be even more eye-catching. I'd – *we'd* – really love you to create some drawings that we can use.'

Juliet inwardly raised an eyebrow at Sylvia's self-correction and wondered just how on board with this scheme Léo was. She bet he didn't want her involved at all and was just going along with her aunt to please her. Well, that made two of them. She didn't want to do anything that would necessitate spending time with him, but she wasn't going to say no to Sylvia.

'Of course – what did you have in mind?'

'Perhaps some caricatures of us cooking, little sketches of the building and kitchen, that sort of thing? I did wonder if we might eventually produce some mugs and aprons and so on, what do you think?'

'It's a great idea. I'd be really happy to help. And forget about invoicing me, I'll do it for you for free, to thank you for your support.' She waved away her aunt's protestation. 'Really, I insist. It will be good for me to do something different – and another way for me to help Feywood.'

'Thank you, darling. It's very kind. If we get as far as merchandise, we'll talk again.'

Juliet nodded vaguely. She was already beginning to outline ideas in her head, rubbing out and correcting her first thoughts about Léo, which painted him in a less than flattering way. There was no denying he was handsome, but she hated that shaggy Gerard Depardieu look; it was so hackneyed, particularly in an actual Frenchman. Beautifully easy to caricature, though, even if she would have to tone down her trademark sharp edge for these drawings.

Sylvia went on, 'Well, I've lived with artists for long enough to see that you're in a creative reverie now. I'll be downstairs if you need me, darling.'

'Oh, sorry, I just had some lovely ideas for your website. I think I'd better start getting some sketches down before I lose them.' She pulled a small notebook out of her pocket. 'I'll start getting acquainted with the light in here, too, it's lovely.'

'All right, but don't forget about the bathroom.'

For the next hour or so, Juliet made some preliminary notes and drawings of her ideas. It was possible that none of them would ever be used, especially once she started observing the chefs at work, but it was as blissfully distracting as ever to work. When she snapped the book shut, she immediately started searching online for local bathroom installers and, twenty minutes later, had two meetings set up. Still reeling from her newfound motivation, she creaked down the wooden staircase to say goodbye to her aunt. But when she reached the kitchen, it was not the comforting sight of Sylvia that met her, but the distinctly less welcome one of Léo. He was sitting on a stool at the island, a pile of heavy cookbooks next to him, making notes in an old exercise book. He looked up as she appeared.

'Ah, hello, Juliet. Sylvia told me you would be down soon. So, you think you will move in?'

'Yes, that's right. I want to do everything I can to help save Feywood.'

She could hear the defensive tone of her voice. Why did she let this man rile her so?

'Ah, very noble. I'm sure you will be sorry to give up your glittering life in London, though.'

'Almost as much, perhaps, as *you* were to give up *your* glittering life – and *femme mariée* – in France?'

The look of shock on his face told her that the jibe had met its target.

'What do you know of this?'

Nothing, really, but it wouldn't hurt him to think the opposite.

'Oh, I know... enough.' *She'd better get on to translating some of those articles.* 'No wonder you came to hide at Feywood.'

'I am not *hiding*. The opportunity here with your aunt was too good not to grab. You, perhaps, feel it is more of a punishment to come back to this glorious place?'

How dare he think he had some monopoly on appreciating Feywood and *her* family. But she wasn't willing to get into some tricky argument, when he did, admittedly, have a point that she hadn't exactly been desperate to return and was undoubtedly hugely privileged to be able to call Feywood home, even if it was crumbling. Time to end this conversation, something she excelled at. She summoned up her iciest tones.

'Don't be so *arrogant* as to think you know me – or my family. Feywood has its secrets and its surprises. You've been here five minutes, but that takes a lifetime of living here to understand.'

With a final contemptuous scowl, she turned and left, wondering as she went if moving back home – and living so close to this conceited, judgemental has-been – was a monumental mistake.

SEVEN

With surprising speed, due to a combination of luck and Juliet's sheer force of character – she was used to dealing with London newspaper editors, so a benevolent builder was no match for her – work started quickly on the space above the cookery school: installing the small bathroom, running the electrics up from downstairs and using one of the leftover stable partitions to create a bedroom, and was completed within a month. She had spent that time in London packing her belongings and organising a drinks party in a local bar to say goodbye. When that evening arrived, her emotions bounced around like a squash ball. She had packed most of her clothes but kept out a stunning vintage black corseted pencil dress with a square neckline, and some vertiginous heels that were firmly in the category of 'car to bar' shoes as you couldn't walk much further than that in them. As she put it on, then did her make-up, she felt horrible butterflies in her stomach but couldn't decide if they were due to nerves about leaving London or excitement about the new path that lay before her.

The leaving party itself was fun. A lot of her friends turned up – well, she had to admit that most of them were more in the category of acquaintances – and she found that several gin cock-tails were perfect for banishing the butterflies. By ten o'clock, she was dancing in the precarious heels on a table as her party guests cheered her on, wondering why she had ever wanted to leave the metropolis and her wonderful friends. By one thirty, she was hanging out of the window of a taxi, praying she got back to the flat without being sick, and rueing the day she ever set foot in London. It was safe to say that Juliet was confused.

The next morning her hangover was brutal, and all she could find to try and alleviate it was a couple of Ibuprofen (how she wished Frankie was there with her mobile pharmacy) and the eminently unsuitable breakfast she had left herself when she was sober and healthy – a yoghurt, banana and a handful of nuts. Everything else had been packed and sent on ahead, so she had a glass of water and nearly cried at its deficiency in caffeine. She couldn't even shower to try to fix herself up a bit as she, very sensibly, hadn't wanted to pack a wet towel, so she struggled into her clothes and a large pair of sunglasses, pulled the door shut on her little rented flat and dragged her suitcase – fairly light, thank goodness, as it only contained last night's outfit and some toiletries and make-up – to Paddington Station. She just had time to grab a vegetable pasty and huge hot coffee before scuttling to the correct platform and climbing onto her train. She managed to get one of her favourite seats, a single one, and huddled down in it, scrolling through her phone as she chomped her ambrosial pasty and flooded her veins with caffeine.

The journey wasn't long, and she alighted feeling margin-ally more human but not – she noted, catching sight of her reflection in a window – looking it. Never mind, the taxi would get her home – home! – in twenty minutes and then she could disappear into that lovely little space in the stables until she regenerated into the sleek, impenetrable Juliet she preferred to be. She looked around for the taxi sign.

'Juliet?'

Oh no, had someone seen her? She really didn't want to make small talk with one of the locals. She cast around frantically for a taxi to leap into.

'Juliet?'

Wait a minute, didn't she recognise those accented tones? Juliet turned around reluctantly. Yup, there he was. For the second time, he was seeing her at her very worst and, she was sure, looking pleased about it.

'Oh. Hello. I'm just getting a taxi up to the house. I'm sure I'll see you up there later.'

'No need. Here, let me take your suitcase.'

'Oh... thank you, but I really can manage myself. And I'm perfectly happy in a taxi.'

'But I have the car here now. Sylvia told me which train you were on, and I came especially to give you a lift.'

Léo looked thoroughly confused, and Juliet realised that she couldn't really turn him down, much as she wanted to.

'All right, come on then. Thanks.'

He beamed.

'You're welcome. Now, let me take this...'

He swept the suitcase away from her before she could stop him, and strode over to the car, where he popped the boot and put it in, then opened the passenger door for her. Juliet shuddered. Did he really think he was going to win her over with all this gallantry? She really hated it – it made her feel out of control, and in control was where she firmly preferred to be. Wordlessly, she slid into the car and clicked her seatbelt as Léo shut her door and got into the driver's seat. As he started the ignition, he continued talking.

'I think we got off on the wrong foot. If we are to be in close proximity, and you are to help us with our website, we need to try to get along, no?'

'Yes, I suppose so. I doubt we'll see that much of each other, though; I'm going to be frantic with work.'

'As am I, so you are probably right.'

Good, she was glad they'd got that straight.

'Which is a shame.'

She glanced at him out of the side of her sunglasses. His eyes were on the road, and he had a small smile – *smirk* – on his face. Wordlessly, she turned to look out of the side window at the green scenery flashing past, and they remained in silence for the rest of the journey. When they arrived at Feywood, Léo was quicker than her and was already bearing her suitcase off towards the stable block before she could stop him. She felt fury rising inside her at his peremptory manner and walked at her own pace, rather than scurrying to catch up with him. She would *not* be railroaded by another man, fooled and confused into submission and gratitude by gentlemanly gestures. A full minute later, she strolled in and up the staircase, where she found him waiting on the tiny landing beside the newly installed and firmly locked door.

'Thank you for carrying my suitcase, but I can take it from here.'

He shrugged and squeezed past her on the small staircase. She caught a delicious scent of a light cologne mixed with some sort of herb and a faint waft of garlic, which she loved. Mingled in was a distinct smell of – well, just of *man*, and her stomach gave a little tug of pleasure in response to it. She stiffened her back and glared at him even more icily when he spoke.

'I do not understand why you dislike me so much, Juliet. I am sorry about it. I try to do nice things – to collect you from the station, to carry your bag – but it seems to make things only worse.'

Don't fall for it, Juliet, you're being manipulated.

His face looked open enough, and for a moment she felt bad that she had upset him, but then she remembered all the times she had taken the blame for Toby's sorrows, and where that had got her. The chink in her armour clanged shut.

'I'm... sorry you feel that way. Thank you for your help.'

She pulled a key from her pocket, opened the door and slipped into the room without looking back at him. Gazing around the light-filled space, Juliet felt a sense of relief and peace flood her. Although there were boxes to be unpacked, the furniture she had either bought or had sent from her studio was in place and the big bed had been assembled. The builders had sent photos of the bathroom, but this was the first time she had seen it for real, and she pushed open the door to admire the tiny space with its glass-walled shower, white sink and loo and neat little cabinets. Content, she returned to the main space to start unpacking and creating her new life.

By the evening, Juliet had not only straightened out the flat, making the bed with brand-new linen, positioning her drawing table just so by one of the sloping windows and arranging the sofa and TV so that another defined little space was created, but she had found an hour to sit quietly with a cup of tea and just gaze at the view. The windows looked out over the lawn and down to the wood that lay at the bottom, with the fields and towns beyond just discernible. It was mesmeric, and deeply relaxing, and she suddenly felt full of good resolutions: to work tirelessly and enthusiastically, to take walks through the dew at dawn and maybe – just maybe – to give Léo another chance.

At seven, she reluctantly pulled the door shut behind her and walked up to the main house, where she knew she was expected for supper. Feeling oddly shy, she slipped in through the boot room and pushed open the sitting room door.

'Juliet! You're here.'

Juliet smiled. Trust Martha not to have realised; she would have been lost in one of her detailed portraits, unaware of the time or any of the comings and goings of the household around her.

'Yes, I'm here, hello everyone.'

Supper was a large gathering at Feywood, and everyone currently living there was expected to turn up, although a kindly eye was turned towards forgetful artists who wandered in late or not at all. Today there was just Martha and Frankie, Rousseau, Sylvia, Will and, of course, Léo. Juliet nodded around at them all and went to join Frankie who was the only one not in conversation; instead, she was tapping away at her phone.

'Sorry, Juliet, won't be long. I'm exchanging *hair*-raising texts with my new man. I'll just finish this one and then I'll put it away – it'll do him good to wait for me.'

She pressed 'send' with a flourish and then stuffed the device down the side of the sofa.

'So, how are you settling in? Did Luscious Léo come and pick you up from the station? He was *very* keen to beat off all the competition – well, when I say "competition", Will offered, but probably just to be polite. Don't you think he's gorgeous? I'd have a crack at him myself if it wasn't for this hottie.'

She gestured vaguely towards the buried phone.

'Shh, he'll hear you,' hissed Juliet, then whispered, 'No, I do not think he's gorgeous, I think he's bloody pleased with himself, and a bossy-boots.'

Frankie flicked an eyebrow at her sister but replied in a lowered voice, 'Oh yes, I forgot you don't go in for any sort of chivalry after that nasty bastard, Toby. I can't blame you, I suppose, but he was really oily. Léo's masculine – he has just the right sort of arms for swooning into.'

'Don't be so ridiculous.' Juliet knew Frankie was winding her up but reacted anyway. 'I'm not looking for a man and certainly not some sort of archaic Romeo who thinks all women want is to be told what to do. If – *if* – I ever get involved with anyone else, it will be someone who sees and respects me first and foremost as a person, not a girlfriend or a wife.'

'Doesn't sound exactly brimming with passion, but whatever floats your boat. Oh look, it's time to go in.'

Sylvia had been popping in and out but was now ushering everyone through into the dining room, where the large table was laid with a haphazard selection of plates, glasses and cutlery. It was a wonder, thought Juliet, that with so much crockery, glassware and silverware, there was barely a piece that matched another. She was glad to sit between her father and Martha, but nearly let out an audible groan when Léo appeared directly opposite her and beamed warmly. She gave a small smile in response, one which didn't meet her eyes, then turned in relief to her father, who was banging his knife on his glass.

'A toast!'

No one had had time to pour any drinks, so there was a scramble to pass around the wine bottles before Rousseau finished speaking. Luckily, reflected Juliet, as she waited her turn, his speeches tended to be on the long side, so she probably wouldn't still have an empty glass by the time he finally got to the point. Indeed, it was a couple of minutes before he concluded:

'... very glad to have Juliet living back with us here at Feywood. To Juliet!'

'Juliet!' said everyone and gratefully started necking their drinks. Juliet's appreciative smile and muttered 'thank you' were as brief as etiquette allowed before she took a welcome slug of her wine.

The food was absolutely delicious, and it was a few minutes before anyone spoke again as they devoured the starter of delicate cured salmon with herbs from the kitchen garden and crumbly savoury shortbread biscuits. Frankie and Will jumped up to help clear the plates and bring in the main course of spring vegetables and nut filo pie, then Martha cleared her throat.

'Everyone, there is something I would like to discuss.'

Every eye swivelled to look at her. It was unusual for Martha to speak up, and she reddened as she continued.

'It's nearly a year now since Mum… since Mum died…' She paused and swallowed hard. 'I think we should arrange a memorial service for her. I mean, I'd like to.'

'But we already had a funeral,' said Juliet.

Out of the corner of her eye, she could see Léo looking at her, his eyes wide and his brow crumpled, doubtless with disapproval.

'Well, yes, but I do feel that I would like to do a proper memorial and invite more people. The funeral was so small, and we did say we would do something later.'

Rousseau rose and came to stand behind his eldest daughter, his hands on her shoulders.

'Martha is right. I, too, would like to honour Lilith with a special occasion in her memory, and maybe we could all create some special art as a tribute to her. Will you organise it, girls? I'll help you write a list of people to ask. Thank you, Martha.'

As he sat down, most of those assembled started talking quietly, congratulating Martha on her idea and discussing what could be done. Juliet had lost her appetite, even for the beautiful food her aunt had cooked. How could she create some art in memory of her mother, when that memory was so sour? Her mother had despised Juliet's art, and she had never hesitated to make that clear, as well as attacking many other choices she made. And now, here she was living back at Feywood because Lilith had put the house at risk. What tribute could Juliet possibly create? The funeral had been bad enough, as she had tried to tackle feelings so mixed that she didn't think they could ever be pulled apart and released, while the few mourners that had been at the small service expected her to show some sort of dramatic grief. The tears hadn't come then but were pricking now. She didn't want to upset the others or stop them honouring the woman they had all had such different relationships with, but she couldn't see what her contribution might be. Pushing her chair back, she whispered her apologies and slipped out of the room.

Grabbing a discarded shawl from the newel post at the bottom of the stairs, Juliet ran out through the sitting room to the terrace beyond and sat at the wooden table they used for meals in the warmer weather. The spring evening was growing chilly, and she tucked the shawl around herself tightly, only now noticing that it was shocking pink. She wondered who had left it in the house, as it wasn't something any of them would wear, but at the same time she was grateful for its soft warmth. Her mind was clearing from the fog of panic and anger that had risen, when she heard the French window open and close softly behind her and footsteps approach the table.

'Hi, I thought you might be sorry to miss your supper.'

Léo placed a tray on the table with her filo pie, two bowls with squares of chocolate brownie and raspberries, two full glasses of wine and, bless him, half a bottle more.

Juliet looked up, wondering if he was laughing at her again, but he smiled with what seemed liked genuine warmth.

'Oh, thank you. That's really nice of you,' she said.

'May I join you?' asked Léo.

She nodded and he pulled out a chair and sat down, taking one of the puddings and a glass of wine.

'You seemed very upset in there.'

'You probably think I'm horrible. I didn't get on with Mum, so I don't know what I could contribute to a memorial.'

'I don't think anything. I don't know you and didn't know

your mother. I do know that mothers can be difficult, very difficult. Your sisters and father, perhaps, feel differently?'

'Oh no, they feel exactly the same. They know damn well how difficult and selfish and narcissistic and controlling she was.' Juliet had a drink of her wine and warmed to her theme. 'They are *well* aware, but somehow, they don't seem as conflicted about it. Maybe Martha feels too guilty – my mother manipulated her nicely into that. Frankie probably got on with her better than the rest of us – their screaming arguments were probably the healthiest dynamic in our house growing up – and Dad... well, Dad always opted for the easy life, let her have her way and retreated into his art.'

Léo nodded.

'And you?'

'My mother despised me. Why she didn't just stop talking to me, I don't know – it would have been kinder. Instead, she did everything she could to criticise me, control me and try to force me to be who she wanted me to be.'

Juliet was furious to feel tears rolling down her cheeks. She was angry at Léo seeing them, angry at her mother for causing them, even from beyond the grave, and angry at herself for being so weak as to succumb to them. She rubbed them away with the pink shawl and glared at her brownie. Léo sat quietly, sipping his wine, and, for a moment, Juliet wondered what it would be like to spill it all out to this sympathetic man, to tell him some of the cruel things her mother had said, the ways she had found to shame her middle daughter. She felt a sudden dizziness as she thought she was going to open up to Léo, perhaps even lean her head against one of his sturdy shoulders and let him comfort her as she reopened the hundreds of little wounds her mother had inflicted, letting him heal them. But almost as soon as the urge had come to her, she pushed it away with a sharp inward breath. Léo looked at her earnestly, apparently unembarrassed by her tears.

'It sounds as if you had a tough time. I'm so sorry you went through that.'

Juliet dragged her eyes up to meet Léo's, wondering if she would find more mockery there, but all she saw was kindness. It was more than she could bear. Grabbing the bottle and her glass, she stood up.

'Thanks. I'm going to bed now. I'll start work on the website in the morning.'

And with that, she hurried back to the sanctuary of her little hayloft.

EIGHT

Léo reached for the discarded brownie and ate it thoughtfully as he watched Juliet march away across the lawn, that wildly incongruous pink shawl flapping around her otherwise impeccable silhouette. She was certainly beautiful, and chic, but he also felt drawn to her rage and sadness, emotions he realised she usually suppressed fiercely but which tonight had spilt over into what he suspected were rare tears. He had wanted to reach out to her, hold her, let her sob out all that pain and frustration, but she hadn't wanted to be supported or even seen with her guard down. He let out a small 'tsk' as he finished off the brownie and picked up his glass to go back inside. He knew he was attracted to complicated women, but now that he was settled at Feywood, he didn't want another drama and certainly not a second scandal that would see him have to leave this life behind him and move on again.

The next morning saw Léo in the kitchen early, pummelling bread and marinating hake in a delicious-smelling concoction of olive oil, lemon and four different fresh herbs, picked from the garden on his way in. He hadn't spent much longer last night with the family; once he had reassured them that Juliet was all right and had returned to the stable block, he went up to his room. Gladly distracted by work, as ever, he had played around with some recipe ideas for a book he was considering and after a couple of hours felt more clear-headed. However attracted he felt to her, he would approach Juliet as a friend only, which would surely be most beneficial to them both.

He was just laying a tea towel over his dough and placing it in the sun on the windowsill when Sylvia came in.

'Good morning, Léo, you've made an early start today.'

'*Bonjour*, yes, I wanted to try this bread. I think my final tweaks might just set it apart. We're nearly ready for the weekend.'

'I know. I do hope they like it all. Is that the hake? It smells wonderful. I'm going to work on the finishing touches to the passionfruit mousse this morning. Shall we go over to breakfast first, or have you eaten?'

'No, I haven't had anything yet – let's go. My dough should be ready by the time we return.'

They were just leaving when they heard a tread on the stairs, and Juliet appeared. *She looks different*, thought Léo, *softer somehow. There's power, perhaps, in crying in front of someone else, no matter how reluctantly...*

Sylvia went to hug her.

'Good morning, darling, how are you feeling today? I must say, you look very well rested. Are you coming over to breakfast?'

'Yes, I will. I slept so well, Aunt Sylvia, it's so quiet here. I'm sorry about the upset last night, I shouldn't have walked out like that. I'll sort it out with everyone this morning.'

If Sylvia was surprised at this apology, she didn't show it, just patted her niece warmly on the arm. Juliet continued, 'Morning, Léo. Thanks for looking out for me last night.'

He smiled broadly.

'You are most welcome, Juliet. Come, let us go and see what your father has prepared for breakfast.'

It was a long-running routine at Feywood that Rousseau prepared breakfast most mornings for everyone staying or living at the house. Sylvia had only stepped in on the day of Juliet's birthday because Rousseau had been so agitated about the family meeting. He was always up with the lark, no matter how late he had worked or caroused the night before, and enjoyed pottering around the large kitchen making steaming pots of coffee and tea and assembling treats that he thought people would like. And they did. Every day they came in to a sideboard heaving with food. The basics were always there – cereal, toast, fruit and yoghurt – but beyond that you never knew what you would find. Sometimes, Rousseau would be feeling continental and there would be croissants and pain au chocolat, sometimes it was pancakes, sometimes a savoury feast with eggs, tomatoes, golden hash browns and vegetarian sausages. Now and again, he would have been reading P.G. Wodehouse and you would be in for kedgeree, and on one memorable occasion, he came over all Japanese and produced a spread of hot, tightly packed triangles of sticky rice wrapped in seaweed, with octopus on the side. Today, as Juliet, Sylvia and Léo stepped in, they saw a vat of creamy porridge and a rainbow of pick-your-own toppings, ranging from dried fruit to granola to a tempting heap of tiny multicoloured chocolate sweets.

'I do wish Rousseau would teach a session at the cookery school,' sighed Léo as he filled a bowl with the porridge and added some of every topping. 'He is so creative, an artist in everything he does. I'm sure he would inspire our students.'

'Don't forget he will continue providing breakfasts on the days our guests are here,' said Sylvia, balancing a plate of toast on top of her bowl. 'Just sharing in his wonderful breakfasts will give them ideas, and knowing Rousseau, he'll pull out all the stops for them.'

'Like he doesn't already,' said Juliet, smiling slightly. 'No wonder there's no money for the roof; these breakfasts must cost a fortune. Not that I'm complaining,' she added hastily. 'I'm all for Smarties on porridge, although the octopus was going a bit far.'

Léo grinned to himself. Already she was showing a different side, more... mellow, and a sense of humour starting to show through. *Intriguing.* He pulled himself up quickly, remembering his resolution to be friendly, nothing more. As the three of them sat down, in came Martha and Frankie, who served themselves porridge and joined them at the table without more than a murmured 'good morning'. A few moments passed, and then Juliet cleared her throat.

'Look, I'm sorry about yesterday evening. I... I understand why you want to do a memorial for Mum.'

A voice came from behind her.

'And will you contribute an artwork, my darling?'

Rousseau had come into the room and now moved to serve himself some breakfast. Léo could see how uncomfortable Juliet was and he longed to reach out to her in some way. He could see her wrestling with what to say in reply and guessed that she didn't know whether to keep her head down and agree, as she had as a child and adolescent, or whether to speak her mind, as the adult she was now. She glanced over at him, and he smiled at her encouragingly, nodding.

'No, Dad, I don't think I will.'

Faces turned to Juliet in surprise, but she kept her gaze steadily on her father, who had paused, porridge spoon in hand. She continued, 'Look, since Mum died, I have battled with how I feel about her and about me. I'm not going to go into it all now, and I don't want to spoil the memorial for all of you. But I don't want to promise something I'm not sure I can deliver. Mum didn't appreciate what I do anyway, so it doesn't feel right to create a cartoon for her. What I will promise is that I will think about it, see if I can come up with something else that I am comfortable with.'

There was a silence as Rousseau continued serving his porridge. Léo tried to catch Juliet's eye to smile again. He felt proud of her for speaking so calmly and honestly, but she stared down miserably into her food and didn't look at him. Rousseau sat down and poured some coffee.

'Darling Juliet.'

Every eye at the table swivelled to look at him.

'My darling girl, I understand.'

Juliet looked up sharply.

'You do?'

'Yes. You've spoken truthfully, and I see how you have grown since you left Feywood. I did so worry that coming back was not the right thing for you, even though it was essential. But now I see that the changes that have been made do not only hold true in London, away from us. Well done, my dear.'

Léo could see Juliet's eyes brimming with tears and, remembering the distress that crying in front of him had brought her the previous evening, he knew that this was the moment to shift the attention away from her and give her a chance to compose herself.

'I wonder,' he said, addressing Rousseau, 'if you might allow me to collate some of your marvellous breakfast ideas for a section in the new recipe book I am planning? In fact, anyone here who has a special recipe or idea could share it with me. This cookbook is going to be a love letter to Feywood and to you all, for the welcome you have shown me.'

Immediately there was a hubbub as Martha and Frankie started chattering about favourite childhood dishes that could be included, and Rousseau agreed willingly to having his breakfast ideas documented. Léo saw Juliet take a moment to dab her eyes and breathe deeply before she turned to him and smiled again, a more natural, relaxed smile this time.

'Thank you, Léo. I think I might have a few ideas too.'

'But your aunt said you couldn't boil an egg?' He grinned at her.

'Oh no, she's right, I can't, but I can mix a wicked cocktail. Wouldn't your recipe book benefit from a few of those?'

'Now that really is a *bon idée*. Play to your strengths, I like it.'

Everybody laughed and the rest of breakfast was spent in relaxed chatter as they all made their suggestions for the book, received gratefully by Léo – but most of which, he thought privately, would never make it to the pages. Particularly Frankie's revolting-sounding suggestion of cold baked beans mixed with Marmite and cheese. Hardly *haute cuisine*.

A short while after breakfast, Sylvia, Léo and Juliet assembled in the cookery school kitchen.

'Juliet, darling, we do appreciate your offer to do the artwork for our website and other literature for free, but we really feel we should pay you.' Sylvia looked uncomfortable, and once again Léo was so pleased that he had gone into business with someone who had such integrity.

'I knew you'd say that,' said Juliet, with something of her previous sternness, which was already melting away, returning. 'I am perfectly happy to do it for free, but I understand that you find that hard to accept, so I would like to offer you a deal.'

Léo wondered if the softer-seeming Juliet had been nothing more than a fleeting image: maybe now they would see the tough city girl reappear. A 'deal' sounded ominous, and expensive. Juliet continued.

'I am exploring photography with various subjects, but one thing I have been short of is people. In return for my drawings, may I have access to you both preparing and cooking the food, and even to the food itself? I don't know how good my pictures will be, I think I have a lot to learn, but you would be welcome to use them if you wanted to. It's the experience I need, it would be invaluable to me.'

So, not a monetary request, but a generous offer, tied up in terms that he and Sylvia could happily accept. Léo reminded himself for at least the third time that morning that he was *not* going to let himself feel attracted to this beautiful, difficult, surprising girl, but *mon dieu*, she was making it hard for him. He shook himself and beamed at Sylvia, who was looking at him questioningly.

'I think that sounds like a very good exchange, *merci* Juliet for your offer. Don't you agree, Sylvia?'

'You're a clever girl, Juliet, thank you, we'd love to take you up on it.'

'Good. Like I said, don't expect Annie Leibovitz, but I might get good enough to make something of it, with practice.'

'Are you thinking of moving away from the cartoons, then, and into photography? I must say, my darling, I think it would be an easier path. I know you've fought to get where you are, but don't you want to, well… relax and enjoy life a bit?'

A look came across Juliet's face that took Léo straight back to when he had first met her. Her lips tightened into a mutinous line and her brow creased like a cross child's. He was annoyed to realise that, whereas previously he had found this expression off-putting, it was beginning to seem endearing. He wanted to poke or tickle her to snap her out of it, but that probably wouldn't go down so well.

When she spoke, her voice was edgy, the warmth and humour of before dissipated.

'I'm not making any decisions. I know you all think that my London life was some kind of bear pit, but I enjoyed it and I'm enjoying the success. It's hard work, yes, particularly for a woman, but I can do it.'

'Oh dear, I'm not suggesting for a moment that you can't.'

Sylvia looked worried. 'I'm really not trying to tell you what to do, darling, I just want the best for you.'

Juliet's face relaxed a fraction.

'I know, Aunt Sylvia, sorry. I just don't want to be pigeon-holed one way or another.'

Léo tactfully removed himself to the sink area and started making coffee, which he considered a good idea most of the time, even just before bed, but particularly when some busyness was needed. Since he had been living at Feywood, he had watched his English hosts go through the same routine with tea, over and over again, but he never found quite the same satisfaction in squishing a teabag against a mug as he did from brewing fresh, aromatic coffee. He had even tried making tea with loose leaves, in a pot, but found it more fiddly than the result warranted, and he didn't like stray tealeaves in his teeth. As he ground and poured and swished, he kept a surreptitious eye on Juliet and her aunt. Juliet must have regretted her harsh tone of voice because after a few more exchanges, which Léo could not hear over the bean grinder, he saw her reach out to Sylvia and then melt into the older woman's kind embrace. She looked so tense but yet so vulnerable; a complicated woman, he reflected again as he gave the pot a single stir, then pushed down the plunger.

'Is that coffee nearly ready, Léo?' asked Sylvia, giving him the cue he needed to turn around and join the women again. 'It smells wonderful.'

'Good! These are the beans I roasted myself – hopefully rather more rich and sweet than last time I tried.'

'You roast your own coffee beans?' asked Juliet. 'How do you do that? I didn't know you could do it yourself.'

'Oh yes, it's very easy. There are lots of ways to do it, but I just use the oven. It's taken me a few tries, but I think this is a good batch. I'll show you how to do it, if you like?'

There was a small silence. Juliet looked taken aback as if he had asked her out to dinner, not just offered to show her a simple kitchen procedure, but he reminded himself of how touchy – or maybe, he revised, a better word would be sensitive – Juliet could be.

'Er, yes, all right, thank you. It would make an excellent subject for photography.'

'*Bon*, then we shall include it in the schedule. Come, let's all sit down and decide where to start.'

NINE

Juliet quickly began work on the drawings for the cookery school website. Although there was no deadline, she felt enthused by the new project and wanted to earn the photography sessions that she felt in her gut were a doorway to a career expansion. For a week, she sat unobtrusively as Sylvia and Léo worked, sketching them as they chopped and stirred, assembled intricate pastries and burnt sauces that had to be started again from scratch. She also caught them laughing together, grimacing in frustration, picking herbs in the kitchen garden and sampling wines to match them to their dishes. It was only a few days before their first students came for the weekend, and the feeling in the kitchen was intense and purposeful, so she stayed in the background as much as possible. When she reviewed her work at the end of the week, she was thrilled with what she had achieved. Her acerbic political cartoons were more about lampooning people she had never met, exaggerating their flaws and idiosyncrasies and making sly, satirical digs. These cartoons, while humorous, were much gentler and more in tune with their subjects. She had drawn out the relationship between them, and amplified it, so that Léo looked particularly flamboyant and Sylvia steady and calming. Her favourite showed him weeping dramatically over a failed sauce, she serenely adding a touch more salt, whilst patting him on the shoulder.

On the weekend the students came, Juliet removed herself from the cookery school completely, knowing that both Léo and Sylvia were nervous, and assuming they wouldn't want her getting under their feet. She considered going back to London – she had the offer of a spare bed and an upcoming party – but although she toyed with the idea, she found herself more drawn towards the flowers budding in the rose garden and the shafts of sunlight playing across the mossy tree trunks in the wood. She had been in touch with some country lifestyle magazines who wanted further examples of her work, and this seemed the perfect opportunity to prepare something, when everybody else was occupied with the cookery school students and nobody would start quizzing her about what she was doing, and why, and how it defined her as a person.

'I don't know why you keep disappearing,' said Frankie, folding towels into messy lumps, which Martha patiently took and refolded, one after the other. 'We could do with some help in the house. I know they're only staying a couple of nights, and thank God they're making their own meals, but they manage to generate a lot of work. Helping with the guests was meant to be part of the deal.'

'I'm not really the welcoming B&B owner type. Look at the disaster when I tried to make the beds, Martha had to redo them all.'

Martha pulled a face.

'Yes, and you still haven't found time to let me show you how to do it properly. It's not difficult, Juliet.'

Juliet felt a pang of conscience. She may hate these domestic duties, but she knew that getting on with them – and getting better at them – was an important part of helping out.

'Sorry, M, we can do it later, yeah? And I'll be all right at cleaning up after they've gone. We should play to our strengths.'

But Frankie wasn't letting up.

'You're going to have to learn how to do everything, we all are. We're lucky to be living here, but look at the place. Every time you move a piece of furniture, there's black mould behind it, and the attic is going to be a swimming pool in the winter if we can't fix some of the leaks. You know how to use a washing machine, don't you? At least go and put these towels in – programme five.'

With a sigh, Juliet scooped up the pile of towels and took them through to the small utility room that was off the kitchen. She stuffed them in, added detergent and fabric softener and set programme five running, although she was briefly tempted to choose something different and inappropriate, so that the towels all came out stiff as cardboard, or the size of handkerchiefs, and her sisters gave up on asking her to help. But, checking the time so she knew when to come back and put the towels in the drier, she knew that she would put in more of an effort, however much she hated it. She wanted to help save Feywood, but housework, she reflected as she walked back to her little studio, was not her forte; she had better hurry up and make a success of herself one way or another so that she could double her contribution to the household finances and skip the domestic labour part.

She slipped quietly into the old stable block, nodding a greeting to the students, who were gathered round Léo and hanging on his every word regarding *crème fraîche*, whatever that was, and went up the stairs, feeling the usual sense of peace and relief when she shut the door behind her. After boiling the kettle, she spent twenty minutes in her new favourite pursuit – drinking a cup of tea while staring out of the window thinking of nothing in particular – before getting to work on honing some of the soft watercolours she was sending to the magazine that afternoon.

By Sunday afternoon, when the students were preparing to leave, Juliet couldn't fail to notice how tired Léo and Sylvia were looking, how tight their smiles had become. The normally pristine cookery school was now in need of a good scrub and tidy, which even Juliet felt she could tackle. Juliet smoothed down her black silk shirt and reasoned with herself that she would probably only break something, or not get it clean enough, making more work for the others in the long run, so she restricted herself to stacking the dishwasher. Then she ran down to the village and bought a couple of bottles of Prosecco and some nibbles, and was waiting with them apprehensively when Léo and Sylvia trudged back from waving their new protégées off up at the house.

'Juliet, what's all this?' Sylvia's tired face lit up.

'Look, I've seen how hard you've both worked this weekend. Your students looked like they were having the time of their lives, and I just wanted to say well done. Sit down and have a drink; I'll start work on some of the cleaning.' She shrugged, feeling awkward now at having made the gesture.

'That was very thoughtful of you, *merci*. I could murder a glass of Prosecco.'

Juliet busied herself ripping the foil off the first bottle and pouring the wine. Not wanting to add making a toast to her embarrassment, she waved her glass vaguely at the other two, muttered a well done and took a big gulp, then turned away and busied herself spraying down the work surfaces. As the Prosecco wound its way down her body, she started to relax. Maybe this hadn't been a terrible idea; they seemed pleased and surprised, both of which she had hoped for.

'I also wondered if we could put in a time for our first photography session, now that the students have gone?'

To Juliet's surprise, Léo roared with laughter and held up his glass in an exaggerated toast.

'Ah, an ulterior motive. Of course.'

Stung, Juliet put down her cloth and squared her shoulders.

'Not at all. I wanted to congratulate you on the weekend. But now that it's over, isn't it time to think about the next thing?'

'Can we not just enjoy the moment, even for a moment?'

Juliet glared at his laughing face – laughing at her, again.

'I know you think I'm some sort of workaholic, but it's not true. I'm perfectly capable of enjoying myself, but I also don't see why we shouldn't get the next thing in motion. Time just slips away, otherwise, and all you've done is drink champagne and chat, rather than *achieving* anything.'

'Sounds okay to me right now,' said Léo, topping up his glass. 'I do not think I can be accused of frittering away time, after the work I have put in to get this school up and running.'

'Juliet, Léo.' Sylvia's calm voice drifted across the table. 'You are more alike than you think, both with admirable work ethics and plenty of drive. Juliet, darling, I know that you will feel calmer if we put in a time to start the photographs. Léo, that can be done quickly and easily and then we can toast our success until dawn if you like. Well... you can at least. I'm exhausted, but you take my point.'

Juliet bristled at her aunt's swift dissection of the situation but couldn't deny the truth of it: she *would* feel less panicked knowing that there was a firm date in the diary for the photos to start; she didn't like nebulous arrangements that might never happen. But it was Léo who spoke first.

'Of course, Sylvia. We can do that. Tomorrow will be spent sorting out the school, and on Tuesday, I have business in Oxford. What about Wednesday?'

'I can't do Wednesday, I'm afraid, and the latter part of the week is busy too, but why don't you and Juliet make a start then? We can always arrange another time for my close-up, darling, and this would get the ball rolling.'

For a moment, Juliet wrestled with her opposing feelings: she wanted to get working on the photographs as soon as possible but didn't really want to spend time alone with Léo – she had been relying on having her aunt there. Her need to work won.

'All right,' she said, regretting the grudging tone of her own voice but unable, somehow, to lighten it. 'Wednesday it is. We can start after breakfast. Thanks.'

Léo grinned that infuriating grin again and lolled back in his chair.

'*Parfait*. I always knew my model looks would be put to good use. I look forward to working with you, Juliet.'

Juliet spent the next couple of days rigorously planning the photo shoot. She didn't want to give Léo any more reasons to be so enragingly smug, although she suspected that he would probably manage it anyway, without any help from her. It was the way he looked at her as if he saw straight through her that she hated the most. She'd had, she thought as she wrote out her list of suggested shots for the third time, quite enough of men who thought they had some sort of superior knowledge of her. Briefly, she let her thoughts wander to Toby, who not only had asserted that he knew her better than she knew herself, but that he also knew what was best for her. And she had believed him, at first. How *could* she have? she berated herself for the thousandth time. Why, *why* had she let him control and manipulate her to the point that her head spun with confusion? For a while, she had truly believed that he had her best interests at heart and that she was a poor judge of how she should run her own life. She had believed him when he told her what her failings were, then clung gratefully to any shred of a compliment he might have tossed her way, even if it was always qualified with a nasty dig to water it down. Her talent had been nothing more than inherited; her beauty not to everyone's taste and of the sort that needed a lot of help anyway; her sense of humour too caustic and spiteful, revealing her true nature, even if people did laugh and *pretend* to like her. She threw her pen down and dropped her face into her hands. Why did she still let him get to her? He was gone, and she was never going to fall into a trap like that again. She called to mind the words of a therapist she'd seen and of the books and articles she had read about coercive control, reminding herself of their insistence that it had not been her fault, but his. Slowly, she started to pull herself away from the memories, and the blame, and stuffed away that tiny kernel of contempt for herself that remained, and returned to her work, her blessed work.

On Wednesday morning, she felt nervous as she got dressed and gathered her equipment together. She had decided against going to breakfast up at the house that morning, buying in some pastries and fruit instead, which she ate curled up in front of some mindless morning TV, which gave her the space and comfort she needed to keep her anxiety under control. But now she could hear Léo moving around downstairs, and she berated herself for her nervousness, firmly reminding herself that this was just another professional job, nothing to get worried about. A final check in the mirror reassured that, if nothing else, she certainly looked the part. She had chosen to wear a pair of black, three-quarter length trousers, with a crease down the front so sharp you could cut yourself on it, and a boat-necked jumper she had pinched from Frankie a couple of years ago, also black. She slid her feet into some black ballet shoes, applied minimal make-up and brushed her dark hair until it was sleek and shiny. The rituals calmed her, and she was pleased with her appearance when she looked in the mirror: professional and businesslike.

She stepped out of her door and was downstairs on the dot of nine o'clock. The smell of fresh coffee wafted across the room, and she saw Léo sitting at the central island.

'Good morning.'

'Good morning, Juliet. I have made some coffee, again from my own beans. I hope you will have some?'

'Thank you. I've brought a list of shots I would like to try, so maybe we could go through it?'

'But of course.'

As they drank their coffee, Juliet took him over the list of photographs she wanted to try, some she thought would work on the website, if they were any good, and some that she needed practice with.

'These close-ups of your hands chopping and sprinkling herbs and so on will be highly effective, if I can get them right, and the formal portraits should be straightforward, as long as I can figure out the lighting. The sun this afternoon should be right for the kitchen garden shots, but they're the ones I'm most worried about, as they're a real departure for me. I do want to try some of you looking as if you're teaching, but if that feels too awkward, then I can ask Martha and Frankie to come down and pretend to be students.'

Léo nodded and drained his coffee cup.

'Juliet, you have thought all this out so carefully, but all you do is worry about what might go wrong. Come, we will have a good day and these photographs will be *magnifique*. And if they are not, we can try again, no matter. I am developing a sauce which will be delicious when it is ready – when I have 'cracked it', as you say – but I have made at least thirteen different attempts and still it does not taste right, or it curdles, or splits, or otherwise misbehaves itself.' He shrugged melodramatically, and Juliet wondered if that really was a French 'thing' or if he was playing a part. 'But it doesn't matter. I am a chef, and the sauce is a sauce. I will win in the end. And so it is with you. You are an artist and will conquer this new form, even if not immediately.'

Juliet didn't know what to say, feeling that any of her own words would be inadequate after this lyrical outpouring, but she appreciated his kindness, and even felt reassured. She still felt she had something to prove – to herself and to everyone – but maybe that didn't have to be accomplished instantly.

'Thanks. Right, let's get started. I'd like to make the most of the light coming in through that window, so if you could start over there?'

Obediently, Léo went over to the window and the shoot commenced. Barking orders and following her plan rigorously, Juliet was pleased with how things were progressing and felt that, regardless of the photos she produced, she had at least managed to organise everything in a professional manner. But studying him and working with him for several hours, she also couldn't help but notice how pleasant and accommodating Léo was, how he treated her like a pro, how his sense of fun shone through. Like it or not, the time spent staring at him also revealed what she had, up till now, tried to avoid – that he was, as Frankie had said, extremely attractive. His eyes were friendly and merry when they darted towards the lens, his smile warm and easy. He had great cheekbones and a well-shaped face in general, and with her artist's eye fully engaged, she couldn't keep pretending that he was unappealingly scruffy, as she had done up until now. She did a series of close-ups of him chopping onions and so deft was he with the scimitar-sharp knife that she had to ask him to slow down so that the photos were not a blur. His skill was admirable, but she was distracted by his hands: they were big and strong, but nimble, and showed the rigours of his job in their old and new scars left by burns and blades.

By lunchtime, they were both tired and went up to the house to eat.

'How's it going?' asked Martha, as they piled their plates with local cheese, homegrown salad, Sylvia's perfectly sweet and sharp pickle and some bread Léo had brought up with him.

'Really well,' answered Juliet. 'I won't be able to tell properly until I can look at the photos on my computer screen, or develop the ones I've taken with film, but it's been useful. I hope there's something for the website too.'

'Have you got much more to do?'

'Kitchen garden this afternoon, then some portraits, and that should be it for now. I'm going to do Sylvia next week, I think.'

'How about you, Léo?' asked Frankie, with her sly cat's grin. 'Is our Juliet cracking the whip?'

'She is wonderful. I have done several photoshoots in my career, and she is tremendously professional and organised. It puts me at ease. I just hope that I am a good subject?'

He looked at Juliet with a single raised eyebrow, and she felt an unwelcome dart of desire in her stomach. Pushing away the image of those capable, rough hands, she tried to distract her mind by thinking about shutter speeds.

'Yes, excellent. Have you finished eating? We've got lots to get through this afternoon.'

With a smile that was difficult to read, he nodded, and they left to continue their work.

TEN

The afternoon in the kitchen garden passed quickly. Léo could tell that Juliet was worried about these shots as she was less confident and, if it were possible, brisker than ever. But he admired the way she worked: the care she took but also the drive to create a beautiful, pleasing end product. It was deeply important to her, he could see that, and it reminded him of himself as he strived in the kitchen. He did not just want to make something edible, that filled you up, but something in which the flavours sang on your tongue, making you want to linger over it and laugh with joy at the pleasure it brought. The portraits, which he sat for back in the kitchen, were quicker and more easy-going, and Juliet relaxed, moving the lights and reflector around confidently and gaining her shots with ease.

'Right, I think that's it,' she finally said, squinting at the little screen on the back of her camera. 'Thanks, you've been really helpful. Sorry it's been such a long day. I'd better get out of your way now.'

She started gathering her things together, but Léo stopped her.

'Hey, you can't leave without trying what you've watched

me cook. All that chopping this morning wasn't wasted. Please, sit down, I'm in no hurry.'

He took the camera out of her hand and put it to the side. He was a little surprised that Juliet acceded so willingly, but she looked worn out and he suspected that the thought of letting someone else do the work for a while was too tempting, even for someone as determined as she seemed to be to accept no succour.

'Are you sure? I don't want to put you out; I've kept you all day.'

'Absolutely. I can call up to the house and tell them we're still working and will eat here, that way we will have peace and not have to share.'

She nodded.

'Okay, thank you. It does smell good – what is it?'

'Can't you guess?' He took a bottle of wine from the fridge and started removing the cork.

'Well, you chopped a lot of onions and made pastry... some sort of onion pie?'

'*Exactement!* Onion tart, with the thyme we picked in the garden, cream and Gruyère. And to go with it, this pinot gris from Alsace.'

'Did you just knock that all up while I was upstairs changing the batteries over?'

'Yes! The finished product is impressive, but so easy. Maybe one day I will show you how to do it?'

She gave him no answer other than a flicker of the eyebrows, and he decided not to push it. After all, however attractive he found this woman, hadn't he promised himself nothing but friendship, however much he wanted more?

'Here, try this wine.'

She sipped it, sniffed it, then sipped again. Then she wrinkled her nose.

'I'm sorry, but that's not for me at all. Too sweet.'

'Ah! I thought you might say that. But let's see what happens when you try it with the food.'

With a flourish, he pulled the tart from the oven and placed it in front of her. It was perfect. Crumbly, golden pastry, glistening onions which had caramelised and sunk gently into the creamy cheese filling. Léo watched Juliet's face and was thrilled to see how delighted she looked. For all that she presented herself as austere and spartan, he knew in that moment there beat a passionate, sensual heart beneath the stern exterior.

He cut into the tart and slid a generous piece onto a plate for her. She went to pick up her fork, but he stopped her.

'Allow me, indulge me, just one moment.'

She looked up at him, her hand hovering in mid-air.

'Why? Don't tell me I have to leave it to cool for half an hour?'

'*Non*, you can eat, but you must savour it, taste a little bit, sip some wine, allow the flavours to reveal themselves to you slowly. We have no rush. It is, maybe, just a simple onion tart, but it is complex and, I hope, delicious.'

Her eyes gleamed and he felt strongly drawn to her, wishing he could push aside the food and kiss her, then apply his slowly, slowly philosophy to peeling off her shirt, revealing that pearly skin...

'Léo?'

He jumped.

'Are you all right?'

'Ah, yes, yes, sorry, I was just thinking about...'

'Yes?'

'Salad! You mustn't forget the salad.'

'Right.'

He sensed he was losing his audience.

'*Bon*, time to eat, come on.'

They both took a fork, and he was pleased to see that she

paid attention to what he had said to her, taking her time over the first mouthful, then letting the wine complement it, in silence. He tried some himself and was happy with what he had made. It was soft and sweet but still tangy, and worked so beautifully with the delicate wine. Heaven. He looked at Juliet again, finding it hard to read her face. But then a glorious smile spread across it, one he wished he could see or, even better, bring about more often.

'Oh, Léo.'

Her voice cracked and she cleared her throat.

'Léo, that is unbelievably good. I was humouring you, really, with the bite thing but... wow. How on earth do you get so many flavours just from some pastry and a few onions?'

He didn't want to point out, while things were going so well, that there were a few more ingredients, and twenty-five years' experience behind the onions and pastry.

'I'm glad you like it. Very glad. And the wine?'

'Amazing. I've never really believed it could make *that* much of a difference. I mean, I'm usually happy to swig down whatever I'm given, but these flavours *work* together. Even an amateur like me can tell that.'

Léo gave an exaggerated shudder.

'*Mon dieu!* Philistine.'

To his relief, she laughed.

'I know, bad, isn't it? But you're going to spoil me; now I'm going to have to learn about more delicious food and wine pairings.'

She flicked him the briefest of glances from behind her lowered lashes, and he felt a jolt in his stomach. Was the ice queen *flirting* with him? He kept watching her, but it was as if he had imagined it, as she carried on eating and changed the subject to start talking about the photographs she had taken that day. Maybe he *had* imagined it? Maybe it was better to believe that he had. His good resolutions to avoid Juliet – and all women, particularly ones he wanted to rescue – were fast dissolving, and he knew that would do nobody any good at all.

ELEVEN

The next morning, despite being tired from the day before, Juliet woke early. When she glanced at the clock, she groaned and tried to snuggle down for another couple of hours' sleep, but after flinging herself from one side to the other, plumping and flipping her pillow and feeling as if her pyjamas were twisting themselves around her like a determined boa constrictor, she conceded that she was going to have to get up. Even then, she found herself pacing the floor of her small dwelling, dissatisfied with anything on TV and throwing her book across the room in frustration as she read the same paragraph four times and didn't take in what was happening even once. Work might help, she supposed, but when she flicked on the laptop, she was faced with row after neat row of photos of Léo, and she slammed it shut in irritation. Eventually, she settled for standing twitchily in front of the window with a coffee, staring at the unfolding morning and trying to push away images of the previous day, which flashed persistently into her head. She could see Léo vividly, one moment his face still with concentration, the next crinkling with laughter. She felt the touch of his hand burning into her arm as he reached out to stop her eating and exhort her to savour her food, not rush it. Her stomach flipped again, as violently as it had at the time, and she wished she had something stronger than coffee to try and suppress it. Although, she conceded, it was a bit early. Realising her cup was empty, and with nothing to occupy her, she decided to go up to the house. Breakfast preparations would be underway by now, and she could pretend she had had a fit of helpfulness. Anything to stop her standing there agitating for a moment longer.

'Morning, Dad.'

'Juliet! Good morning.' Her father came over and gave her a kiss. 'It's very early for you, are you feeling well? We missed you at supper last night.'

'Yes, Dad, I'm fine, just woke up early. I thought I'd come and help with breakfast.'

Rousseau bellowed with laughter.

'Did you indeed? There really must be an emergency. Ah well, I suppose you'll tell me in your own time. Or not.'

'I don't *have* to help. I thought it might be appreciated, but if you're only going to laugh at me—'

'Come on, come on, enough of the wounded martyr. I'd love your help. You can keep an eye on this porridge, if you like. It's only got a couple of minutes to go, and I don't want it sticking to the pan.'

Juliet poked at the bubbling mass with a wooden spoon, wondering how on earth she would stop it doing anything it wanted to do. It looked to her like it had a life of its own. Rousseau bustled around the kitchen, piling up trays with food and suddenly vanishing to take it through to the dining room. Eventually, the porridge was the only thing left, and he came over to inspect it.

'Looks good, Juliet, thank you, my dear.' He took the

wooden spoon from her and turned the mixture one more time. 'Now, grab that tureen, will you, and we'll pour it in.'

When the saucepan was scraped clean, he picked up the porridge, and Juliet followed him through to the dining room, where Frankie and Martha were waiting.

'Ah, here she is,' said Frankie. 'We missed you – *and Léo* – at supper last night.'

Juliet ignored her and sat down.

'Oh, come on, spit it out. What were you two up to? You can't have been working *all* that time.'

'Knock it off with the insinuations, will you, Frankie? We worked until late, then had something to eat. No story, no gossip, no excitement. Sorry.'

Frankie pouted.

'Oh, shame. I was hoping you were going to have something to tell us, even if it was only about the *femme mariée*—'

She stopped talking as the door opened and Léo came in with Sylvia. They looked puzzled at the guilty breakfasters and loaded silence.

'*Bonjour.* Everything all right?'

'Fine. My sisters were just asking how the photos went yesterday.'

Oh God, he probably thinks I've been talking about him. I knew I shouldn't have simpered all over him last night. Juliet could feel that telltale flush come to her cheeks.

'It was good. Very good. Your sister is a professional as well as an artist. Sylvia, I'm sure you will think the same when you do your session.'

That was kind of him.

Juliet didn't look at him but ate her breakfast as quickly as she could. Not quickly enough, alas, for Frankie, who had smelt blood and wasn't going to let her quarry go that easily.

'Juliet was just telling us how you had a cosy supper together after the photos. Wasn't she, Martha?'

Martha flushed. 'Well, no, not really—'

'Oh, shut up, Frankie.' Juliet shoved her chair back and dropped her spoon on the table. 'Stop trying to cause trouble. There's nothing to see, nothing to talk about, do you understand? *Nothing.*'

'Are you quite sure? Very defensive...'

Frankie was intolerable in one of these moods, like a cat with a mouse, playing with it just for spite. Well, Juliet wasn't going to stay in those velvet paws with their barely sheathed claws a second longer.

'This is ridiculous. I've got work to do. Sylvia, maybe we can catch up later to arrange our session.'

Without waiting for an answer, she snatched up her half-full bowl, having learnt her lesson from the growling stomach she had suffered the last time she had stormed out of a family meal, and retired to the kitchen. *Bloody Frankie*, she somehow always knew which nerve to touch, like a sadistic dentist.

Juliet hadn't cooled off much once she had finished eating and decided to try to walk off some of her fury before starting work. Leaving the house, she went to collect her bag and jacket, as the spring morning hadn't quite warmed up yet, then set off towards the woods. They started to work their soothing magic as soon as she stepped into their shady gloam. She had never felt frightened in these woods, rather reassured and somehow protected as if any enchantment they might hold was more nurturing than threatening. Once out of sight of Feywood's gardens, she paused and took some deep breaths, letting the earthy smell fill her lungs and expelling the toxic anger and worry she had let consume her. A woodpecker drummed somewhere overhead, and a blackbird appeared to look at her inquisitively before hopping away. Why had she let herself get so confused and overwhelmed? Léo had been nothing but kind and respectful yesterday, she had enjoyed the day and yes, she had felt attracted to him. It was only natural, he was gorgeous, she wouldn't pretend to herself any longer that she thought differently, although she'd die rather than admit it to her sisters. But what had shaken her, she knew, was not the attraction itself, but the repulsion and fear that squirmed alongside it. She had seen herself soften and melt as he guided her senses with the food and wine, and while that felt divinely sexy, and she longed to sink into it luxuriously, it simultaneously jolted her awake. Was this how it had been with Toby? She had locked away the memories of just how he had led her into such submission to him, but she remembered what it had become, how she had been disallowed, eventually, to choose things for herself, make her own decisions, have her own likes and dislikes, her own opinions. Everything was under subjugation to Toby, and if it wasn't, it was wrong. And she would suffer then, from cruel, cutting words reminding her that she was too stupid, too lacking, too rigid to think for herself. He would laugh at her, question her round and round in circles until she found herself agreeing with him, apologising. But how had it started? Maybe it had been like this, with honeyed words and her own glad capitulation. She stamped her foot on the soft moss, scaring a robin that had been inspecting her from a branch. Well, it couldn't happen again. Léo didn't *seem* anything like Toby, she had to admit that, but he had seduced a married woman, and wasn't that how these men operated? Clever and subtle, knowing how to manipulate you and exploit your insecurities. Juliet picked up her bag and began striding through the woods again, this time letting them fire her up rather than calm her. No, he would *not* worm his way in. This time she would be her own fierce advocate. She would have to be professional but no more, no more.

Passing through a final small glade that she knew well, as a favourite place the three sisters had come to as teenagers to drink disgustingly sweet alcohol and practise snogging on their local boyfriends, she soon left the wood and crossed the boundary of her family's land, emerging onto the road into the village. She made straight for the village shop where she bought some food that she could keep in her room, so that she didn't always have to go up to Feywood for meals if she didn't want to. Admittedly, the choices were scant, but she wasn't planning on doing it regularly; she just wanted the option to make her own choices once in a while. It had only been a short time, but she was starting to find the sense of obligation stifling. And besides, it was the perfect way to avoid Léo. Non-perishable items started stacking up in her basket: melba toast, jam, long-life milk, cereal, tinned tuna pasta salad that reminded her of aeroplane food and some biscuits and crisps. She almost avoided the latter, as she had no off-switch when it came to crisps and her tailored trousers were already tighter than they had been when she was living in London on a diet of coffee and gin, but she had a sense of rebellion – against what, she wasn't sure: her family, Feywood, her old life, herself? She shrugged and threw in another brightly coloured tube of delicious reconstituted, salted potato. She knew this stuff wasn't good for her, but *hell*, it felt good to be in control of it. No mother or Toby peering over her shoulder and asking her if she *really needed* it. She dropped in a bottle – wait, two bottles – of wine and headed for the counter. Oh God, it was the shop's owner on duty – a particularly odious man who had sneaked to her parents on more than one occasion over her purchases. He smoothed his few remaining strands of hair across his bald spot and peered at her over his glasses with his small, dark eyes.

Juliet glanced at him, still wearing the same beige, bobbly cardigan he had sported for the last twenty years, its pockets stuffed with half-used tissues, and sighed. 'Hello, Brian, lovely day.'

Brian peered into her basket.

'Hmmmmm. Having a party, are we?'

'Nope! All for little old me.'

'Won't be so little if you eat all *this* by yourself.'

'No, maybe you're right. It is an *awful* lot. Actually, quite hard to carry. Perhaps I'll put it back and get the big super-market to deliver instead.'

Juliet knew that one of Brian's biggest hatreds – and fears – was the competition from delivery services. She believed in shopping locally when she was at home but missed the blissful anonymity of some non-judgemental delivery driver turning up at the front door with her guilty pleasures. Even the one who had delivered nothing but a bottle of champagne, some pretzel sticks and a sixteen-pack of loo paper – the time she had preloaded her online trolley to save her delivery slot then forgotten about it – didn't bat an eyelid.

Brian glowered at her and snatched the basket towards him, scanning the items at speed and stuffing them into bags, before she could make good on her threat.

'Enjoying being back at home, are you?' he asked pointedly, as he slid the wine bottles into a bag.

'It's marvellous,' said Juliet, touching her card to the reader. 'I'm so glad I chose to return.'

'Nothing to do with Feywood crumbling around Rousseau's ears, then, and you being the last hope of providing some money to prop it up for another few years?'

'Not at all. Thank you!'

She trilled a goodbye as she swept from the shop, as confi-dently as she could pretend to, then marched down the road and turned into the nearest place she could sit down and gather her thoughts. That happened to be the graveyard, which suited her dark frame of mind perfectly. She sank onto a convenient bench and contemplated the stone in front of her, some poor unfortunate who had, at twenty-five years of age, 'drowned while bathing in the Boca Grande, Mexico' in 1860. She was unable to dwell on this, or anything else, as a deep voice drifted across the cemetery.

'Juliet! Marvellous to see you.'

She looked up, a smile at the corners of her weary mouth. She would recognise that dear, familiar voice anywhere.

'Father Benedict!'

The vicar came bounding towards her, and she stood up to be enveloped in his enormous, warm hug. The smell of frankincense, furniture polish and old books lingered, as ever, on his vestments, and she thought of how much she had paid in the past for a candle to evoke that very thing. It seemed ridiculous, now, to have burnt a forty-pound candle in her London flat, when all she had needed to do was to come home.

'How are you, my dear, dear girl?'

The tall, bearded vicar held her at arm's length and inspected her. She never minded his scrutiny, his advice, his occasional admonitions. Never had. It was funny how some people you just *trusted*.

'I'm all right, thanks.'

'Okay being back at home? Bit different living there without Lilith.'

'Yes, very. I'm enjoying it, getting plenty of work done.'

'Hmm, good. Well, I was going to come up to Feywood this week to seek you out, as it happens. And look! Put in my path, right here on church land. I wonder who could be responsible for that, eh?'

Juliet wasn't sure where she stood on the subject of God and his interventions in the world, but she loved the way Father Benedict always credited the Almighty for every 'God-incidence', as he called them. Today, she wasn't going to argue.

'I needed to get away, and this was the perfect sanctuary.'

'Of course it was. Now. What did I want to talk to you about, you might wonder?'

'I do.'

'Well, it is something of a favour. You are aware that Lammas is fast approaching?'

Juliet frowned as she delved into her memory for this particular reference.

'Lammas? Oh, isn't that something to do with bread? Isn't it also called Loaf Mass?'

'That's right. I knew you'd remember. You loved it when you were a little girl, trotting up to the altar with your plaited loaf.'

Juliet did remember. It had been her favourite of the church's festivals, beating even Christmas for her, which had always been fraught due to her mother's pernickety, critical attitude towards presents. It was almost impossible to get her something she liked, and she would never hide her disappointment that *you* thought *she* was the kind of person who would like... *that*. Even if you pushed the boat out and found something special, she would complain that she had no use for it, and that you shouldn't have wasted your money. If you got nothing at all, she went into a monumental sulk about not being loved, and if you got a pretty or amusing token gift, then she would be deeply offended at your lack of care. One year Juliet knew for a fact that she had hit the jackpot with a particular pair of earrings she knew Lilith had admired, were a reasonable price and she had to take a special trip to buy. True, her mother couldn't find anything to complain about, but she had never once worn the earrings, and after her death, Juliet had found them stuffed down the back of a drawer. She knew that the issue, whatever the hell it was, was to do with her mother and not with her, but the memory was still painful. Lammas, on the other hand, she remembered with joy.

'Yes! Every year Aunt Sylvia would patiently help me shape the dough, and every year we said we would practise for next time, but we always forgot. I used to love putting it in the church with all the other loaves – there were some amazing shapes. My little plait was very simple in comparison.'

'But nonetheless welcome.' Father Benedict smiled warmly at her. 'I do hope that, now you're back, you're going to bring a loaf to the church on the first Sunday in August? It's only a month away. Maybe try something a little more ambitious this time?'

'Oh, gosh, I don't know about that. I mean, I haven't made bread for years – probably not since the last time I did it with Sylvia.'

'Well then, this is your golden opportunity. Sylvia always brings something down, but I had very much hoped it might be you again. I'm sure Sylvia would be as willing as ever to guide you, but I know that she does have a lot on at the moment. She might be glad of a year off. I'm sure you could make a wonderful loaf, dear Juliet.'

Juliet couldn't help but smile at the vicar's gentle but very persistent manner. And he was right. Sylvia was so busy and had been looking tired and pale. Maybe it would be fun to join in with this aspect of community life again. It had always been 'her' thing and brought back no memories of her mother, who had been completely uninterested, much to Juliet's relief.

'All right, Father Benedict, I'll give it a try. But I can't guarantee it will be edible.'

'Process not product, my dear, process not product. I have a feeling it will be nourishing for you no matter how it tastes. There is more to our daily bread than flour, yeast and water, you know.'

The vicar patted her hand and stood to go. Juliet sat for a while longer, feeling calmer and even enthusiastic about making her Lammas loaf. The idea crept into her head that she could enlist Léo's help, but she huffed loudly at the thought. She didn't need him; she could do this on her own. It would be the best loaf in the village.

TWELVE

Léo put down his pen in satisfaction. Despite the ruckus at the breakfast table and the conflicting emotions he still felt over Juliet, he had managed to do a good morning's work. It had been partly administrative, processing the details of the next group of guests coming for a cookery weekend, and partly creative, pulling some ideas together for different breads he wanted to try. He was even contemplating starting up some bread master-classes – one-off days rather than whole weekends – but he wanted to talk to Sylvia about it before he started doing any solid planning. Working with Sylvia, let alone starting up this school together, had been a steep learning curve for him. They had met several years ago through a mutual friend, and he had instantly liked and admired her, so when he was looking to leave France, it had seemed like fate had come knocking when he learnt that she was embarking on this venture and hoping for a partner. Much of the initial planning had been done while he still lived in Paris, working out his contract at the restaurant, and in the early stages the bulk of it had concerned which ovens to install, which pans to buy, whether they would need two fridges or three, and these things were easily decided. But when they started creating recipes and actually cooking together, Léo had needed to check himself more than once. He was used to being completely in charge of a frantically busy kitchen, issuing orders and having them obeyed immediately and without question. Now he found himself making suggestions rather than giving commands, and sometimes being corrected or challenged by Sylvia. She did it with the utmost grace and respect, and he had hidden his occasional annoyance – he hoped – but sometimes he missed the simplicity of having complete autonomy, if not the daily problems that he had also faced. Sharing issues that came up had been one of the best things about working with a partner, even if he had had to be persuaded into it, at first. One day, early on, he was wrangling with a supplier and Sylvia had found him, head in hands, groaning.

'Léo, what on earth's the matter?'

'Please, do not worry, I can sort it out.'

'I know you can,' she had replied patiently. 'But we are partners in the difficulties as much as in anything else.'

Yes, working with Sylvia had taught him a great deal.

He stood up and switched the kettle on to make coffee, allowing his mind to wander back to the previous day. Although Juliet was still hiding behind a façade of brisk professionalism, which he admired in its own right, he had seen the occasional flicker of a different woman, one who wanted to have fun, who was willing to listen and to laugh. Someone softer. It intrigued him, and he wanted to peel away the layers and find out who was there when the steel doors were allowed to open. Something about the way she fought with herself – one minute opening up, the next with that hard shell snapped shut again – made him think that she was wrestling with it herself, that she knew she was more than a tough city girl but wasn't yet ready, or confident enough, to shed that particular skin. Shrugging, he picked up his coffee cup and turned to go and sit down again, when the door opened and in came Juliet, carrying bulging bags. She stopped when she saw him, then nodded a greeting and pushed the door shut behind her, making straight for the stairs.

'Hi there,' said Léo. 'Can I get you a coffee? I've just made one for myself.'

She paused with her foot on the bottom stair and turned her head slightly towards him, not meeting his eye.

'No, thanks, I've got to get on with some work.'

She resumed her ascent.

'So have I, but a coffee in your hand never hinders that, does it?'

This time when she stopped, she turned around to him completely, shifting the heavy bags across her reddening fingers and meeting his eyes full on. He recoiled at their flintiness.

'It's fine, thank you, I'll make something upstairs. I have to get on now.'

He didn't ask her again, just watched as she stamped purposefully up the steps and heard the door open and then shut with a decisive 'click'. Any glimmer of friendliness had clearly been extinguished, and Léo felt irritated as he sat down and picked up his pen, then tossed it down and drank some coffee. *Stop worrying yourself over whether this girl is some poor, vulnerable soul in need of fun and love. It seems more obvious that she is just a spoiled madam, a complete pain. Don't waste your time on her, Léo, you don't need that kind of complication.*

The talking-to he gave himself helped, and soon Léo was absorbed once more in his recipe creation, shutting out the sounds of Juliet moving around upstairs, no doubt making herself substandard instant coffee. His stomach told him it was nearing lunchtime when he put down his pen and switched on his tablet to check his personal emails. He deleted the usual influx of rubbish – advertisements, newsletters he didn't realise

he'd signed up for, exhortations to upgrade various things – and
was about to log out when he saw an email from a friend of his,
Mathias, titled 'I think you should see this.' Intrigued, he clicked
on it and read:

Dear Léo,

I hope things are going well for you in England and you have
found some peace. I don't know how much you look at the
gossip news – probably not at all – but I did think you may want
to see some of the things that Veronique is doing and saying. I
don't want to disturb your equilibrium, dear friend, but you may
wish to defend yourself.

Your friend,
Mathias

Léo paused, hovering over the link below Mathias's note.
Did he want to know? Veronique, with her high public profile
due to the reality shows she had appeared on, had done and said
so many damaging things over the last year; did he want to read
any more of her toxic, narcissistic lies? After all, he had come
here – to England, to Feywood – to escape the fallout of their
affair.

He knew he couldn't heal the wounds he had inflicted, but
Veronique seemed determined to keep them open and even to
create new ones. Leaving the whole sorry mess behind him
seemed the only sensible thing to do – for the preservation of his
mental and physical health as well as of his professional
reputation.

She had attempted to shred that, but thankfully he had built
up enough recognition and appreciation of his culinary skills
that he had been able to work with Sylvia, who couldn't care
less about scurrilous gossip, as long as it didn't affect their busi-

ness. His publishers were also keen for him to write this new cookery book about Feywood and didn't seem to think that sales would be affected, although he still privately harboured reservations. After all, the publication of the book would reveal his English hiding place, and he wasn't sure if – or when – he would be ready for that. He turned his attention back to the email; he should know what was being said about him. Mathias was a good friend who had seen the aftermath and would not have sent him something distressing without good reason. His finger fell like lead to touch the link, and immediately a garish pink and yellow webpage sprang onto the screen, its headline in French screaming:

LONELY VERONIQUE REVEALS MORE ABOUT LÉO HEARTBREAK IN THE CASTLE OF LOVE!

He groaned. So, she had gone onto the most lurid show on French TV – *Le Château d'Amour* – and was taking the opportunity to say God knew what about him. The programme was one he had seen only a few clips of, and that was enough for him. It was not, however, easy to avoid hearing about the exploits of the 'guests' who went to stay in the ultra-luxuriously appointed castle, being filmed at every moment. They were all single and all minor celebrities in desperate need of airtime to keep the feeble flames of their careers flickering. The premise was not an original one, but still managed to draw in thousands of viewers a week: six men and six women were locked up together and either encouraged to play silly games and challenges or to get bored and drink too much. This, coupled with their drive to be famous, inevitably produced repeated opportunities for showing off, having arguments and falling into each other's only too welcoming arms. Four series in, all the contestants knew from watching their predecessors that the best way to secure future projects was to be as outrageous as possible, and they all engineered ways to snatch screen time from one another. This must be Veronique's latest bid for attention. He read on:

Last night in the Castle of Love, Veronique broke down in Gilbert's arms, after they had shared a kiss. She sobbed as she told him that although she found him attractive, she was still pained by her heartbreak after her affair with renowned chef Léo Brodeur.

'He treated me so cruelly,' she wept, clinging to Gilbert as her body shook with sobs. 'He always knew I was married but promised me we would be together. I was so weak, I should never have gone with him, I regret every second of what he led me into. When the story broke, he said it would all be all right, that he would stand by me and, like a fool, I trusted him. Instead, he coldly packed up and left for England, where he is living now in luxury in a stately home. I didn't even hear from him when my darling husband left me, even though that is what he said he always wanted. He used me and I feel bereft.' When Gilbert asked what had attracted her to Brodeur, tempting her from her marriage, her voice dropped to a whisper.

'I don't know, Gilbert. He was very... persuasive. He had a way of telling me, rather than asking me, what I wanted. I have never spoken about this, but I had suffered several miscarriages and I suppose I was weakened, and vulnerable, and he saw his opportunity.'

Veronique's marriage collapsed a few weeks after news of the affair with Brodeur became public, and shortly after he fled to England. Veronique has always maintained that he wooed her relentlessly, promising her the world and urging her to end her marriage of four years to be with him, only to abandon her once this dream became attainable, but this is the first time she has spoken of her miscarriage trauma, or hinted at Brodeur's methods."

His face creasing in disgust, Léo cast a glance at the grainy pictures. There were several of Veronique nestled in Gilbert's muscly arms and two of himself and her kissing on a bridge. They were the photos that had revealed the affair when they were sold to a similar rag and splashed across the front cover with no warning. Despite his revulsion at what was written, he read it through one more time, then tossed his tablet onto the table. Why was she peddling these vicious lies about him? He understood that she craved fame and attention – God knows he had learnt that to his detriment – but surely she could achieve that, or at least the sort of notoriety that was apparently enough to satisfy her, without dragging his name through the mud at every opportunity?

It may not have even been lunchtime yet, but Léo felt the need for something to fortify him as he chewed over the contents of the article. He knew that there was an open bottle of red wine and went to pour himself a small glass, sipping it as his mind rolled around the words he had read. So, the marriage had ended. That was news to him, although he wasn't surprised. Her husband's humiliation had been public and comprehensive, and although the couple had initially stayed together – Veronique ringing to tell him regretfully that she would never see him again as if he wanted to by that point – he hadn't believed her declaration that she and Charles were closer than ever and deliriously happy. After all the untruths she had told *him*, he wouldn't have believed anything she said. But he was sorry, again, for Charles, who seemed like a decent man. A fresh wave of guilt broke over Léo, and he wondered if yet another apologetic message would go ignored, like the many before it. He couldn't blame the man, but he would have been so grateful for absolution. He drank some more of his wine, which helped to calm the hot flush of shame at the memories of his own gullible stupidity. No, he did not deserve forgiveness from Charles, and this shroud of guilt was a small price to pay for the part he had played in the destruction of a marriage.

Léo went to have another sip of wine, then looked at his empty glass in surprise. How did that happen? He was feeling a little light-headed, his stomach empty and beginning to rumble, but he wasn't prepared to go and have lunch at the house, not with the rest of the article to think over. He refilled the glass and got out some bread and cheese. The bread was homemade and the cheese a wonderful local blue, mild yet tangy and extremely moreish. He even felt a pang of guilt at his lunch. Surely he should be suffering more than to be eating beautiful local produce in this gorgeously located old stable block, the home of his new, successful business? Maybe Veronique was right and he was cold and self-serving? But these self-criticisms, once so easy to believe when his mind whispered them to him in the middle of the night, were becoming harder to stomach, especially in the light of articles like this which were, frankly, slanderous. He tore off a hunk of bread and flicked the screen on again with a shudder, to remind himself of her vicious words. What was this, about miscarriages? Apart from one miscarriage, of what she said was his baby – he swallowed the lump that came to his throat whenever he remembered this – she had never mentioned any others to him. He felt tears begin to well up in his eyes and wondered if more wine would help or hinder, and would he even know which either looked like? *In vino veritas* was the best approach, he decided. The wine would maybe bring forth the truth of his feelings, and even if that *was* a bit messy, it was probably good for him, cathartic. Veronique had disliked what she witheringly called his '*tendance trop émotionnelle*', his over-emotional side, but what could he do, he asked the empty room, tipping the rest of the bottle into his glass. He was who he was, and if that meant he felt his feelings, in all their technicolour glory – pah!

'Is something the matter?'

Léo jolted round on his chair, nearly dropping his glass.

'Juliet! I didn't hear you come down.'

'Are you all right? I thought someone was down here with you. I thought I heard you talking?'

'Ah, no, just maybe thinking out loud. I am working on recipes, it helps sometimes.'

'Is that one of them?'

Juliet nodded towards the brightly coloured gossip page open on the tablet in front of him. He hastily switched the screen off.

'No, no, that was just something a friend sent. Nothing... nothing at all.'

'All right. Are you going over for lunch?'

'I think I'll just have a simple lunch here.' Juliet said nothing but raised an eyebrow pointedly at the empty wine bottle. 'What about you?'

'Yes, I'm going to see if my sisters are around. Enjoy your... lunch.'

When she had left, Léo stopped himself from groaning out loud, in case she heard him through the door and thought he was even crazier – or drunker – than she already assumed him to be. What must he look like, sprawling at the table reading trashy rags, rambling out loud and tucking into the red wine? It would do nothing to improve her low opinion of him. He might as well finish looking at the article. Where was he? Ah yes, the miscarriages. Poor Veronique, if only he had known. Would it have changed anything, though? This he could never know. It had been she who had pursued him so vigorously, no matter what she said in the Castle of Love, but maybe that was some dreadful emotional reaction to her trauma? Maybe he should have been more sensitive, more questioning. A tear escaped and he brushed it away, steeling himself for the final paragraph, which was for him the most painful. To claim that he had made such promises... how could she?

This was not the first time she had accused him in this way, but no matter what he said, still the accusations came. He had racked his brains to try to unpick the truth, torn between his memories and her insistence that he had badgered her to leave her husband and threatened reprisals if she didn't: his so-called 'methods'. Because the situation was so obviously wrong and he had ultimately contributed to the collapse of a marriage, although Veronique had lied to him as comprehensively and skilfully as she had to Charles, he felt a terrible weight of guilt. His feelings of remorse were so strong that they overwhelmed reason, and he wanted to take all the blame, in the hope that by doing so, he could somehow put things right.

Reading articles like this one, which he finally closed, did little to help. He just felt bad that he had played a part in Veronique ending up where she was now, a bitter and desperate woman making an exhibition of herself for a few crumbs of attention.

The door opened and Léo jumped off his stool to try and look busy, but it was not Juliet who walked in but Sylvia. Her quick eyes took in the debris on the table and the expression on Léo's face.

'Are you all right?'

He sank back onto his stool.

'I'm afraid I have had something of a shock. I do not think that wine was, perhaps, the best way to manage it, but...'

He shrugged and looked hopelessly at her. She dropped the bag she was carrying, pulled herself up onto another stool and took his hand.

'What's happened? You look awful. Can I help?'

'Nobody can help. What is done is done, but oh, how I wish

it wasn't. It is Veronique. You know I told you about her when I first came to England, when you rescued me?'

'I rather think *you* rescued *me*, I couldn't believe it when you agreed to come. What's happened?'

He flicked on the iPad and opened the article for a second time, holding it out to Sylvia, who looked at it briefly, then back up at him.

'I can't understand a word of this, Léo, you'll have to explain.'

He took a deep breath.

'Veronique, she has entered a show where she lives in a castle with others, to find love – *Le Chateau d'Amour.*'

'A reality TV thing?'

'*Oui*, that is right. She has said that I treated her with great cruelty, that I had always known she was married, that I abandoned her when she needed me most.'

'And are those things true?'

'It is true that I left France – but she had left me, returned to her husband, and I was being vilified in the press. I thought it was best for us all that I go. I have caused so much pain.'

'So, the things she has said in this article – they're lies?'

'Yes, yes. I did not know she was married when we met. I did not abandon her. I did not treat her in the way she says. It is true she had a miscarriage when we were together, but she says she had several and I did not know of any others. Maybe I should leave here too.'

'What!' Sylvia's hand flew to her chest. 'Léo, you can't go. I need you; Feywood needs you. What good would leaving do?'

'It is clear that I bring misery when I do not mean to. If she says these things, if she hates me as much as she seems to, found me controlling and cold... maybe I do not realise the damage I do? I do not want to risk bringing this to you.'

'Oh, poppycock,' said Sylvia, relaxing her hand and looking annoyed now. 'It sounds to me as if this Veronique is doing everything she can for column inches, and blaming you is the perfect way to go about it. Tell me what you did right.'

'I beg your pardon?'

'What did you do *right*, in all this mess? You are doing what she wants you to do: taking the blame and guilt for everything. So, what did you do right?'

Léo thought for a moment.

'When I found out that she was married, I ended things.'

'Good.'

'But I was still responsible for finishing their marriage...'

'Why? It sounds to me as if that responsibility lies firmly at Veronique's door. What else did you do right?'

'I – I – I tried to apologise to her husband. And I am sure I did not treat her badly, but I should have been more careful, I should have known things. I rushed in with passion and should have been more careful. You say in English that "fools rush in", I think?'

'Yes, "fools rush in where angels fear to tread". But Léo, feeling that way about someone and failing to do a full background check is hardly a crime.' He smiled. Sylvia's brisk approach was making him feel better. 'It was *her* responsibility to tell you about her marriage. You cannot take all the blame.'

'Maybe. But she is clearly vulnerable, and I wish I had been more careful. I have not only left all this hurt and hate behind me in France, but I risked my reputation. What if this news surfaces when more people learn about the cookery school, or when the book is published? I will bring with me a dark cloud.'

'You'll do nothing of the sort. I'm glad to have you here, and we can worry about any of that stuff when and if it happens. For now, I'm going to put the cheese I just collected from the farm in the fridge before it melts all over the floor, then I have an appointment to get to in Oxford.'

When she had gone, Léo was encouraged, if not wholly convinced by Sylvia's practical approach. The temporary soothing and numbing effects of the alcohol, carbs and fat were beginning to wear off and he felt tired and sick. It was tempting to go up to the house, to his room, and lie down for a while. For a moment, the image of collapsing onto the large, comfortable bed, having drawn the curtains against the afternoon sun, was mesmerising, but instead he stood up and marched to the sink.

Non, Léo. A sleep in the afternoon won't do you any good. Fresh air is what you need, fresh air and water, then work.

Maybe he should try to bump into Juliet, to check she was all right and try to prove that he was not an afternoon drunk, but reason piped up again.

Tiens! Stop being a fool. Yes, she is beautiful, and intriguing, but you know she is hurting. Given your past, must you wade in and, in trying to save her, ruin more lives? You have come here to work and, yes, to hide, to recover, to atone. Learn your lesson.

He drank a pint of water and not stopping to clear away his lunchtime debris, marched out of the house and into the kitchen garden, where he hoped he might find some peace.

THIRTEEN

Lunch up at Feywood was a quiet affair that day. Sylvia was away in Oxford again, Rousseau was working, and Will was at some boring conference on estate management, so it was just the three sisters who gathered together some bits from the kitchen and sat down at the big, faded table in there to eat, rather than bothering with the dining room.

'Where's Léo today?' asked Martha, sawing wonkily at a cucumber with a blunt knife.

'Here, give me that.' Juliet took both items from her, discarded the knife for something sharper and began slicing efficiently, while Martha redirected her efforts to buttering bread. 'I don't know, last I saw of him he was drinking wine and looking sadly at some article on his tablet.'

'Maybe it's his *femme mariée* again,' said Frankie. 'Did you see anything?'

'No.'

In fact, Juliet had noticed some of the photographs, but something stopped her telling Frankie about them. She would only want to rush off and try to find the article, and it felt intrusive somehow, to be scrabbling around for salacious details.

'We all should have tried harder at school with French. Who knew it would have come in so useful? That's very good cucumber-cutting, by the way, Juliet. Been taking lessons from the charming chef?'

Juliet looked down at her handiwork in surprise. It *was* rather good. Maybe being around the cookery school so much was beginning to rub off, but she didn't welcome Frankie's lazily snide comments.

'Oh, shut up, Frank. You could always try doing something other than waiting for me and Martha to fill your plate.'

'I don't mind, girls, I'm too much in love to eat.'

She immediately countered this comment by breaking off a large hunk of cheese to go with her crackers and perfectly sliced cucumber.

'Ooh, Frankie, who is it?'

Martha's eyes lit up. For someone so hopeless with men, thought Juliet, Martha was irrepressibly romantic.

'Haven't you noticed? It's Will, our gorgeous estate manager, of course.'

Martha's hand flew to her mouth, then she tried to compose herself.

'Oh... that's... that's lovely news. I hadn't realised. Well... erm... great, good luck.'

She produced a smile, then busied herself with some left-over quiche. Juliet glared at her sisters in turn. Frankie could be cruel at times, lolling in her chair and grinning at her older sister's crestfallen face.

'Frankie, give it a rest. Martha, of *course* she's not in love with Will, and he's certainly not in love with her. He's got far more sense than that. She's winding you up.'

Martha raised her gentle face to look at her sisters with renewed hope.

'Really? Wonderful! Erm, I mean, that is, I would have been happy for you, but I'm not sure you're really a perfect match...'

She trailed off, reddening.

'There, there, big sis.' Frankie patted Martha's hand. 'I know he's your dream man, I wouldn't do that to you. But I wish you'd get on and tell him, rather than mooning around. It's been two years now.'

'I... did you know as well, Juliet?'

'You might as well paint it on the side of the house, it's that obvious.'

Juliet felt sorry for Martha but was glad of the distraction.

'Oh no! Do you think he knows too?'

Her cheeks were now aflame, and tears had risen in her eyes. Frankie stretched and yawned, then took pity, as she always did.

'Nah, he won't have noticed. He's far too busy counting bricks in old stone walls and helping wickle hedgehogs find a cosy bush to snuggle down in. You should tell him, though.'

'I couldn't! I mean – oh! I just couldn't.'

'Why the hell not? It's the twenty-first century, you don't need to sit around with your smelling salts waiting for him to come and sweep you off your feet.'

The idle bickering carried on like this for the next twenty minutes or so and, to Juliet's relief, they did not return to the subject of Léo. She walked back down to the stable block, wondering if he would be in the kitchen, but when she pushed the door open, the room was empty. The tablet lay discarded on the table amongst a debris of crumbs and an empty wine glass and bottle. She was tempted to turn it on, just to have another quick glance at the page he had been reading, but remembered firstly that her French was appalling, so she would learn no more anyway, and secondly how kind he had been yesterday during the photos and teaching her how to taste the food with the wine, and she felt disinclined to pry. Instead, she went upstairs and pushed open the door to her little studio. In the short time she had been living there, it had become 'home' more comprehensively than anywhere she had ever lived, including Feywood itself. She wandered over to the kettle and made a cup of herbal tea, something she thought she would never do, but which she found oddly empowering, as if she was making a positive decision to take care of herself. Then she sat down and switched on her computer. It was time to tackle those photos.

As ever, work helped the dust storm in Juliet's brain to settle, and after an hour and a half, she pushed back her chair and sighed in satisfaction. Although many of the photos hadn't worked, the most problematic being the ones she had taken in the kitchen garden, some of the others gave her a great rush of pride. The close-ups of Léo's hands working the dough and chopping onions and herbs were almost perfect and would enhance the website, along with her drawings, which she would be able to finish soon once she had completed some other, paid, commissions. She felt shy looking at the portraits. When she was taking them, she had had the detachment of a surgeon, checking light levels, working out the shadows and angles with absorption. But now that she looked at the finished photographs, Léo gazing into the lens with calmness, confidence and humour, his personality fizzed off the screen and she felt as if she could reach out and touch him. This alone made her feel all hot and cold, and she returned to some compositions of oil bottles on the windowsill for a while, before returning to the portraits. Unfortunately for poor Juliet, the effect hadn't worn off. His warm, brown-eyed gaze held just the slightest hint of sexiness, with a definite invitation teasing her. Even in the more serious shots, his lips curled upwards, with a natural inclination towards joy and fun. Her clever lighting had picked up the tawny highlights in his thick hair and shadowed his face flatteringly. Not, she had to admit, that he needed much help. He was a very handsome man, but not in a bland, polished way;

not, she thought, like Toby with his sculpted hair and pampered skin. No, Léo had the look of someone who had lived; not dissipated, just well-adventured. Despite her reservations about him – partly because he was a man and therefore not to be trusted, but also because of the magazine article which was unfair, she knew, because none of them had understood enough French to know what was going on – when she looked at these honest portraits, she saw a kind, friendly, open face. It was a shame about the bossiness, she reflected, but maybe she shouldn't jump to the conclusion that this made him controlling. She could decide *that* once she knew him a bit better.

Juliet knew only too well how it felt to be misunderstood, or labelled as something you knew wasn't 'you', to the extent where everyone else seemed to believe it, and you doubted the tiny remaining nugget of certainty deep inside.

The screen had now become a swirling mass of colours as the screensaver kicked in, but Juliet didn't nudge the mouse or tap a key to bring it back to life. She stared at it meditatively for a few moments, letting these thoughts wash across her brain and take form. Yesterday's proximity to that most masculine of men, his calm authority when he had guided her to eat mindfully, his gorgeous eyes gazing into hers, albeit through a camera lens, had unsettled her. She had, she mused, believed her own publicity for too long and her confused push-me-pull-you reaction to Léo was a far cry from the cool, impervious ice-queen image she had cultivated for so long. *It's bloody Feywood, it does this to you. How can I be anyone but myself here, and how can I allow that when it caused me so much pain for so long?* An image of Juliet's mother flicked into her head, of her scorn at her middle daughter's developing talents and interests and her mocking criticism and sudden, unexpected rages which had driven Juliet up several different pathways before she left altogether, only to realise years later that she still wasn't allowing herself to be, well, herself. How ironic that it was being back at

Feywood that was finally bringing about the softening she had secretly craved. *The ice queen melts*, she thought to herself, and laughed.

Juliet didn't see Léo for the rest of that day. She didn't go up to the house for supper, preferring to eat some of her village store treats in front of the TV. She would have to get some more comfortable clothes, she thought to herself as she once again pulled on the only soft joggers and sweatshirt she had; this new lifestyle didn't really call for tight waistbands and sharp tailoring.

The next day, after breakfasting in her pyjamas whilst taking in the glorious golden morning view and wondering how difficult it would be to capture on camera, she dressed quickly and set out to look for Léo. She hadn't heard him downstairs, but on passing through the kitchen noticed that everything from the previous day had been tidied up, and the tablet removed. She had a brief twinge of regret that she hadn't looked at the webpage when she had the opportunity, but remembered her new resolve to let Léo show her who he was, and not second-guess or jump to conclusions. She found him in the kitchen garden, tying up some sort of plant to conical bamboo structures.

'Morning.'

'Ah, good morning, Juliet.'

'What are you doing?'

'These are some beans I am trying to grow. The plants seem to shoot out fast all over the place, but there isn't a single sign of a bean yet. Please can you help me? Just hold that piece of string there... *bon*! It is done, thank you. What brings you out here? More photos?'

'Well, actually, the photos I took out here didn't go well, but I'm pleased with the others. I've got some more work to do on them and then I'll show you. No, it was something else I wanted to ask you about.'

'Is everything okay?'

'Yes, yes, I actually wanted your help with something. Something for the village.'

'Of course, I will help you if I can. As long as it does not involve singing. I do not sing well.'

Juliet laughed with surprise.

'No, not singing! Absolutely not. No, it's something much more up your street actually – baking.'

'That's more like it. Are we going to enter something in the famous village fete scone-making competition? I have heard a lot about this, it sounds extremely competitive.'

'No, not that, I wouldn't dare. Agnes reigns supreme over the scone competition, and I certainly don't want to get on the wrong side of her by entering, let alone winning, with a professional chef to help me. No, this is just making bread. Well, sort of.'

Léo narrowed his eyes suspiciously.

'Sort of? Go on...'

'There is a celebration coming up in a few weeks' time called Lammas – lots of English villages mark it.'

'Okay... I haven't heard of it. Lammas?'

'That's right, it means 'loaf mass' and is a sort of early harvest festival. It celebrates the first wheat harvest of the season, I think. Something like that. Anyway, we always took a loaf down to the church when we were children – well, I did. It was sort of my thing. I bumped into the vicar yesterday, and he's asked me to revive the tradition.'

'It sounds wonderful. In France we have celebrations for the grape harvest, with plenty of wine, of course.'

'Of course. I'm afraid there's no booze at this one, but the bread is fun. It's traditional to make it into interesting shapes. I always just made a plait, but owls and corn sheaves are popular.'

'You want to make bread in the shape of an owl?'

Juliet snorted with laughter at Léo's bemused face.

'It wouldn't *have* to be an owl, but I thought it might be fun if it was. I mean, if you don't think you're up to it, then that's fine, I'm sure I can do it on my own.'

Juliet wasn't sure of anything of the sort and would really rather not present the vicar with a burnt lump of rock-hard bread on Lammas, which was all she was confident of producing by herself. But she suspected that needling Léo with a challenge might be her quickest path to getting some help. She was right.

'*Non*, Juliet, of course I will help you. An owl it will be! Your vicar will be delighted, and *you* will learn to bake bread.'

'Steady on, I wasn't really thinking about a lesson.'

'*Ah, non?* Perhaps you thought you would sit and celebrate the grape harvest with a nice glass of something while I knead, and shape, and bake, hmm?'

'It's like the story of the Little Red Hen!' said Juliet in delight.

'Hen?'

'Yes! You know – the hen keeps asking everyone to help her make the bread, but no one will, so she does everything herself and then she eats it herself too.'

'Okay, so you see the benefit of working together then.'

Juliet screwed up her face.

'Well, not really, because this bread is going to the church... but I will help you,' she added graciously.

Léo looked at her as if he wasn't sure whether to feel amused or appalled. She smirked at him, for once enjoying playing up to her image as a spoilt princess. His confusion just added to her merriment, but she decided to put him out of his misery.

'Oh, come on, I'm joking. I'm very grateful for your help, I'd be absolutely hopeless doing it on my own.'

Léo threw his hands to his face.

'*Merde!* Caught out again by the English straight face. I never know when you are joking. Okay, okay, we will make your owl bread together. It will be magnificent.'

'I hope so, the vicar has terrifyingly high standards. We don't want a repeat of what happened in 2009.'

Juliet shook her head sorrowfully and gazed at the ground.

'What did happen in... Oh, wait, I am being joked with again, right?'

She let a naughty smile creep across her face.

'I'm afraid so.'

The next few weeks passed uneventfully for Juliet. She finished the photos for the cookery school website, including the difficult kitchen garden shots of Léo and a terrific daylong session with Sylvia. She had become concerned by her aunt's repeated absences, and thought she had been looking pale and tired, but as the shoot went so well and Sylvia seemed upbeat and chatty, Juliet decided not to ask any questions. After all, she hated being grilled about her private life and was sure that her aunt would open up to her in good time if, indeed, she needed to. She had also decided to take some pictures of the house itself, but each time she examined them in high resolution on the screen, she felt more depressed.

'Poor old Feywood,' she murmured, looking at them. 'It'd take more than some Vaseline on the lens to cast you in a flattering light.'

She wondered if Rousseau had noticed half of what her camera showed up, or if he was just focused on fixing the roof and windows. The photos showed brickwork that urgently needed repointing, floorboards riddled with woodworm, damp creeping through the ceilings and ivy taking over the ancient guttering. Juliet had tried to draw a heavy velvet curtain that was pulled over a little-used window behind the stairs, and it had fallen to dust in her hands. The electrics and heating were unpredictable, and they often resorted to expensive plug-in heaters in the winter. The only thing that worked properly was the upstairs plumbing, which had been fixed as an emergency about five years ago. You could always be guaranteed a good, hot shower, but never knew if you'd be washing up downstairs in cold water. It was amazing to call a house of such history and character home, but Juliet knew that they all had to be a lot less romantic and a lot more pragmatic about it if they wanted to keep it, let alone have paying guests staying. It was all very well giggling together when you got showered with plaster at the dinner table if someone walked across the room overhead, but people would expect luxury – and working radiators – when they had finished a day in the cookery school.

Juliet had finished several commissions for editors in London, one of which, in particular, had paid handsomely, so she felt justified in taking some time to work on her floral art. Her sisters were also busy. Frankie seemed obsessed with the new boyfriend, but nobody had met him yet; rather, she would go away for several days at a time looking gorgeous and bouncing with excitement on her departures but returning more withdrawn and with dark circles etched under her eyes. Only once had Juliet commented:

'Frank, you look like you've been up for three nights in a row. Glad to see the new man has some stamina.'

'Shut up, I've got work to do.'

It was an uncharacteristically brusque reply from the normally expansive Frankie, and Juliet hadn't commented again but noted that Frankie wasn't doing much work and was more likely to be found in bed until lunchtime and mooching around aimlessly in the afternoons. Martha was too distracted by organising their mother's memorial event to be much help, so Juliet filed Frankie away with Sylvia, resolving to keep an eye on her but not pry where it wouldn't be welcome. *Who would have thought it? I'm becoming quite the family woman. I'll be checking to make sure Dad's taking his vitamins next.* But with Lammas on the horizon, her attention was soon stretched even further.

'Juliet, what do you think about adding olives to the bread? An olive branch is a Bible symbol after all.'

'Juliet, do you think the vicar would mind if we used *French* flour? I know it's not quite in keeping, but it makes a superior loaf.'

'Juliet, I was wondering what sort of owl would be most suitable? I have been researching them and a barn owl is so typical, but a snowy owl so beautiful. What do you think?'

'Honestly, Léo, I think you're overthinking all of this. Can't we just mix together a bit of flour and water, squidge it up, make a sort of owllike shape and bung it in the oven?'

He looked at her as if she had suggested opening a tin of beans for the king.

'No, Juliet, we cannot. I have been reading about your Lammas, and it is a wonderful and very old festival. I have spoken to Father Benedict, who is most keen that the celebrations should be expanded over the next few years, and sees this year as the perfect time to launch that plan. Our owl is to be the centrepiece in the church, it must earn that place. So please, stop grumbling at me with your squidging and bunging, and help me think about how to achieve perfection.'

A single arched eyebrow was Juliet's only response, but the call to perfection appealed to her, and that evening she began sketching owls, wondering just how wise she had been to ask for Léo's help.

FOURTEEN

'Okay, Juliet, today is the day. Are you ready to make the owl bread?'

She could hardly believe it was already the first of August and that she had been back at Feywood for three months. Her life in London had already faded to nothing but a murky memory, other than those times when she was just drifting off to sleep and a sudden flashback came sharply to mind, awakening her with a jolting shock and, more often than not, a rush of shame. But today couldn't be further away from London; today was about the village, about Lammas and about this damn owl bread.

'I'm ready, but I'm also rather wishing I'd never got myself into all this.'

Léo laughed.

'Do not worry. Between us we will make something to be proud of. But *vite!* We must get on or the vicar will not get his loaf.'

Juliet tied on an apron and rolled up her sleeves, wondering what her London acquaintances would say if they could see her now. Mind you, most of them didn't surface till midday at the weekends, sleeping off the excesses of the night before. It was early still, and she glanced out of the window as the morning sun streamed in, thinking that she would prefer to be here, in flat shoes with a clear mind, even if it did mean getting covered in flour. And it clearly would. Léo was lifting a huge, dusty bag of the stuff onto the counter.

'*Bon*. We need a kilo of this, but only a small amount of yeast. We do not want our loaf to rise too much and lose the beautiful shape we are going to create. Cold water, also. Please get half a litre.'

Juliet rolled her eyes.

'I have no idea what half a litre is, but I suppose I can work it out.' She pulled out a measuring jug and examined it theatrically. 'Ah, you mean a pint, now I see.'

As she had hoped, Léo visibly bristled.

'I do not *mean* a pint, I *mean* a half litre...' He trailed off as he saw her grinning at the running tap. 'Oh, I see, I have fallen into your trap once again.'

'Sorry, you're such an easy mark. Here's your water.'

Léo soon got his revenge, it seemed to Juliet, as within minutes she was elbow-deep in the huge bowl, trying to wrangle the mixture into a smooth ball.

'It's hopeless, it's just all sticky.'

She held up a hand webbed with dough.

'Juliet, you have been kneading for about thirty seconds, you have many minutes left to go. Bread is not an instant thing, it takes time and sweat, but it will be worth it.'

'Yuck, I'm not sure anyone wants my sweat involved.' She glowered at him. 'I don't see why we can't just use a bread machine.'

'That would not be in keeping with the spirit of Lammas,' said Léo sententiously. 'Rather, maybe you should reflect upon the blessings and many abundances of your life as you work.'

It seemed to Juliet there was no adequate response to this

other than to work her irritation into the dough. Bloody man: he always made her feel simultaneously ignoble and self-righteous. She tried to keep up the momentum of her feelings as she pulled and scraped at the sticky gunk, but as the dough started to take shape, she found that her annoyance ebbed.

'Look, it's real dough!'

'Indeed, well done. That is the first part of the job finished. Now comes the real work.'

Juliet swiped her forearm across her face.

'What do you mean? It's a ball now, isn't it? Can't we make the owl?'

'We are a long way off making the owl, which is why we had to start so early. Okay, more flour.'

Léo dipped his hand into the bag and sprinkled flour liberally over the work surface, dusted his hands, then lifted out the ball of dough.

'It has to be worked now, very hard, very well for at least five minutes, maybe more, to activate the yeast and gluten and get the rise and texture we want. Now watch my technique.'

Juliet bristled at Léo's didactic tone but was intrigued and leant to observe more closely as he slammed into the dough with the heels of his hands, turning and folding it as he went, keeping up a string of instructions. She was just beginning to feel hypnotised by the repetitive, unrelenting motions, when he stepped back.

'Voila. Now it is your turn, you can show me if you have learnt well.'

Bossy-boots, thought Juliet. *I'll show him all right.*

Pushing her sleeves up, she attacked the dough, resisting as she did so the temptation to picture Léo's face as she pulled and pummelled. *Whack, thump, bang.* It was certainly satisfying. She lifted her hands away and looked triumphantly over at the French chef.

'There. Even got my heart rate up a bit. What's next?'

'What's next? What's next is that you keep going for another four and a half minutes.'

'I beg your pardon?'

'Juliet, you have been working that dough – vigorously, I agree – for no more than thirty seconds. You must carry on.'

'Can't you do it?'

'Don't tell me you are worn out already?'

'More bored really.'

Now she sounded like Frankie, but it was hard to keep the petulance out of her voice when he was glaring at her like a stern headmaster.

'Well, you cannot be bored with your dough. Come on, or it will never be ready for your vicar. Your technique was good.'

'Oh. Well. I expect it was, yes. All right then.'

She resumed what she was now considering to be her daily workout when Léo added:

'Yes, a good technique, you listened well.'

Juliet refrained from throwing the dough at his head but relieved her feelings instead in her *technique*. She was sure he was dragging out the five minutes but determined not to ask if it was up. She was relieved when he finally announced, '*Bon*. Let us see if it's ready.'

He leant over and pressed a finger into the dough.

'Good. You see the way the press mark – what do you call it, is there a special word?'

'The dent?'

'Ah bon, the dent, it rises again quickly. That means it is ready.'

'Great. So, how do we make the owl shape?'

'Juliet, have you truly forgotten everything in the years since you last made your loaf for the vicar? The dough must be left now to rise – an hour at least.'

'Oh right, yes, of course. Actually, this might be a good time for something else. An idea I had.'

She suddenly felt shy. Maybe he would think it was stupid, but he smiled encouragingly as he draped a cloth over the dough and placed it on the sunny windowsill.

'I just wondered, maybe it would be fun to present the owl in a sort of summery nest – look, I did some sketches.'

She pushed some pieces of paper across the work surface, which he picked up and scrutinised. Each showed a different arrangement of flowers, fruit, foliage and even hay to make a dreamy bed for the owl to nestle in.

'Juliet, I think this is a wonderful idea. I have a deep tray we could use – but where will we get the leaves and things we need?'

'I'm sure we'll be able to find everything we need down in Fey Woods – the woods at the bottom of the garden, that is, not the house. Have you ever been there?'

'No, I have not. I am not really one for tramping around in woods, but today I will make an exception for you.'

Juliet disdained to answer, just flicked an eyebrow at Léo and turned to leave.

Five minutes later, they were entering the woods. They never failed to cast their spell on her, thought Juliet, feeling the familiar shiver of anticipation as they stepped between the first few trees and the quality of the light changed. It was one of the few things left in life, particularly once she had started living in London, that felt so purely and peculiarly seasonal. There was no need of particular pop songs, or artificial scented candles, of the same tired old articles about getting your body ready for this or that or buying a new coat. In Fey Woods, you instantly knew by the filtered light what season it was. Now, in mid-summer, the woods were golden-green and the pine needles dry underfoot. There was a sensation of movement around them, of life nearby, and Léo must have noticed it too, for he asked:

'What animals are there here, Juliet?'

'Well, you're unlikely to spot anything more exciting than a grey squirrel, but the woods are home to a huge range of wildlife. Masses of insects of course, but also foxes, hedgehogs and badgers – the usual sort of English woodland fare. Frankie says she spotted a deer once, but no one else ever has. Lots of birds too, and there's a pond over on the east side that's simply stuffed with frogs and toads and things. Our father has a policy of benign neglect, and it seems to be good for the nature here.'

'A little like rewilding, we have some projects in France.'

'Yes, here too. We haven't really needed to rewild Fey Woods, though, just leave them alone.'

'Often that is the best way, I find. Oh, and what does the word 'fey' mean? I have been meaning to ask.'

'It means "fairy", and that's what these woods are – fairy woods.'

'Of course! We have the same word in French – *fée*. But surely Juliet does not believe in fairies?'

Juliet slid him a sideways glance, to see if he was laughing at her, but found just a friendly – if teasing – expression on his face. She took a deep breath.

'Look. You're right that I'm impatient with people who aren't – well, straightforward, I suppose. But even for me it's difficult to come into these woods and *not* let a tiny part of myself believe that there's some sort of magic twined around these trees.' She shrugged. 'I know it's silly, but there it is.'

'*Non*, not silly; I agree. And it is the perfect place to find nesting materials for our wise Lammas owl. Come, let us start looking, or the dough will be ruined.'

A companionable silence fell between them as they started to fill the basket Juliet had brought with her. Soon it was brimming with scented sprigs of pine as well as cones and feathers.

'We don't want it to look too Christmassy,' said Juliet, looking at the basket. 'I think we'd better get some flowers from the borders on the way back. There's some gorgeous love-in-a-mist there, or even some dahlias might look pretty, if we can find some smaller ones.'

'You know a lot about flowers,' said Léo. 'Somehow I did not expect this of you.'

Relaxed by the walk and the spell of the woods, Juliet did not deflect his comment, but smiled.

'I love flowers, I always have. In fact...' She hesitated.

'Go on.'

'In fact, I have been working on some flower paintings. It's a bit different for me, but I'm enjoying it.'

Léo nodded, his face serious.

'For an artist, it is so important to keep trying new things, even better if they are things you love. I hope maybe you will show me these pictures?'

Juliet felt all at once glad and shy. Léo did have a way of looking at you that made you feel very *seen*, and she wasn't sure how much she wanted this bossy French chef to know of her.

'Maybe. And I'd be grateful if you didn't mention the flower pictures to my family.'

'Of course. And now, how are we going to get back? I have lost all my sense of direction. I should have laid a breadcrumb trail.'

Juliet smiled.

'Getting lost in Fey Woods isn't something you have to worry about if you're with one of the Carlisle sisters. We've all be running around here since we were tiny. Come on, this way.'

Within minutes, they emerged from the milky green of the woods back into the bright August sunshine. After a quick detour along the borders, where they cut some wispy blue love-in-a-mist and spiky red dahlias, they returned to the kitchen.

'Okay, let's see the dough.'

Léo fetched the bowl and brought it to the central island, then removed the tea towel with a flourish. Juliet couldn't help herself letting out a delighted squeak.

'Oh! It's risen, look at that.'

'It's like magic, huh?'

'It really is! Can I touch it?'

'Not just touch it, you have to knead it again, I'm afraid, until it is firm. Come now, Juliet, roll your sleeves up at the same time you're rolling your eyes so hard. It will only take a few moments, and we will be ready to create the owl.'

Without comment, Juliet washed her hands, dusted flour around liberally, then lifted the fat ball of dough out of the bowl and resumed her kneading, breathing in the fresh, yeasty smell as she did so. Ignoring Léo's dig and focusing just on the task in hand felt soothing, and she was surprised when Léo broke her reverie.

'That's five minutes, let me see if it is ready.'

He leant in and began pulling and pressing the dough, his hands brushing hers, which she snatched away as if she had been burnt. He was standing very close to her, but looking only at his work and, for once, the normally confident Juliet felt confused. His proximity was discomfiting, but only in that it was making her blood run faster, her heart beat harder. Part of her wanted to stalk off around the kitchen island to safety, another part wanted to slip an arm around his broad shoulders, press herself into his warm body, feel his lips on hers...

'*Bon.*'

She jumped guiltily.

'It is ready.'

'Oh, er, good, good. Right, I've looked into this a bit. We have to divide the dough more or less in half – half for the basic shape and half for the decoration. I've got some pictures, hang on.'

Soon the owl began to take shape on the baking tray as they

added feathers and other features to it. Juliet forced herself to concentrate on the job, rather than allowing herself to become mesmerised by Léo's strong, skilled hands as they gently shaped dough into feathers and curved claws. When it was finished, they stepped back to admire their work.

'Now,' said Léo, 'it just needs a short time to prove, and we have to hope that we have got our quantities right so that the shape is not lost.'

During the second proving and the baking, they cleaned up and prepared the 'nest' on a large tray, and when the timer sounded, Juliet had a rush of excited anticipation; better, she thought, than any thrill she had felt at the prospect of yet another boozy night out with her London friends.

'Please,' she said to Léo as he handed her the oven gloves, 'you do it. I feel too nervous. What if I drop it?'

'What if *I* drop it?'

'You are not remotely worried about that, so don't pretend you are.'

'*Oui, c'est vrai.*'

With steady hands, he slid the tray from the oven and placed it on the cooling rack.

'Oh, it's fab! Aren't we clever?'

'We have created something beautiful together, yes.'

They stared at each other, delighted with the perfect, golden-brown loaf that had emerged. The shapes had all been maintained beautifully, and the feathery owl gazed back at them from round eyes. Suddenly, Léo scooped Juliet into an embrace. For a moment, the euphoria of the successful bake swept through Juliet and she hugged him back, but it was quickly followed by a rush of other feelings, which confused and dizzied her. Being so close to Léo, so suddenly, the sensation of his rough cheek against her face, his arms around her body, his woody scent mixing with the smell of the bread... she was thrilled but also panicked. As they pulled away, his hands lingered on her shoulders and those deep brown eyes looked intensely into hers. Juliet knew that she could kiss him, right then, and felt her body propelling her towards him, longing for nothing else than to feel his mouth touch hers. But then she felt the doors slam shut within her and she pulled away with a sharp inhalation of breath. She turned back towards the bread, trying to cover her confusion.

'I suppose it needs to cool a bit, then let's get it into the nest, and then I want to take some photos before it goes down to the village. The vicar must be wondering where on earth we are.'

Léo turned away, too, and busied himself tidying oven gloves and spatulas; Juliet wondered what he was hiding, what emotions were being put back in place before he gathered himself and returned to their work.

The next hour was spent professionally as they cooled, arranged and photographed their masterpiece. At last, it was time to carry it down, and Juliet texted her sisters:

> Come on you two, it's lunchtime, time to get dressed and come to the church for the Lammas celebrations. You promised, remember?

The replies were typical: a winking face with a sticking out tongue from Frankie, who probably *was* still in her pyjamas, and an apologetic essay from Martha, who had been ready and waiting for hours, sorry, she'd just got caught up in her latest portrait, wouldn't be a sec, promise.

They met at the front of the house, Léo carrying the bread which was now carefully wrapped. Rousseau and Sylvia were there too.

'Good to see you baking the Lammas bread again, darling,' said Juliet's father. 'Can I have a look?'

'When we're at the church. Come on, we'd better get moving or we'll be late.'

They walked down together, Frankie glued to her phone as usual, smiling a secret smile at each new text she received, and Martha needing regular chivvying as she stopped to wonder at the colour of a leaf, or the way the sun caught a spider's web.

'Honestly, I don't know why you two can't get a move on,' grumbled Juliet. 'Everything around here takes so long. I've been waiting all morning for the bread to organise itself and now a ten-minute walk is going to take half an hour if *you* keep stopping to text and *you* insist on marvelling over every blade of grass.'

'You're not in London anymore, Dorothy,' snapped back Frankie, deliberately pausing to select an emoji. 'Chill out, there's no rush.'

'Well, I would like to be on time, that's all.'

'Try not to worry, Juliet, we have time,' said Léo. 'But you and I can walk ahead if you prefer?'

Remembering the almost-kiss, Juliet felt herself going pink at the thought of strolling on ahead with Léo, and then pinked further at the thought of the comments that Frankie was bound to make, never able to resist the opportunity for a jibe. She replied more sharply than she had intended, 'It's fine. Let's just keep moving.'

When they reached the church, it was rapidly filling with people from not just that village but several other local places. The Lammas celebrations, forgotten now by so many churches, were famous in these parts and followed by a jolly lunch in the meadow next to the church, which Juliet could see was already bright with bunting and dotted with chairs and trestle tables. They were greeted by the vicar.

'How wonderful, the whole family. Welcome, welcome! And is this our loaf?'

'This is it,' said Juliet, suddenly feeling a little shy. 'I hope you like it.'

'Was it made with love?' asked Father Benedict, staring at her earnestly.

Juliet wouldn't have known where to look, had Frankie's snort of laughter not given her an excuse to glare in her direction. Léo intervened.

'Of course!' he said neutrally. 'All the best bread is.'

'Then in that case I will like it very much,' he replied. 'Now please let me see.'

Trying as hard as she could not to let her hands brush Léo's, Juliet helped him to unwrap the loaf and reveal their owl to the little group. For a moment, no one said anything, but Martha was the first to recover herself.

'Juliet, Léo, it's *beautiful*,' she breathed.

Everyone agreed, and Juliet found the courage to meet Léo's eyes for the first time in several hours, finding them smiling warmly right back at her, causing her stomach to turn several not unpleasant somersaults.

'Come,' said the vicar, carefully taking the tray. 'It is time to begin.'

FIFTEEN

The next couple of weeks were busy for Juliet, and she had little time to wonder about her feelings for Léo. She barely saw him, despite their proximity as they both worked, for he rose early and she slept late and worked late, often into the early hours. Sometimes, she had a project to finish – the newspaper work had tight, rapid deadlines – but sometimes, she got so carried away with her own projects that she didn't glance at the clock until she realised her eyelids were drooping and dawn was creeping up over the quiet trees of Fey Woods. But now and again their paths did cross, and it was on a day towards the end of August, a day when Juliet thought she had detected the first faint smell of autumn on the summer breeze, that she wandered downstairs to see if they could spare some milk.

'Why don't you join us for a coffee, Juliet?' said her aunt, smiling. 'We hardly see you these days, you're barely even up at the house for meals.'

'I know, it's been manic. I thought some of the newspaper work might dry up when I left London, but it's been busier than ever. Mind you, that's mostly down to politicians doing stupid things, not my moving away.'

'I enjoy your cartoons very much,' said Léo, putting a creamy, brimming mug of coffee in front of her, then turning to take a tray of golden, flaky pastries out of the oven. 'How you see right to the very centre of these people, what they have done, what they think, so... *concis*. Is the English word "succinct"? It is a good word.'

'Thank you,' said Juliet, accepting a plate laden with the pastries. 'It does get to be something of a knack over time, but most of these people are much more transparent than they believe themselves to be. Mmm, these are delicious, what's in them?'

'It's a new recipe we're trying for the school,' answered Sylvia. 'They're classic croissant pastry, but the paste filling is a mix of roasted hazelnuts, honey and thyme.'

'Well, they're incredible,' declared Juliet, hoping her chin wasn't bristling with crumbs. 'Can I take a few with me to London tomorrow? I think I'm going to need some comfort food.'

'I didn't know you were going,' said Sylvia. 'Is it for work?'

'Yes, my editor wants me to meet a couple of people to talk about a project we've got in mind. I don't see why it can't be done over Zoom, but she's always preferred a face-to-face meeting to a computer screen. Frankie was going to come with me, but of course she's chosen this week to have a bloody big bout of gastroenteritis.'

'I'm not sure she had much choice in the matter, darling.' Sylvia's words were reproachful, but her eyes glittered with amusement. 'Why was she going with you? She won't usually stray from the county now she's met her mysterious boyfriend. I wonder if he has family locally? I can't help being curious.'

Juliet licked her finger and started dabbing up the crumbs on her plate. She chewed her lip.

'Well, the thing is...' She glanced at Léo, sipping his coffee. 'Look, Frankie was coming as something of a bodyguard. I'm scared of running into Toby, all right?' The words came out in a rush, and she quickly reached for another pastry to busy herself with.

'Toby?' said Léo.

Juliet didn't answer, the familiar feelings of shame and anxiety coursing through her. She wanted Léo to know, but she didn't want to have to explain. Sylvia came to her rescue.

'He was an unpleasant man that Juliet was unlucky enough to get involved with,' she said, taking a croissant herself. 'Managed to hide his real nature quite well, as I understand it, but clever Juliet realised and got herself out before he could do too much damage. He is persistent though, like a nasty rash, and it makes sense to have a buffer when possible – they work in similar industries, see. Do you want me to come, darling?'

Juliet smiled gratefully at her aunt and her elegant explanation. Whenever she tried to talk about Toby herself, she always ended up making excuses for him, not thinking people would believe how badly he had treated her, or that they would blame her for staying with him as long as she did.

'No, Sylvia, I wouldn't dream of it. The last thing you need is a long day in London. I'll be fine, and if I do run into him, I'll deal with it.'

'I'll come with you, if you like?'

The two women turned to Léo in surprise.

'You?' said Juliet. 'Oh, well, that's very kind of you, but I couldn't possibly impose on you—'

He waved her words away.

'*Non*, it would not be any imposition at all. I am always glad to go to London and very happy to be your buffer to this unpleasant Toby. But only if you would like me to? I'm sure you are more than able to manage him alone, but it is always nicer, no? To have an ally?'

Juliet hesitated, but Sylvia spoke up.

'He's right. Take him with you, you'll feel much better.'

'Okay. Thank you, Léo, I'd be glad if you came.'

'Good, then it is arranged. And, if you don't mind, I will think of somewhere we can have lunch?'

Juliet laughed. Somehow, what she had seen before as Léo's bossiness was starting to feel quite comforting.

'Why not?'

The train journey to London wasn't long, just over an hour, and Juliet found that it went by in a flash. Now that she had relaxed in Léo's company, she found him funny and interesting, with his stories about life in Paris and his passion for cooking. Rather than overbearing, he was charismatic, but there was true character there as well, not just a charming, glamorous shell with nothing beneath, as there had been with Toby. *Toby*. How she hoped not to see him, but her editor's office was in the same development where he worked, and she wouldn't be surprised if he had heard on the grapevine that she would be in town. Every time she thought about him, her stomach lurched, and she found herself tugging at her hair or clothes nervously, potential conversations running through her head.

However, they reached the office without incident.

'My meeting will probably be two hours, are you going to be all right?'

'I will be fine, I'm in London. Plenty to do, don't worry about me. I will see you back here at one and we will go to lunch.'

She nodded.

'Great, see you later.'

The meeting was one that Juliet had been looking forward to; finally, she was getting the opportunity to discuss her idea for a children's book with the editors in another department of the media group which owned the paper she worked for, and when she emerged just over two hours later, it was with a smile on her face. Léo was sitting in the enormous glass and marble atrium of the building and rose when she emerged from the lift.

'It went well?'

'Very well, I can hardly believe it.'

'Wonderful! Come, tell me about it over lunch, I think I have found the perfect spot.'

Juliet was about to ask where they were going, when the voice she had so dreaded hearing snapped across the hard, shiny space.

'Juliet.'

She dragged her eyes around to look at Toby as he strode towards her, the heels of his polished black shoes clicking sharply on the floor. She felt herself shrinking inside as he got closer, and then a sense of panic began to rise. *What to do?* It was too late to get away. *What to say?* Her mind was empty. And then she felt Léo's hand on her shoulder. She jumped, then leant into him and looked Toby squarely in the face.

'What are you doing here?' he rapped out. 'I thought you'd left London. You might have told me you were in the city. That was very hurtful of you, Lettie, you know I would like to see you.'

Her first instinct was to apologise; he always made her feel like she was in the wrong. And she might have done, unable to stop herself, had it not been for one thing: he had called her 'Lettie', which she had always hated and he knew she hated – she had told him many times. But he had always insisted, saying that *he* preferred it, it was softer, and anyway, didn't she *want* to please him, and to have a secret, special pet name? Hearing it again provoked a cold rage in her, and she drew herself up, shaking off her fear and guilt.

'I'm here for work, not to make social calls. And now

Monsieur Brodeur and I have a lunch appointment to discuss another project.'

'And that's *for work* as well, I suppose,' sneered Toby, looking pointedly at Léo's hand on Juliet's shoulder. Léo did not remove it.

'It's time we left,' Léo said. 'Lunchtime is busy there, and it would be a shame to have to wait long.'

'And where is this "working lunch"?' said Toby. 'You should know that Lettie does get uncomfortable anywhere too smart. Remember that time you spilt your champagne everywhere in Le Gavroche because you were so terrified of the waiter?'

Juliet remembered it well, but it had not been the waiter who had unnerved her; he had been kind and, she knew, slightly pitying. No, it had been Toby's cruel and humiliating attitude that had caused her to fumble with her drink. He had told the waiter in ringing tones that she only got confused looking at menus in French, and he would order for her, so they weren't waiting until midnight while she figured out what she wanted. Toby had then demanded that she thank him for his thoughtfulness, and sulked for the rest of the meal because she hadn't been grateful enough. But Juliet couldn't say any of that now. Instead, she bit her lip, and wished the whole encounter could be over.

'We're going to Cornucopia. It is quite new, in Soho.'

Toby barked out a derisive laugh.

'Oh yes, I know of it. And you don't want to wait long? You do know the waiting list is about six months, not fifteen minutes, don't you?'

Juliet wanted to die on the spot, but Léo spoke up calmly.

'Indeed, about six months for most people. But as luck would have it, the proprietor is a friend of mine and will make a table available, *pas de probleme.*'

Toby's face was instantly suffused with a deep, blotchy red.

Recognising this a harbinger of anger and spite and realising that she didn't have to be on the receiving end of it anymore, Juliet decided it was time to go. She muttered a goodbye and turned to leave before anything more could be said. She and Léo put a couple of hundred yards between them and the apoplectic Toby before she burst out in slightly hysterical laughter.

'I have to say, that was brilliant.'

Léo shrugged, grinning.

'It was simply the truth.'

'Ah, but that makes it even better. I suppose I ought to feel sorry for him, but I don't.'

'No, don't waste your pity on a man like that,' said Léo, hailing a taxi. 'Although he is surely unhappy and deserves pity. Instead, let me tell you about this wonderful – and very difficult to get into – restaurant.'

When they arrived, Juliet did a double take as she got out of the taxi. Léo had explained that the place was opulent, but nothing could have prepared her for the glorious façade. The restaurant was quite small, but the front was spilling over with fruit, vegetables, corn sheafs and leaves. She would have loved to have photographed every inch but settled for a few snaps on her phone. The door was barely visible through this tumbling waterfall of plenty, but Léo led her in confidently. He was immediately greeted with great delight by a tall man, also French, who had a thick thatch of russet hair, greenish-brown eyes and a booming voice. He and Léo conversed briefly in French, of which Juliet couldn't understand a word, then they turned to her.

'This is Emile, the owner of this fabulous place,' said Léo. 'And this is Juliet.'

She went to shake hands but was immediately enveloped in an embrace.

'Juliet, it is my pleasure to welcome you here to Cornucopia. I have the best table ready for you and I hope you will enjoy whatever you please from the menu. Come!'

They were led to a corner table, from which they could see the whole room and take in not only the décor, which continued the theme of arcadian splendour from outside, but also the glamorous diners who she would certainly take pleasure from observing. Her desire to be at the heart of things had diminished and she was happy to just be with Léo at their table, watching the glitterati do their thing. There was also a small voice at the back of her head telling her that having a good view of the room could be useful if Toby suddenly turned up; she wouldn't have put it past him to come barging in and demand a table.

Emile came over to hand them menus. They were in French, but had an English translation underneath, Juliet saw with relief. She remembered what Toby had brought up earlier and felt a rush of panic, her eyes darting across the different options, trying to decide quickly, then she felt a hand on her arm and looked up at Léo, who was smiling at her gently.

'Take your time. There is no rush in choosing. This is lunch, the best meal of the day, and should be enjoyed at leisure.'

He returned to studying his own menu, and Juliet, with a new sense of calm, went back to hers, reading it carefully in order to decide between all the mouth-watering dishes on offer. Emile seemed to intuit when they had decided and came over to take their order and suggest some wine.

'And as we are celebrating Juliet's good news, I think we should start with some champagne as well,' added Léo.

The champagne arrived, followed by their first course – both had chosen the same marvellously garlicky prawn dish, flecked with green parsley and bright red chilli – along with a brimming bread basket. As Léo offered it, Juliet hesitated. She dearly wanted a hunk of the seeded sourdough, but this had always been a test with Toby and the only way to pass it was to wave the bread away in bored disgust. As if one would *dream* of eating carbs! But now, she took some. She tried to tell herself she didn't care if Léo minded, but the truth was that she couldn't help but feel drawn to him, and she wanted him to find her attractive. Even as she broke off some of the bread to eat, conflicting thoughts coursed through her mind: he would never fancy her anyway – he was probably into sexy, dishevelled French women, like the one she had caught a glance of in the photos, not hard-edged Brits like herself, who preferred squashing their emotions to be as tiny as possible, rather than expressing them flamboyantly. Toby had been right about one thing: no one but him would be patient enough to put up with her, and generous enough to try to help her be a better person.

It had only taken seconds for all of this to flash through her mind, but when she drew her eyes up to look at Léo, terrified of finding a look of horror on his face, she saw that he had finished his first piece of bread, soaking up some garlicky juices with the last of it, and was reaching for another, seemingly unaware of her turbulence, shame and carb habit.

'Do you like the food?' he asked her, temporarily abandoning his bread in order to seize a prawn and start peeling off its shell.

She felt like laughing. All this anguish over a piece of bread. Dipping some into the oil, she popped it into her mouth and revelled in the explosion of flavours.

'I love it,' she said, allowing a grin to break out across her face. 'Absolutely delicious, and this bread is divine.'

'My recipe,' said Léo, reaching for a third piece. 'I will show you how to make it when we return to Feywood. No good for shaping into little owls, I'm afraid, but worth it anyway.'

As the meal went on, Juliet relaxed more and more. The conversation ranged from art to politics to food, of course, but with barely a pause until when the pudding arrived, Léo said:

'Juliet, I want you to know some more about the *femme mariée* you mentioned.'

Reddening, Juliet felt some of her old defensiveness return in order to conceal the embarrassment she felt about poking into his private life.

'Oh, don't feel you have to explain yourself to me...'

'I do not feel this, but rather that I would like you to know.'

She shrugged, on the one hand desperate to understand what had happened, on the other terrified that he would tell her how much in love he was with the woman, and that it was only a matter of time until they were together.

'I did not know at first that she was married, she kept this a secret. When I found out, it was a very confusing time, but I ended things with her, with Veronique, and I apologised to her husband. The marriage, it broke down anyway, and she has made some accusations about me in the press. They are all untrue, but I decided to leave France for a while, to hide away, I suppose. To be where I was not questioned about these painful things and to try and put some space between us. Please, think carefully about what you have read. I would rather you asked me than believed it.'

The first silence of the afternoon stretched out between them, and then Juliet spoke.

'Thank you, Léo. I haven't really read anything – my French is *trop mal* to understand – but I had seen enough to... to...'

'To question my integrity?'

She shrugged again.

'You were right to do so. All of us make mistakes, but it is how we deal with those that matters, I think. My conscience, it bothers me, but I have done everything I can now.'

She nodded, then smiled.

'Well then, maybe we should drink to doing our best.'

Despite her inclination to mistrust others, particularly men, Juliet looked across the table at Léo's open, worried face and started to wonder if this might be a man she could rely on.

SIXTEEN

As they enjoyed a coffee after the meal, Emile came to join them and regale them with scurrilous and thoroughly indiscreet stories about the celebrities who had visited his restaurants over the years. The room emptied around them, and when they finally emerged, blinking, into the street, the light was fading. Juliet looked at the time and gasped.

'Léo! I didn't realise how long we'd been in there. We've missed our train by an hour.'

He laughed.

'Ah well, poor horrified Juliet, what matter? We can find alternatives. Would you have made that lunch any shorter?'

'Well, no, of course not, but how can it possibly have got so late?'

'You are not used to forgetting to watch your clock.'

It was true. Even at some of the wildest parties she had been to, if she wanted or needed to leave by a certain time, Juliet kept control of things and made sure she was out on the dot, discarding a string of disappointed friends in her wake. Never before had she simply *forgotten* to check the time, especially with a train to catch.

'That's true, but we can still sort it out, there must be other trains we can catch.' She took out her phone and started tapping away. 'Oh yes, there are several. If we hurry, there's one that will get us back to Feywood by about eight. What do you think?'

'What I think is that we are having such a pleasant day, and that we are still celebrating your good news. Why not prolong it, rather than rush for a specific train?'

'Oh! I suppose we could, but...' She tapped away some more. 'The trains get infrequent later and then it's harder to get home from the station.'

'Juliet, I am suggesting that we don't go back to Feywood tonight.'

She looked up at him in surprise.

'Not go back?'

'*Non*. Why do we not stay here and enjoy London? We could find an hotel, it will be an adventure.'

Juliet bit her lip. Because the plan had been to go back... yet the idea of staying in London for the night, with Léo, felt somehow irresistible. Her stomach fluttered with a combination of anticipation and nerves. *A hotel?*

'All right,' she said slowly. 'Let's stay.'

'*Super*! What would you like to do, now we are not running for a train? A walk, perhaps, it's a lovely afternoon?'

And then what? Still not ready to confront the reality of this hotel, Juliet stalled, for a moment considering whether to forget the whole thing and bolt for the station. But looking at Léo standing patiently smiling at her, she knew that here was another opportunity to dip her toe in the waters of courage, to continuing probing to find out if Léo's benevolent exterior concealed a monster beneath. God knew Toby had seemed amiable enough to begin with, but it had all been a façade to lure her in.

'Yes, a walk would be nice. And then... there is an art deco cinema I would like to visit in Kensington. They normally have a showing of a classic film at six thirty, and you can order food, although I'm not sure I'll ever be hungry again.'

'Wonderful idea! We can walk through Hyde Park and be rewarded for our exercise with dinner, wine and a movie. Do we need to book?'

Juliet's face broke into a real smile, the little muscles that had been twitching with worry finally relaxing.

'You're not the only one with contacts, Léo. Let me make a quick phone call.'

The walk took just under an hour, and it was one of the most pleasant Juliet had ever spent in London. No noisy crowds, no banging music, no demands to be cutting and witty, just a stroll through a beautiful park with Léo as her companion, a companion who made her laugh, pointed out things he thought she might enjoy seeing and listened attentively as she spoke.

'Did you walk here often, when you lived in London?'

'You know, I don't think I walked through once, although I did come to a few shows at the Serpentine Gallery – including one of my father's.'

'And how was that?'

Juliet drew breath to give her normal answer – that it had been wonderful, she had enjoyed every second, she was so proud of Rousseau – then paused. Léo was asking for real – how was it? – and he wanted a real answer.

'I like my father's art, although I don't always understand it, and I am very proud of him, but I find the exhibitions difficult sometimes, and that one in particular was a horrible evening. We were surrounded, as usual, by a throng of Dad's admirers – critics and fans. Some of them are great – genuinely interested in him and his process – but so many are just gushing, pretentious sycophants with less interest in art and more in having their photo taken next to some art or, even better, an artist. And failing that, an artist's daughter.' She paused and glanced up at Léo, wondering if he would challenge her, suggest her criticism was due to her own insecurities, but he merely nodded, his eyes kind, and she continued. 'My mother was on her finest form, telling anyone who asked me about myself not to bother, as I was the Cinderella of the family talent with my little cartoons, and Toby was busy sucking up to her and telling me oh-so-sympathetically that we should probably go soon, as it must be *too* upsetting for me to be highlighted as the mere shadow to the rest of my family's talent.'

'It sounds miserable.'

'It was, but the unhappier I felt, the more I was sure it was my own fault, so I stuck it out until the end, then ended up drinking too much and giving Toby another reason to tell me off. No wonder I was known as an *enfant terrible*,' she said, giving Léo a wry grin. 'I felt bloody terrible and just like a child, however sophisticated I may have seemed.'

'You are smiling about it now, which means you are healing. Do you think that coming back to live at Feywood has helped?'

Juliet shrugged.

'Maybe. I don't know yet. It's exorcised some ghosts and raised a few more. I'm glad to be out of Toby's immediate reach, I'm rethinking my career without anyone interfering and I'm experiencing home and the rest of the family without Mum being there. Well, mostly – I can still hear her voice sometimes.'

'Ah, isn't that the truth? The voices of those behind us in our lives still echo loudly at times, don't they?' Juliet was just going to ask him what voices he still heard, when they came to a junction. 'Which way from here?'

'We need to go right, up past the Albert Hall and then it's about five minutes more from there. I can't believe we've been walking for almost an hour.'

'Indeed. The time seems to pass very quickly with you.'

. . .

They arrived in good time for the film which was, to Léo's delight, the classic French movie *Plein Soleil*.

'Have you seen it, Juliet?'

'No, what's it about?'

'It is the story of *The Talented Mr Ripley* – you know that one?'

'Yes! It's a favourite of mine.'

'*Bon*, then I hope you will like this French version. Do we need more champagne to enjoy with it?'

'Maybe later, but for now I could murder a cup of tea.'

He laughed.

'Tea over champagne, of course, and I will join you.'

They found their seats, which had been reserved for them by Juliet's friend, and settled down to enjoy the film. Juliet had been prepared to concentrate carefully, and hoped that later she would be able to draw some sage comparisons between this and the English language version of the story she had enjoyed, but just a few minutes in, Léo's rough, warm hand closed gently over hers where it lay on the armrest, and she lost at least the next twenty minutes ricocheting between excitement from the electric sparks that were shooting randomly from his touch all over her body and panic about whether her hand felt sweaty and he was now only being polite not pulling away. As soon as she remembered to breathe and relax, and managed to start focusing on the film again, he started rubbing his thumb along her little finger, and the confusing fireworks were set off all over again. When the film finished, she wasn't sure if an eternity or a split second had passed. She busied herself collecting up her bag and pretending to look for a lip balm, but eventually had to meet Léo's eyes. He smiled gently at her.

'Did you enjoy the film?'

'Er, yes, yes, very much.'

'Good. What would you like to do now, about spending the night?'

'I... I don't know. I'm not sure... you know...'

She tailed off, furious with herself. Why couldn't she just pull out sassy old Juliet, who would have led the way to the swankiest hotel in town, taken charge, seemed confident, no matter how she felt inside? *Because*, whispered a small voice, *because you have to be honest with Léo, and you know it.*

'I do know. And that's all good. I have a suggestion.' She nodded. 'We have to sleep, yes, and it is late now to go back to Feywood. We go to an hotel, we sleep, we return in the morning, nothing more – except of course more tea...'

She looked to see if he was teasing her, and he was, but kindly.

'Yes, I'd like that. Especially the tea.'

They both laughed and the awkwardness melted away.

'Come then,' said Léo, 'I think I know a good place near here.'

They walked for a short time before arriving at a small, but utterly exquisite hotel. It would have been easy to walk past if you weren't looking for it, thought Juliet, with its frosted glass door and discreet sign whispering, rather than announcing, its name: Pulchra. Inside was a luxuriously renovated Victorian townhouse with gleaming marble floors, deep velvet armchairs and the enveloping scent of orange blossom. An immaculately dressed young man stood behind the polished wood reception desk and greeted them politely.

'Good evening, madam, sir. How may I help you?'

'Unfortunately, we have missed our last train and were hoping for a room for just tonight?' said Léo.

'Of course. I have our Amabilia Suite available, if that would be suitable, consisting of a bedroom, sitting room and spa bathroom as well as a small, private roof terrace where you may like to take a cocktail, or breakfast in the morning?'

'That sounds ideal,' said Léo, handing the man his credit card.

'Léo!' hissed Juliet, as the card details were entered into the computer. 'How much does a hotel room like that cost? You must let me give you half.'

'*Non*, not this time. It was I who insisted we stay in London. You can insist next time, if you like.'

The receptionist was out from behind the desk before Juliet had a chance to argue, handing them a key card and directing them towards the lift, which rose three floors before depositing them outside a large wooden door. Léo swiped the card, and they went inside.

'What an absolutely gorgeous room,' said Juliet, forgetting all the awkwardness she had endured over the past hour. 'And look at the view. You can see all along the Thames – oh, it's beautiful.'

'This furniture is worthy of a French chateau,' said Léo, running his hand along the back of a mahogany chaise longue. 'And the mini bar is more maxi – *regarde*.'

He opened a painted cabinet to reveal a dazzling array of miniature glass bottles as well as a further door which turned out to be a tiny built-in fridge, stuffed with mixers, white and rosé wine and champagne.

'Shame I don't feel like another drink,' said Juliet, 'but look at the choice of tea. There must be twenty different types. This is amazing, Léo. How did you know about it?'

He shrugged.

'Just one of those things. Come, let's see what else there is.'

The bedroom was as beautiful as the sitting room, with a huge bed, plump with pillows and another window offering not just the same spectacular view but access to a large roof terrace, furnished with table and chairs. A door led off the bedroom, and when Juliet pushed it open, dusky lighting gently rose to reveal the bathroom.

'Oh wow, they weren't kidding when they said it was a spa. Look at it, Léo! This is a waterfall shower – you could fit about five people in it. And the bath as well! And look at all the gorgeous products, there's everything we could possibly need.'

Léo grinned.

'I think a fancy bathroom might be more your thing than mine, so I'm going to leave you to enjoy it.'

Although she felt a stab of disappointment at his departure, Juliet didn't need telling twice. Within seconds of the door closing, she had pulled off her clothes and was standing under the hot stream of water in the shower, pressing a different button every couple of minutes to change the force or pattern of the deluge. It had been a wonderful day, but a lot had happened, and the peaceful drenching was blissful. Eventually, feeling revived, she emerged and wrapped a bath sheet around herself, then started investigating the tub. She started the water running and poured in a luxurious amount of a foaming bath oil she had seen rave reviews for in magazines but couldn't bring herself to pay forty-five pounds for. The scent of patchouli and bergamot filled the air and she breathed deeply. She was about to climb in when she noticed a small sign above some white cotton bags, saying 'Laundry'. Closer investigation revealed that she could bag up her clothing, alert Reception and have it washed and pressed by morning: ideal. She decided to take the bags and a robe out to Léo to see if he wanted to avail himself of the service as well and found him stretched out on the sofa listening to quiet music flooding the room from hidden speakers.

'Hi, just leaving this here in case you want your clothes washed.'

'Ah, *merci*, I will do that. I will call down. I must say, this sofa is very comfortable, I shall spend a pleasant night here.'

'You don't have to do that.'

'Of course, I do not mind – that was the understanding, *non?*'

'I didn't mean, well... I mean, you know, you don't have to

sleep out here. That bed is massive, it would be silly to waste half of it. Obviously, do whatever you want. But I don't mind.'

Ugh, so awkward.

'Then I shall gladly share, thank you.'

'Great! I mean, fine, whatever works. Oh look, magazines! I might take one for the bath.'

Grabbing a copy of *Vogue*, Juliet scuttled gratefully back to the bathroom, wishing she could get her head in order around Léo. It was infuriating how much he unsettled her, yet how calm and accepting he was of her obvious fluster.

When she emerged some forty-five minutes later, Juliet felt she had regained some composure. Léo was still in the living room but soon showered and joined her in the bedroom.

'I have had a wonderful day getting to know you, Juliet. I feel as if we could stay in this hotel room forever.'

'I know. London has been very different with you. But I have to say – something I never thought I *would* say – I am looking forward to going home. And Feywood is feeling like home for the first time in a long time.' She yawned lavishly. 'I'm sorry, I'm dropping off.'

'Not at all. Good night, lovely Juliet.'

* * *

Léo dropped a kiss on Juliet's forehead and watched as her eyes closed and her face relaxed. The softening effects of sleep changed her beauty, blurred the edges somewhat and gave him a glimpse of the child she had once been. All signs of wariness left her, and he wished that the same was true for when she was awake. How he longed for her to share all her vulnerability with him, to allow him to smooth away the hurt of the past. His anger flared at the thought of the pain that her mother and Toby had put her through, and he had to relax the fists that had involuntarily clenched. He was suddenly gripped by the fear that he would only become another bad interlude. *Maybe I'll also hurt her, but how could I, when I feel such a protective instinct? Maybe that will save her – and me?* He hoped so. Neither of them needed any more anguish in their lives.

SEVENTEEN

When she awoke the next morning to the stunning room and Léo's sleeping form on the bed beside her, Juliet couldn't contain a shiver of pleasure. He had honoured her wishes without any attempt to persuade her otherwise, either through flattery, cajoling or irritated half-threats, and she felt that was one of the most heroically romantic things anyone had ever done for her. She raised a sardonic eyebrow as she wondered if maybe she had set the bar a bit low, but then remembered the overblown gestures she had been subjected to in the past from Toby. Flowers, a trip to Paris, even a hot air balloon ride – but never the gift of respect. All his offerings had come with a hefty price tag, and she had been the one to pay it. For the second time in recent months, she felt a sense of homecoming – this time to a person rather than a location. Still wrapped in her cosy bathrobe, she wriggled across the bed and snuggled into Léo's chest, resting her head and feeling the rise and fall of his body as he breathed. He lifted his arm and closed it around her shoulders, pulling her closer into him.

'*Bonjour, ma chérie.*'

'*Bonjour*. Did you sleep well?'

'I did, beautifully. And you?'

'Very well. I'm hungry now, though.'

'As am I.' He twisted his arm around to look at his watch. 'It is quite early still; shall we call down for breakfast and enjoy it on the roof terrace?'

Juliet agreed to this, and soon they were sitting in the morning sunshine enjoying coffee, pastries, yoghurt and fruit and grinning at each other.

'I'd better turn my phone on,' said Juliet. 'I messaged Martha last night to let her know we were staying in London, but then I thought I'd better try to preserve the battery. Mind you, this amazing hotel would probably have lent me a charger.'

'I'm sure, but it is also nice to be free of these things once in a while, *non*?'

Nodding her agreement, Juliet lit up her phone, then grimaced at the flurry of beeps.

'Look, there's Martha, oh, and bloody Frankie thinking she's Britain's next top comic with all her unfunny messages about us staying over. God, I forgot we'd have to run that gauntlet when we get back.'

'Do you prefer to keep our friendship a secret?'

'No, no, I don't want to, but I don't want them asking loads of questions and going on about it. What am I supposed to say?'

Léo shrugged.

'The French do not stumble over these things as you do. We are happy to announce an affair, and people are often happy to hear it.'

'An affair? Is that what this is?'

Léo looked confused.

'*Oui* – I hope so? A love affair – *une histoire d'amour*.'

'Oh!' Juliet flushed. 'Um, well... *histoire* is story, isn't it?'

'Yes, that's right. Is affair the wrong word?'

'Well, in English, it usually means something casual or illicit, like...'

She stopped abruptly, and Léo continued.

'Like the one you saw in the magazine? Ah. No, I hope this is something very different – a story, yes, and not a *cinq à sept*, which is how we describe your "affair" – a relationship that happens between five and seven p.m.'

Juliet burst out laughing.

'Is that really what it's called in French? That's so funny. I suppose it tells it like it is.'

'Well, quite. But all this talk of love and affairs and stories has made me realise something very important.'

'What's that?'

'*Une histoire d'amour* this may be, but I have not yet kissed you, and that is definitely not very French.'

'Not very English either,' said Juliet, smiling at him.

'Perhaps not.'

Léo leant forward in his chair and slid one hand into Juliet's hair; the other took her hand gently. She could feel her pulse pounding and, as she gazed into his eyes, realised that never in her life had she wanted anything more than to be kissed, now, by Léo. She leant forward fractionally, without meaning to, and he responded instantly, bringing his lips to meet hers. Their touch carried infinite tenderness, but also sent a shockwave throughout Juliet's body and the combination of sensations was dizzying and compelling. Her arms sprang up to wind around his neck, and she yearned to feel his body against hers; impossible sitting in chairs, as they were. She pulled away a fraction.

'When do we have to check out?'

'Not for another three hours yet.' A teasing tone came into Léo's voice. 'Aren't you in a hurry to get back to Feywood?'

Juliet grinned at him.

'Not anymore.'

She stood up and kissed him again, now pressing her body against his, feeling the shared heat and urgency. Together they stumbled back towards the bedroom, the view and the breakfast forgotten.

By the time they drifted back through the front gate of Feywood, it was three o'clock and the place seemed deserted. But if there had been a welcoming party of her entire family ready to quiz and josh her about her night in London with Léo, she wouldn't have cared; in fact, she was more likely to start volunteering information to any passing neighbour, she felt so buoyant. They started walking up the drive, hand in hand, when Léo suddenly stopped.

'What was that?'

'What?'

'Listen.' He pressed a finger to his lips and there came the sound of a pathetic, whining cry.

'It sounds like an animal or something that's been hurt,' said Juliet. 'It came from back here.'

They turned back towards the road, stopping again to listen for the noise, then Léo darted into the hedges next to the road, agile for such a large man. Juliet peered through but couldn't see anything, just heard him speaking gently and cajolingly to whatever he had found. In a minute or two, he emerged, his jumper wrapped around a small form that he cradled in his hands.

'What is it?' asked Juliet.

He pulled down the jumper to show her.

'Oh, it's a puppy! God, Léo, it's tiny, what on earth was it doing there?'

She looked up to see his normally friendly face looking grim.

'Abandoned. It was not alone – the mother and another puppy are there also, but I'm afraid they have not survived. It was obvious that the mother had been mistreated.'

Tears sprang to Juliet's eyes.

'How awful. Let's get it up to the house and call the vet.'

They dashed inside, smack into Frankie, who was coming down the stairs. She drew breath, doubtless to start a barrage of fun, when she saw their faces.

'What's happened? I thought you two would be sickeningly lovey-dovey, but you just look sick.'

'Frankie, can you call the vet? We've found a puppy.'

She took one look at the pathetic bundle and whipped out her phone.

'I'll call now and get him up to the house. Take it into the kitchen, it's warmest in there.'

In the space of a few minutes, the sleepy teatime house was alive with action. All the Carlisles were ardent animal lovers, and Juliet was touched by their collective determination to save the little dog. By the time the vet, Henry, had arrived there were six people clustered around, plus a concerned-looking Moriarty, the family's own small dog. Léo was still holding the puppy, wrapped now in a soft towel that Rousseau had seized from the downstairs bathroom. Martha was warming milk in a pan and Sylvia and Frankie were hunched over a phone, frantically Googling 'how to save a new-born puppy'.

'Right, let's have a look,' said Henry, putting down his bag. He took the little bundle from Léo and placed it gently on the table, then unwrapped the towel and gave a sharp intake of breath. 'This is a very young dog, not even twenty-four hours old. There, there, poor little thing, let's see how you're doing.' After a few minutes' examination, Henry wrapped the puppy up again and turned to the assembly of concerned faces. 'Okay, so you have a little girl puppy. She's in pretty good shape, considering, but she'll need a lot of care for the next few weeks. Are you able to do that here, or should I take her with me?'

An immediate chorus of replies came back: *oh no, we'll look after her, we'll do it here.*

Henry smiled and nodded.

'All right then. I'm going to leave you with strict instructions for her care as well as some powdered puppy milk and a special whelping box for her to sleep in, with a heat lamp. She'll need feeding every three hours or so, but it looks like you'll be willing to do that in shifts, so it shouldn't be too much of a problem.'

Twenty minutes later, with the vet gone, having promised to remove the bodies of the other dogs, the family sat around the kitchen table.

'I don't mind doing the night-time feeds,' said Juliet, stroking the puppy's head tenderly with one finger. 'I'm often up working into the early hours, so it won't be a shock to the system.'

'Looks like your motherly side has been brought out recently,' said Frankie with a sly smile. 'Look out, Léo, she might get a taste for this.'

Juliet opened her mouth to tell Frankie, as usual, to shut up, but Léo was too fast for her.

'I think Juliet is a wonderfully nurturing person and that this puppy is just one of us in this room who is lucky to have her.'

She beamed at him, and he gazed back at her, while the rest of the family stared in astonishment. Even Frankie didn't have a quick reply. It was Martha who recovered herself first.

'Well, I think it's great. Good for you, Juliet. I'm willing to do anything that's needed to help – shall I write up a rota of when she needs feeding and who's going to do it? And we ought to think of a name for her.'

'I think that honour should go to Léo,' put in Rousseau. 'After all, it is he who found her.'

'*Merci*. I have been thinking about this. I wondered whether her name should reference that she was lost and orphaned, but we do not want this to be her legacy. It is more important to look forward than back in life. So then I wondered about the future – the word for this in French is *l'avenir*. That does not make much of a name, but what about Ava?'

'Perfect,' said Rousseau, and there was a murmur of assent around the table. 'Ava it is, well done, Léo. And now, I must attend to my own future and return to my work. Put me down for a feeding shift, I am best in the early morning.'

'I'd better go as well,' said Sylvia. 'I've got to get something in the oven. I can do any time, but maybe not the middle of the night.'

'And I'm going out,' said Frankie, looking at her phone. 'Is that the time? I'm going out *now*. Look, I'd love to help with Ava, but a regular shift might be asking a bit much. Maybe I could help on a more ad hoc basis. Ciao for now.'

And giving a wave, she slipped out of the room before anyone could argue. Martha also returned to her work, leaving Léo and Juliet to nurse the little scrap, while Moriarty bustled around their legs.

'I think he wishes he could help too,' said Juliet, patting his head.

'Yes, your family is very kind,' said Léo, 'even your dog. Come, let us find a comfortable place to put Ava's box, and I will make coffee. These first few hours will be the most important.'

Juliet carried the box through to the small, cosy library which got little use, as the family generally preferred gathering in the large sitting room. She switched on the heat lamp and settled herself into the sofa to wait for Léo to come in with the coffee, thinking how dramatically and unexpectedly her life had changed in just a few weeks, but how comfortable she felt with that. Maybe – just maybe – she had changed, too, and was ready to leave the past firmly behind her and look to her own future.

* * *

Léo brought in the coffee and some biscuits he had found, checked on little Ava and then joined Juliet on the sofa.

'She seems comfortable,' he said. 'We just have time to drink this before her next feed is due. She is lucky to be nursed in such lovely surroundings.'

'This is probably my favourite room in the whole house,' said Juliet, looking around her at the deep green walls, lined with mahogany bookcases. 'Nobody ever comes in here much, other than me. I loved it when I was a teenager. I used to sit at the desk to do my homework and imagine it was four hundred years ago.'

'Why did the rest of your family not like this room?'

'Martha likes more of a view – I think it makes her feel claustrophobic with its tiny window. Frankie is far too big for a small, quiet room like this. And my parents – I don't know. They liked to be on show rather than tucked away here, amongst the books. I was always glad, I thought of it as *my* room.'

'Have you ever read any of the books?'

'Some of them. There are copies of Dickens and Austen, and some hilarious housewives' compendiums from the 1920s, all about how to mend your husband's shirts and dress "daintily" to do the cleaning.'

'Advice you have taken seriously, I hope?' said Léo teasingly.

'Ha ha,' replied Juliet, sticking her tongue out at him. 'I'm just glad this is one of the few parts of the house that hasn't deteriorated too badly; it would be such a shame to lose these books.'

'Talking of books,' said Léo, peeping in at Ava for the thousandth time, 'there is something else I wanted to discuss with you.'

She dunked a biscuit in her coffee.

'What's that?'

'I told you all previously about the cookery book I am writing, and how I wanted your contributions – you said you would give me some cocktail recipes.'

Juliet laughed.

'So I did! Do you need them?'

'Well, there is no hurry for those, and I may not need them at all, as Sylvia and I have decided to expand the focus of the book from simply recipes. Now it will also include sections based around the items one can easily cultivate in a garden, and which are enjoyable to do. Not so much your potatoes and carrots, which can be hard work digging, but more herbs and edible flowers. There would also be a strong emphasis on sourcing locally produced food, with a guide on what to look for, depending on where you live. I want recipes people can adapt, depending on what is available to them – so if you live in Dorset, you can use Blue Vinney cheese; if you live in Derbyshire, you will choose Stilton.'

Juliet stroked Ava, sleeping under the heat lamp.

'That sounds like a great idea.'

'Thank you. We were also wondering if you would take the photographs for the book, and perhaps do some illustrations as well – of the flowers, maybe?'

Juliet looked up at Léo in delighted surprise.

'I would love to!'

'You are sure you're not too busy?'

'I am busy, but this sounds like a wonderful project. And...' she said with a shy smile, 'I'd love to work on it together.'

'*Bon*, then it is decided. Maybe once little Ava is thriving, we can start pulling some ideas together.'

'I'd like that. And speaking of Ava, I think I'd better go and prepare her milk.'

She was back shortly and soon cradling the puppy and speaking softly to her as she encouraged her to drink. Léo watched her, his heart full, and wondered if maybe at the end of the book he would include a section on romantic meals for two – or maybe even wedding breakfasts. Although, at this moment, he never wanted to leave the cosy room where the three of them were so content together.

EIGHTEEN

Ava went from strength to strength. She responded marvellously to the care and attention lavished on her and three weeks later, she started trying to climb out of her box. Soon she was staggering around the library, making everyone who saw her laugh with delight.

'What sort of a dog do you think she is?' Martha asked Juliet one day, as they played with her.

'I don't know. She's such a mix, isn't she? There must be some spaniel in there, given those silky, floppy ears, but her body is more like a terrier's, isn't it? I'm not sure she'd win any doggy beauty contests, but I think she's lovely.'

Juliet picked the little dog up and cuddled her, and Ava nuzzled into her neck.

'You've really bonded with her,' said Martha, smiling. 'And with Léo. It's great seeing you so happy. How's the cookery book coming along?'

'Really well. Léo has such creative ideas and is doing loads of research – I think people will want to buy it. And it's been good for Sylvia too. It's something a bit easier that she can work on when she's tired.'

'Do you think she's all right?' Tears sprang to Martha's eyes. 'I've noticed how pale she looks, and she keeps disappearing to Oxford. I've wondered if she's seeing a doctor, but I've tried to bring it up with her and she definitely doesn't want to talk about it.'

'I know, me too. I think that all we can do at the moment is quietly look after her and hope for the best.' She handed Ava to her sister for a cuddle. 'And what about you, Martha?'

'What about me?'

'Are you all right? You spend all your time working or pottering about Feywood. I just wondered if you – oh, I don't know.'

'Have much of a life? I'm all right.'

'You should ask Will out for a drink.'

Martha jumped as if her sister had slapped her.

'What! No, no, I don't, I mean, I couldn't possibly. I don't want to, that is. Look, Jools, I'm fine, I'm busy organising this memorial for Mum. Have you decided yet if you're going to do anything for it?'

Juliet set her mouth in a stubborn line.

'Not yet. I know you think I'm mean, but I just can't see what I *would* do. Mum had no time for me and certainly not for my art. What part of her memory am I supposed to honour?'

'I know you didn't get on with her, and I know she was unkind. I'm not saying you have to do something – of course you don't. But maybe if you give it some thought, you will find something that you are grateful to her for, or that holds a happy memory, and that might be a better thing for you to focus on, rather than the, well, the er...'

'The bitterness?'

Martha nodded miserably.

'Sorry, Jools, but that is what it is.'

'Yes, it is. I am bitter towards that woman.' She sighed. 'But maybe you're right. Léo would probably witter on about looking to the future and not dwelling on the past, so I suppose I could try something along those lines.'

'Well, see how you go. But you will come? I think it's going to end up being quite a big event.'

'Yes, of course I'll come. And I'll help if you need it.'

Martha smiled.

'Thank you. I've been trying to rope Frankie in, but she's hardly ever here at the moment.'

'There's a new man on the scene, isn't there? It's obvious from all the texts and secret smiles.'

'I think there must be, but I don't understand why she's being so clandestine about it. Usually, we have to meet them over breakfast about five minutes after they got together, and then just when you've learnt their name, you find a new one there.'

'That's a bit bitchy for you, Martha, even if it is true. You definitely need to ask Will out – or find someone else to fancy.' Seeing her sister reddening, Juliet moved on swiftly. 'There must be something about him she doesn't want us to know – I just hope he's not married.'

'Oh, you don't think so, do you...'

Martha broke off as the door opened and Rousseau came in.

'Ah, girls, marvellous, I was hoping you'd be here. How's darling Ava today?' He scooped the puppy up and kissed her lavishly before continuing, 'I wanted to see if you were both here for supper tomorrow night. It's a yes from everyone else – even Frankie, although we'll see if that comes to fruition. I'm inviting a special guest who I'd like you all to meet.'

'Ooh, Dad, who is it?' asked Juliet.

'I'm not telling you, and you're not to gossip about it, the three of you – although one might as well be Canute trying to hold back the tide,' he added dramatically. 'You can find out tomorrow, just make sure you're free.'

Both girls agreed, and when he had left the room, blowing

kisses to them and Ava – but mostly Ava – they turned to each other and grinned.

'Come on, then,' said Juliet, 'let the gossip begin. Who do *you* think it is?'

The next evening, everyone started gathering in the sitting room at seven o'clock. Léo and Sylvia were missing, as they had promised to cook for Rousseau's mystery guest, but the three sisters were there with Will. Ava was snuggled in a blanket on the sofa with Moriarty lying next to her, keeping a close and adoring eye. Even Frankie had turned up, positioning herself by the cocktail cabinet with a feverish glint in her eye.

'Right, what's everyone having? I have the tiniest feeling that we might need a stiffener before Dad appears with whoever-it-is. My money's on an American magnate who wants to pay over the odds for Feywood and chuck us all out so he can make it into a hotel.'

Martha's hand flew to her mouth.

'You don't really think so, do you, Frankie? Surely he wouldn't?'

Frankie poured a large measure of vodka into the cocktail shaker and shook her head solemnly.

'Well, I wouldn't be at all surprised, Martha, not at all.'

Martha turned towards Juliet, her eyes panicky.

'He won't, oh he *won't*, will he?'

'Calm down, she's only joking. You know Dad would prefer to stand here like some sort of tragic Miss Havisham as the crumbling fragments of Feywood fell around him rather than sell it to anyone. Come on, Frank, stop making trouble and start making drinks. I'll have a Tom Collins if there's any gin left.'

Soon everyone was furnished with a cocktail – even Will, who usually stuck to tea.

'You must be worried,' said Frankie. 'Do you think he's bringing in a new estate manager?'

'Oh, do shut up,' hissed Juliet. 'I heard a car outside – that must be them.'

Sure enough, the living room door soon swung open, and everyone sat up in interest, only to be disappointed when Léo and Sylvia came in.

'Why do you all look so horrified?' asked Sylvia. 'We've just about finished making supper and we've brought canapés; we thought you'd be pleased to see us.'

'Sorry, Aunt Sylvia,' said Martha, jumping up to take the large tray from her. 'We're all just a bit on edge waiting for Dad and his mystery guest.'

'But surely it is a lover?' said Léo, going over to sit next to Juliet. 'What were you all thinking?'

But nobody had a chance to reply, as the door opened again and this time it was Rousseau, hand in hand with a woman. She was of a similar age to him, with silver hair pinned up, soft waves falling around a pretty and intelligent face. She wore a flowing dress patterned with exotic birds and over this a soft velvet duster coat in deep pink, with a turquoise lining.

'Everyone, I'd like you to meet Sindhu. Darling, these are my three daughters, Martha, Juliet and Frankie; my sister, Sylvia; Léo, who is running the cooking school with her; and my estate manager, Will.'

Sindhu smiled and gave a little wave.

'Lovely to meet you all, and to see your wonderful house. Rousseau has told me a lot about Feywood and how much you all love it.'

There was a little ripple of 'hellos', followed by an awkward silence. It was Martha who found something to say.

'I can show you round later, if you like? But maybe you'd like something to drink first?'

'Yes, please. What are you all having?'

'Well, Frankie's making cocktails, but they're rather strong. We've got everything.'

'I'm going to open some champagne,' said Rousseau. 'I'll go and get it, if that's what you'd like, darling?'

She nodded shyly, and Rousseau whirled out of the room. There was another silence as everyone looked at each other, or the dogs, or the floor. Léo stood up.

'Sindhu, come and sit down, try one of our canapés and tell us how you met Rousseau. I think we are all surprised he has managed to keep you a secret: we find such things difficult around here.'

'Thank you, they smell delicious. We met through art, which probably won't surprise you, but originally about a hundred years ago when we were students. We didn't know each other well, but we still have mutual friends and one of them had a party a few months ago. And here we are.'

She popped the canapé in her mouth, and her eyes darted around the room, betraying a nervousness she didn't show in any other way.

'What sort of artist are you?' asked Martha.

'I used to be a sculptor, working mainly with marble, but in recent years I moved into making jewellery – beaded pieces but also silver. This is all mine.'

'It's lovely,' said Martha, going over to look more closely. 'Do you work with silver clay or sheet silver?'

'It depends on what I'm making,' replied Sindhu, and Martha sat down next to her to continue the discussion.

Juliet glanced around at the others, wondering what they were thinking. Will and Léo were talking earnestly about chimneys or something equally boring, so she disregarded them. Martha was now engaged in conversation with Sindhu about her jewellery as Sylvia listened in, and was as warm and welcoming as only Martha, of all the family, could be. Actually, thought Juliet, she was most like Rousseau in that respect;

although she didn't have his confidence, they shared the same open, all-embracing manner that made everyone feel at home. Her glance moved to Frankie, who was now slouching against the bookcase by the cocktail trolley tapping away at her phone. Juliet was surprised to see that, rather than revelling in this new piece of super-gossip, she instead looked cross and upset. She went over.

'Hey, Frank, you all right?'

She did not look up from the little screen.

'Frankie? What's up? You look furious.'

'Oh, it's bloody Dad. He's such an egoist, making a fuss about his *mystery guest,* then producing a girlfriend. I mean, who *cares?*'

She spat out the last word with such vitriol that Juliet took a step back.

'You obviously do.'

'And you obviously don't. Mum's only been dead a year, he didn't hang about.'

Juliet shrugged.

'I had a completely different relationship with Mum from you. Sindhu doesn't bother me in the least. And don't make the mistake of letting her bother *you.* You can't stop him being with someone, it'll only make trouble.'

'Oh, haven't *you* got all wise now you're loved up with Léo?' said Frankie sarcastically. 'Live and let live, is it, Juliet? I never thought I'd see the day *you* stopped fighting. I don't believe it for a second. Oh, sod this, I'm going out.'

She flung herself out of the room, nearly colliding with Rousseau returning with the champagne. He called after her, but the only response he received was the slamming of the front door. He looked at Juliet questioningly, but she had no intention of explaining Frankie's sudden departure.

'You've got the champagne, lovely. Shall I get some glasses?

We've all finished our cocktails, so why don't we drink to the two of you?'

They toasted the happy couple and, as everyone started chatting again, Martha came over.

'What happened with Frankie? She doesn't normally disappear so quickly when there's champagne on offer.'

Juliet glanced around to make sure they couldn't be overheard. No, Will and Léo had resumed their boring conversation and Sindhu was talking to Rousseau and Sylvia.

'She's upset that Dad's got a new girlfriend.'

'*Frankie* is?'

'I know. But she was the closest to Mum of all of us, so I suppose it makes sense. What about you? How do you feel about it?'

Martha glanced across the room.

'Look, I'm happy for him – for them. You know me, I love love, I just can't seem to find it for myself. But I am worried about the memorial service. Do you think he'll invite her?'

Juliet shrugged.

'No idea. I suppose that's up to Dad.'

'Mmm. And you? Do you mind he's seeing someone? Truthfully?'

Juliet opened her mouth to brazen it out, declare her lack of interest in the whole thing, then closed it again and paused. She looked over at Léo, who gave her a big smile, and turned back to her sister.

'Truthfully, I am fine with it for Dad. He likes to have a partner and she seems nice. But...'

She trailed off. Martha smiled at her encouragingly.

'Go on, just say it.'

'Look, the truth is that I have been feeling quite... freed. I'm not saying I'm glad Mum died, but it has been a sort of release for me. I'm not sure I'm ready for a stepmother, to be a mother's daughter again, just as I was finding out what it means to be me.

You probably think that's disgustingly self-absorbed, but that's how I feel right now.'

Martha smiled tenderly and reached for Juliet's hand.

'I think you're doing brilliantly as *just you*, and no amount of girlfriends – whether they become stepmothers or not – is going to change that. And if she *does* stick around that long, well – maybe we'll all learn a different sort of mother-daughter relationship. It won't be the same, Jools, *she* won't be the same.'

Juliet returned the squeeze and smiled.

'Thanks, you're right. And I'm getting ahead of myself, just a bit. Come on, let's get some more champagne before Dad necks it all.'

NINETEEN

'*Bon*, I think it is time we went to eat, yes?'

Everyone looked up from their conversations and nodded.

'Wonderful!' said Rousseau, taking Sindhu's hand. 'And thank you, Léo and Sylvia, for cooking for us tonight.'

They walked into the dining room, which looked lovely with an array of stunning dahlias from the garden adorning the table. Juliet found herself sitting next to Sindhu and returned the older woman's smile as they sat down.

'So, what have you been doing between first meeting Dad and now?' asked Juliet, pouring them both some water. 'If you were at art college together, that's a gap of...'

'Nearly fifty years,' said Sindhu. 'I know, it's mad, but I'm so very glad we met again. What have I been doing? Well, a lot in all that time. The potted history is that I worked as a fairly successful sculptor – not in Rousseau's league, of course – and owned a gallery and shop in Notting Hill. I never married, but I have a son – he must be a few years older than you.'

'Is he an artist as well?'

'Not by profession. He's a doctor, a GP, married with two

little daughters. They live in Oxford, and I sold up recently to be nearer to them and pursue my interest in jewellery making.'

Juliet was about to reply when the food arrived, large platters bearing pomegranate seed jewelled couscous, crispy fried tofu in a dark, sticky-looking sauce, herbed flatbreads and a spectacular salad studded with flowers.

'*Bon appetit*,' said Léo, as he put down the final dish.

'We hope you enjoy it all,' added Sylvia. 'We wanted to showcase the finest Feywood has to offer to our guests – most of this has come from the garden – and we also admit that we are trying out recipes for the book.'

Everyone agreed on how gorgeous it all looked, and Juliet reached for her phone.

'Don't anyone touch it yet, I want to take a few pictures – not proper ones of course, but to help me start collecting ideas.'

When she had finished, she sat down again.

'Sorry about that, I can't help myself sometimes, and I'm determined to do the very best I can for this book they're writing.'

'It's quite a departure for you, isn't it?' said Sindhu, helping herself to some salad. 'I must say I've always loved your cartoons; I look for them in the paper and online these days, of course. There was one of the Prime Minister at the height of that whole scandal over the tax he was – or rather, wasn't – paying that was so vicious and funny and damned accurate I nearly choked on my breakfast.'

Juliet beamed, proud at her work being so admired, but Sindhu's next words took her aback.

'I don't want to speak out of turn, but...' She paused. 'Are you thinking of moving to the country permanently? I mean, if you did, would you still be able to push on with what you're doing, would you be in the right place?' She looked abashed at her own outspokenness, but continued, 'I really am in awe of your considerable talents, it would be terrible to see them wasted.'

Wasted, indeed? thought Juliet. And what makes you think you know so much about it?

After supper, everyone drifted off to various corners of the house: Martha had a painting she wanted to work on, so wished everyone a polite good night, and Sylvia looked exhausted, so Juliet and Léo insisted she go to bed while they cleared everything up. They waved away offers of help from Will, Rousseau and Sindhu and soon found themselves alone in the large kitchen.

'More wine while we tidy?' asked Léo, holding up a half-full bottle. 'Or tea?'

'Actually,' said Juliet, pulling on some yellow rubber gloves, 'I oddly want both. Is that weird?'

'Not in the least,' said Léo, pulling out the cork, then flicking on the kettle. 'If that is what you want, then *c'est ça.*'

They packed the dishwasher and washed the larger and more delicate items and, within ten minutes, were sitting at the old, Formica-topped table with their drinks, Ava and Moriarty now installed in his cosy basket.

'I can't believe this table's still here,' said Juliet, patting it fondly. 'It's hideous, I know, but it takes me straight back to being a little girl.'

'Happy memories?' asked Léo.

'From when I was little – yes, very.'

'I am glad. And what do you make of Sindhu? She seems an interesting woman, and strong. She was telling me about her business.'

Juliet sipped her tea.

'Yes, I agree with both of those. And I'm happy for Dad.'

'But?'

She smiled at him.

'You can tell there's a but?'

'*Oui*. There is something concerning you.'

'There is. Since my mother died...' Juliet stopped and decided on wine this time. Léo waited for her to start speaking again. 'Since she died, I've felt a sense of release, that I have regained control in my life. And I mean that in the deepest sense. For years I was taking a very rigid sort of control, constructing a life and an image that didn't form a complete picture, but which *worked*. I could do it, and do it well, and I could push back against Mum at the same time. Now the control is kind of the opposite of control. Oh dear, I'm not making sense. It's just that for the first time I feel able to let go of that version of myself and try other things, even things which my mother would have approved of. I could never do that while she was alive. In a way, she had control over my rebellion, because I couldn't allow a single chink that might let her think that she had won, that she was right all along.'

Léo nodded.

'You do make sense. You no longer have to fight, and you can relax and truly be yourself. That is good. But what does this have to do with Sindhu?'

'Probably nothing. But I don't want another mother, someone else who assumes they can start directing me. There was already a hint of it at supper; she was giving her opinion on my career.'

She repeated what had been said, and Léo shrugged.

'It sounds as if she is being supportive, not controlling. As I said, a strong woman, so maybe her manner is vigorous, but she has only just met you, and as Rousseau's girlfriend, she will want to befriend you.'

'But maybe she sees herself marrying him, and is establishing her role as stepmother?'

'I am sure she is no wicked stepmother. She is also not

Lilith. And you said yourself, you have come so far, discovered much. This will help, you cannot be subsumed again, you won't let it happen, and neither will I.' Juliet nodded. 'Come, let's go to bed, it has been a long evening.'

'Yes, I'm tired. I think I'll just go to my apartment tonight, Léo, if you don't mind. I could do with some time alone.'

A flash of hurt crossed his face, but he smiled.

'Of course. I'm sure you will feel good about it all in the morning.'

Juliet sat on the edge of her bed and stared out of the window into the dark night. Thoughts and images and snatches of conversation whirled around her head, confusing her. She picked Ava up out of her basket and cuddled the sleepy puppy to her as she tried to calm her mind and make some sense out of the chaos there. When Sindhu had made those comments about her career, she had instantly, instinctively, felt that the older woman was assuming some sort of matriarchal position, that she believed she had the right to give her opinion. But Léo had all but dismissed her concerns. Why? Why hadn't he taken her seriously? Didn't he realise that she needed to defend herself, not just shrug and go with the flow? And what had he said about *him* not letting anything happen? Surely he wasn't going to try to fight her battles for her – she wasn't a helpless princess in need of protection, and she thought he had understood that. *Ugh.* She stood up suddenly, waking Ava.

'Sorry, darling, I didn't mean to make you jump. Here, you go back to bed, it's where I need to be too.'

But once she was lying there, her confusion did not wane. And then another, more worrying, thought crept in. This confusion, it felt familiar. She pulled herself up to sitting.

'It feels like Toby,' she murmured.

Surely, *surely*, she hadn't been stupid enough to do it again, fall for a man who denied her her own thoughts and feelings, then used the ensuing confusion to control her? But as quickly as the thought had come, it disappeared. No, Léo wasn't like that, she knew it deep inside. He was just trying to stop her worrying, when he was right – there was nothing to worry about. She lay down again. If Sindhu started throwing her weight around, she would stand her ground, be who *she* wanted to be. And she would enjoy Léo's support while she did it. Thus comforted, she drifted off to sleep.

The following day Juliet woke feeling more positive. She made coffee and toast and ate it alone in her apartment, watching the morning news on TV and listening to the sounds of the cookery school being opened up. She knew that there was a private class in there later – a man keen to impress his new boyfriend with his culinary skills – so Léo and Sylvia would be busy preparing that. They had agreed to get together at ten to compare notes so far for the recipe book, which gave Juliet a luxurious length of time to get her papers and example photos together and do the preparation sketches for one of the drawings she was going to propose they used.

* * *

Downstairs, Léo checked again that he had everything he needed. He liked the client who was coming that afternoon, Michael, and because of this, and the fact he had booked a block of six lessons, wanted to make the session perfect. They were making a mushroom and truffle soup, with garlic and thyme focaccia, and were going to forage for the mushrooms in Fey Wood, which he felt was a nice touch. They would also cut the thyme from the herb garden and use home-grown garlic.

'I think the private individual lessons were a good idea,' said

Sylvia, selecting the knives that would be most suitable for the work. 'I've had another enquiry from someone who wants to nail some pretty basic baking skills, so I've asked her to come along tomorrow. And we've got a hen party booked in for a few weeks' time – a celebrity bride, no less.'

'That's great,' replied Léo. 'Will there be any opportunity for publicity?'

'I'm going to find a tactful way of asking her, but judging by her Instagram, we're bound to merit a few photos and a namecheck out there to her followers, even if there isn't a magazine deal.'

'Probably better. How many followers does she have?'

Sylvia picked up her phone and tapped a few times.

'Here she is. Oh wow, three hundred and fifty thousand followers. That's crazy!'

Léo shrugged.

'That's celebrity. What is she famous for?'

'She was a model, then she did a reality show, locked in a house with other people and they had to matchmake each other. She's marrying the man she met when she was there.'

For a moment, Léo was taken aback. This was just what Veronique had done, but he couldn't bear to discuss that with Sylvia, not now. He nodded calmly, hoping his emotions didn't show on his face as they so often did.

'Well, hopefully it will be good for us. Right, I think that's everything. Juliet will be down any minute to do the book, so I'll put the coffee on.'

'Marvellous. I've got some rather scrummy-looking lemon puffs I was trying out, so we can road test those as well.'

Juliet appeared a few minutes later, and they all sat down at the kitchen island with their drinks and biscuits.

'How are you feeling this morning?' asked Léo.

'Better, thanks.' She smiled at him. 'I was probably worrying about nothing. Now I just want to get stuck into this book – and these lemon puffs! Aunt Sylvia, they look amazing.'

Léo sipped his coffee as she and Sylvia pored over the photos and drawings that Juliet had prepared. They were for the 'Drinks and Desserts' section of the book, which was more her domain than his, so he had the opportunity to sit back and watch, thinking how much she had changed – or maybe, rather, how much of herself she had revealed to him – since that first meeting in the aftermath of her birthday party. And he knew he was falling in love with this complicated, intriguing, talented woman. A ringing phone broke into his reverie.

'Oh, that's mine,' said Juliet. 'Where is it?'

'Over here,' said Léo, picking it up. 'Oh, it is Toby.'

'Oh *no*. Would you mind answering it, Léo? He'll just ring and ring if nobody does, and I don't want to speak to him ever again. I'd block the number, but he'll find another way to get through. At least this way I know it's him.'

'*Mais oui.*' He answered the call as he left the kitchen and went to sit in the little boot room. 'Hello, this is Juliet's phone?'

'Got you working as her PA now, has she?' came the sneering tones on the other end of the line. 'Put Lettie on, would you?'

'I must say, we greatly enjoyed our lunch at Cornucopia. Have you managed to get a table there yet?' Léo knew he was deliberately antagonising the man, but he couldn't help himself. Toby's superior and bored tone was surely designed to bring out the worst in people?

'No, the cognoscenti have already decided it's rather passé, all those corn sheafs. So I didn't even bother trying. Now put Lettie on, will you? Nice as it is to *parler* with you, it's her I want to speak to.'

'I'm afraid Juliet does not wish to speak to you.'

'Don't give me that nonsense. She says she doesn't, but it's just her way of thinking she's punishing me. If you don't put her on now, she'll only call me back later, so you might as well save time.'

'I'm sorry, but I don't believe that to be true. Juliet made her feelings very clear.'

'Oh yes, yes, I'm sure she did, but I think I know her *fractionally* better than you do. Just put her on.'

Léo paused for a moment. He wasn't going to give the phone to Juliet: he would respect her wishes. But what should he say to this *imbécile?* Anger was boiling inside him, longing for the satisfaction of eruption, but men like Toby thrived on such reactions.

'Hello? Hello? Bonjour? Are you still there?'

'*Oui*, but not for long. Do not call again, please.'

And with that, Léo hung up and returned to the kitchen.

'I do not think that is the last you have heard of him,' Léo started, just as the phone rang again. He tapped the green button. '*Non, merci,*' he said, and hung up. 'But I think he will start to get the message.'

'Thank you, Léo,' said Juliet, taking the phone from him. 'Now I know he's trying, I'll be careful. Surely he'll go away in the end?'

Léo could only hope so.

TWENTY

The next few days felt settled, and Léo was able to concentrate on developing recipes for the book, which he knew was coming along well. Juliet seemed more relaxed about Sindhu, who had been around more but had not offered any further career advice. Toby had called a few more times, but, to his knowledge, Juliet had simply cut off the calls and deleted texts without reading them. But his feelings of contentment were not to last.

It was a Wednesday evening when he received the email. He was working late in the kitchen, Juliet was upstairs trying out some sketches for the book and the rest of the family was at the house or, in Frankie's case, out and about who knew where. He was pleased with the progress he had made and decided to check his email while he waited for the oven-baked risotto he was trialling. Working his way through an inbox mostly clogged up with junk, he saw a message from his friend Mathias, and clicked on it, eager to hear his news. But the news was not what he expected.

Dearest Léo,

I hope this finds you well and still enjoying England. I am sorry to contact you with more news of Veronique, but I do not know if you see the French gossip magazines and I think probably not. It is only fair that you know what is being said about you, so that you can respond if you wish...

Before moving on to other matters, Mathias had provided a link to the same magazine in which Léo had previously read about Veronique's exploits in *Le Château d'Amour*. This time, there was a large photograph of her at home, sitting cross-legged on the sofa, wearing black clothes, minimal yet skilful make-up and looking extremely pale, if undeniably chic. There were a further three inset pictures. One showed Gilbert, the man she had grown close to on the television programme, looking muscly and brooding, the second was of herself looking drunk and distraught, her mascara streaking her cheeks and the third was an ambulance. The headline screamed: 'Desperate and Depressed: Suicidal Veronique Recovers to Share Her Story.' Léo took a deep breath and read on.

After finishing in first place on *Le Château d'Amour*, and leaving with not only the trophy but a new boyfriend, you might have thought that Veronique's future happiness was assured. But, shockingly, she tells us that not only was she not as joyful as she appeared, in fact she was at her lowest point.

"I was so happy to win the show, and happy with Gilbert inside the Château, but when we left and the party had finished, everything started going wrong. I felt so miserable inside. I seemed like the girl who had everything, but I had still lost my husband, my babies and, worst of all, my trust in anyone."

When asked why this trust had been eroded, she at first demurs, clearly unwilling to name names, but soon the tears rise again in her eyes and she confesses, "It is because of what happened with Léo. He made me feel...' Her voice drops to a whisper. 'He made me feel so very bad, so worthless, so expendable. I could not believe that Gilbert could be so different, and I started testing him, trying to prove he really was the wonderful man he appeared to be, a man so different from Léo."

He knew he would have to finish reading the article, but Léo put down the iPad for a moment. The unfairness of what Veronique was saying made him feel as though he was having poison poured down his throat. Tears rose in his eyes as her words sank in, and he let them fall as he steeled himself to continue reading.

She wipes away tears as she continues:

"I didn't treat Gilbert well, always asking him where he was and looking through his phone and his pockets. It is not surprising that he grew tired of this behaviour and left me. I was in despair and then – and then..."

She stumbles over her words as she speaks, clearly struggling to talk about the next terrible event that takes place. But after sipping some mineral water, she carries on bravely:

"It was then that I lost all hope and decided my life was not worth living. I remember sitting on my bed, weeping, and taking tablet after tablet... and the next thing I recall is waking up in hospital."

His face contorting with anguish, Léo clicked to read the second page of the article, which featured a large photograph of Veronique and Gilbert on the sofa, with him also clad in black and looking strained but noble and protective. The article went on:

At this point, Veronique is joined by Gilbert, who wraps his arms around her as she sobs into his shoulder. After a few moments, the tears subside, and he checks that she is able to continue. She nods.

"It was a stupid thing to do, but you must understand that I felt I had no choice, that I had burnt all my bridges. Thankfully, Gilbert found me in time, and I am fully recovered – in more ways than one."

They look deeply into each other's eyes, then share a tender kiss.

"Gilbert and I are stronger than ever. I have shaken off Léo's iron hold on me, and Gilbert and I are ready to move forward as lovers, and..."

She pauses and looks shyly at her man, who nods gently. "...and as parents. Our baby is due soon after Christmas." Their radiant smiles say it all: a happy ending at last to a long, and at times insalubrious, story. Léo Brodeur was not available for comment.

Léo laid the iPad down gently and switched off the screen. He sat for a moment, gazing at the shining utensils hanging on the kitchen wall, his mind a muddle of images and feelings that might never consolidate into coherence. It was only the sound of the oven alarm that roused him, and he went to retrieve the risotto. As he went through the motions, barely noticing the glorious garlicky smell that rose from the dish, one thought floated up above the maelstrom: Juliet. How he loved her! But *mon Dieu*, how toxic would this love end up being to her? With no bad intentions at all, he had apparently driven Veronique first to a sordid reality TV show, which then catapulted her into the arms of this dubious Gilbert who, because of him, she had been unable to trust, which ended in her attempt to take her own life. What worse havoc could he wreak on the life of Juliet? What damage had he already done, unwittingly, unintentionally? Remembering the last time he had read one of these articles, and the way he had spiralled into despair, he drew his eyes away from the half-full bottle of red wine on the counter and instead picked up his phone.

'Mathias? My friend, I'm so glad you answered. Is this a good time to talk?'

'Of course, it's good to hear from you, I miss you. You've received the email I sent?'

'Yes.'

'I'm sorry to be the one to break these things to you, but I think it's better that you know.'

'It is, it is, but Mathias, how can she say such cruel and untrue things? Do people believe them? I'm still so very angry with myself for what's happened.'

'But these things aren't your fault. You did your best, what more could you have done? You're not a mind reader.'

'I suppose not, but somehow, I feel I should have taken more care. And now I've met a wonderful woman, but I worry that she will be hurt by me as well, that – as with Veronique – I'll unintentionally cause her pain.'

'But how would you do that? I know you, you're kind and sensitive. You have always been there for me and never behaved in any way that has done me harm. Quite the opposite.'

'I'm worried that our relationship stops her from being in London, that it would be better there for her and for her career. She wasn't sure about living here at Feywood again, her family home with all its memories and ghosts. Her father has a new relationship, and this worries Juliet, but I'm afraid that I've minimised her concerns and left her open to more pain and confusion. You see, I only wanted to help, but perhaps I can't be trusted not to create a problem.'

'But Juliet is an adult. She won't stay if she doesn't want to. Is it so hard to believe that she chooses to be with you for all the right reasons?'

Léo sighed deeply.

'I don't know. I don't want to treat her as a child, that's true. I'm so anxious that I will stop her being where she should be, with someone more suited to her.'

'I don't understand. Why shouldn't that be you?'

'Maybe it is, maybe not, but she has only recently left her life in London, her friends there, an ex...'

'And what does Juliet say?'

'She says she's happy to have left, and certainly speaks poorly of the ex. I do trust her judgement, but I'm concerned that she says these things with such vehemence to make me feel more comfortable. I don't want her to think she must keep me happy.'

'I know it's hard for you after all the lies Veronique has told, but you must trust Juliet – it's the only way you will go forward. And you must trust yourself. You're my friend, not some angel of darkness.'

This made Léo laugh.

'*Non*, you are right. I will make sure it is all right, all of it.'

They spoke for a few minutes longer, before saying goodbye and arranging to speak again soon. Comforted by speaking to his friend, Léo dug a fork into the risotto and forced his mind back to the present, even though he knew that the worrying shadows still lingered.

TWENTY-ONE

As work on the recipe book and Juliet's own book gathered pace, along with regular customers at the cookery school, it was a busy but satisfying period. One afternoon, Juliet was in the kitchen at Feywood, where she had come to escape from the bustle and work in total silence. She knew that Martha would be as absorbed as ever in a portrait, Rousseau and Sindhu had gone out for the day and Frankie was barely around anymore, off as she was with the mysterious boyfriend she still refused to tell anyone about. Having achieved a pleasing amount, Juliet was standing by the kettle waiting for it to boil and contemplating a chocolate biscuit or two, while thinking how much she liked this room, even though it was badly in need of a facelift. It had last been refitted in the 1970s and had no doubt been the height of fashion then, when it replaced the 1930s boxy painted wooden cabinets that had preceded it. The dark green fitted units with textured brown laminated worktops that had been installed were rather tired, but still exuded a certain dated charm although not, thought Juliet, tugging at a drawer that always stuck, quite as appealing as smooth runners and soft close mechanisms. The kitchen would be very low on the list when it came to sorting Feywood out and who knew? Maybe it would survive long enough to come back into fashion, although they would have to hide the freestanding gas cooker from any officials, who would instantly condemn it. She was wondering how many of her London friends would mind holding their breath whilst leaning into the oven with a match in order to light it, when Sylvia came in.

'Hello, would you like a cuppa too? It's just boiling.'

Sylvia sat down heavily at the table, then leant down to stroke Moriarty's scruffy head as he came over to greet her.

'I'd love one, thank you. I came up to pinch some saffron as we've run out at the school, but it's not a bad time for me to take a break.'

Juliet dropped tea bags into two mugs and looked at her aunt with concern.

'Are you all right? You look awfully tired.'

'I *am* tired. The school is doing well, which I'm incredibly grateful for, and the book is coming on wonderfully, thanks to you and Léo, but it does all feel a bit much at times.'

'I don't want to pry, but is your health up to it all?'

Sylvia smiled.

'Thank you, darling, you know I don't really talk about it much. Yes, I'm okay, but I do get tired more quickly than I used to. I don't want to be a party pooper when everything is going so well, but I think I need a rest. And actually, I think that you and Léo could do with a break as well. We've all been working flat out.'

Juliet nodded.

'I think you're right. Léo has seemed rather... oh, I don't know, *offish* recently. Maybe a break is a good idea, but can we manage it financially?'

The truth was that Juliet was worried. She had found herself acting cautiously around Léo lately as he veered from affectionate to distracted and touchy and, try as she might to ignore it, it brought back memories of how carefully she had had to handle Toby. She wasn't fearful of Léo, or scared that he would rage at her, but the sensation of walking on eggshells was familiar, and unwelcome. Getting away from work sounded like a good idea, hopefully one that would put things back on an even keel.

'We've been very busy,' said Sylvia, sipping her tea, 'but I think Léo mentioned something earlier about a cancellation. Hold on, I'll look on our booking system.' She took out her phone and tapped away for a few seconds. 'Oh yes! We had a group in next weekend, Thursday to Monday, but they've only just cancelled which means we still receive thirty per cent of the fee. Right, I'm blocking the time out before anyone else makes a reservation, and we are all going to take some time out. A friend of mine has been asking me to visit for ages, so I'll see if she's free.'

'Good plan. And I think I have an idea that might convince Léo it's worth taking the weekend off.'

'So, this place is run by a friend of yours?'

'She's more a friend of Martha's actually – they were at school together. But I know her quite well and she was happy to make space for us this weekend. She's keen to swap notes with you.'

Juliet turned the car into a long driveway, past a sign announcing 'Halebrook Hall Hotel and Restaurant'.

'And I with her,' said Léo, peering out of the window at the rolling lawns in front of the large house. 'She has been running a restaurant mainly from her own kitchen garden for many years, has she not?'

'Yes, her father started it – on a much smaller scale, of course – then she and her sister took over about ten years ago. Now almost all the food they serve is grown by them, or if they can't quite manage that, then they source it within twenty miles. They gave over some of the house to hotel rooms and the place is always booked months in advance.' She pulled up next to a grubby Land Rover and turned off the engine. 'We're staying in the family part of the house, so it won't be quite as smart, but we'll be perfectly positioned to find out how they run things.'

Léo grinned.

'Not so smart for you, maybe, but I am still accustoming myself to your country house splendour.'

Juliet rolled her eyes.

'Oh, you know what I mean. But yes, we'll hardly be slumming it. Come on, let's go and find Adriana.'

They eventually tracked down their host in the restaurant, closed at that time of day.

'Hello, Juliet, welcome to Halebrook. And Léo, wonderful to meet you.' She hugged them both warmly. 'I'm so glad you've visited; I've heard all about the cookery school and your own garden, of course, and I'm dying to swap notes. I was also wondering about an apprenticeship scheme of some sort between us, seeing as you're so close by.'

They both smiled at the warm welcome and Adriana's enthusiasm.

'This all sounds great,' said Juliet, 'but I'm going to leave you both to it. Are your parents around? I'd love to catch up with them, then I think I'll take some photos.'

She left Léo and Adriana talking animatedly and walked back to the house contentedly. It looked like this weekend was just what she and Léo needed to relax and forget all about Sindhu and Toby and the memorial service. She hoped so anyway, because she didn't want to ask Léo why he seemed distant and moody: she was too scared of what the answer might be.

. . .

It wasn't until early evening when Léo and Juliet saw each other again, when they both went to their room to get ready for dinner.

'Have you had a good time with Adriana?' asked Juliet, slipping a grass-green dress over her head. 'She is so friendly, isn't she?'

'Very,' agreed Léo. 'She has given me so many tips and ideas – we really have to improve our waste recycling – and she wants some sort of partnership so that we can continue working together. It was a good idea of yours to come here, Juliet, but...'

He paused.

'What?' she asked.

'It was a good idea for me, but what about you? Maybe this is not the first thing you would have chosen for yourself for a weekend break?'

She frowned at him.

'I don't know what you mean. It's lovely here. I can take plenty of photos and I get time away from Feywood and the family. What's not to like?'

He shrugged.

'I just want you to do what *you* want, that is all.'

'It *is* what I want. Léo, I was trying to do something nice for you, I don't see what the problem is.'

He opened his mouth to reply but was interrupted by her phone ringing. She snatched it up, then flicked the red icon furiously and threw it down again.

'Bloody Toby!'

'Is he still ringing? I don't understand why you do not block his number.'

'Look, I don't enjoy it, all right? If I block his number, he'll find another way to call, and at least this way I know it's him, so I won't answer by mistake. It helped for a while when you picked up, but not for long.'

'He is very persistent, is he not?'

'Yes... but he's wasting his time.'

'He surely thinks there must be some possibility you will change your mind, or he would not bother?'

Juliet stared at him for a moment.

'Are you serious?'

He dropped his eyes.

'I – I don't know. I just want to be sure, Juliet, that I am not stopping you from what is best.'

'And you think *Toby* is best? For goodness' sake, Léo, you've *met* him. Do you really think he might be the best thing for me?'

Léo raised his eyes, filled now with tears, and stepped towards her.

'*Mon amour*, please, I am sorry. I just worry, worry that I might spoil things somehow.'

She stepped into his embrace and laid her head on his shoulder.

'Léo, I know that I was with Toby for a long time, but that wasn't because it was good. It was... it was... well, more complicated than that. It's hard to explain.' *Hard to explain when I don't understand it myself, and all I feel is shame for being such a fool.* 'But just know that I would not make the same mistake again, and I know I am not making it with you. I don't understand why you think I might.' *Oh, how I hope I am not making it with you.*

He lifted her chin and kissed her tenderly.

'I am sorry, *ma chérie*. I trust in your wisdom. I just want to be good enough for you.'

'Of course you are. Of *course* you are. Now let's go down to dinner and enjoy ourselves. I think we needed a break more than I realised.'

The evening was wonderful and the food exquisite. Sitting in the candlelit orangery opposite Léo, chatting nonstop about everything from how much borage is too much to whether she should approach Frankie about her recent erratic behaviour, Juliet relaxed. They were so happy together; she mustn't let her experience with Toby make her scared and defensive. No, it was time to move on, and who better to do it with than this funny, passionate, caring man?

The next morning, Léo was invited to work with the chef to discover how he planned his menus, so Juliet took the opportunity to catch up with Adriana over coffee in the magnificent, panelled library.

'You've done amazing things here at Halebrook,' she said. 'Feywood is a lot smaller, and I don't think we could manage things on quite this scale, but I'm glad we've got the cookery school – and I've even got some ideas about how we could build on it.'

'You should. These massive old houses are incredible, and a privilege to own and to live in, but my goodness they come with problems – and responsibilities. Some members of the family were hugely against us opening up at first, but everyone understands now that it was necessary, and most of us enjoy sharing the place with others. You're lucky that you have Léo – he really knows what he's doing.'

Juliet smiled.

'Yes, he does. I thought he was an arrogant know-it-all at first, but he's just really... good.'

They laughed.

'Good is good!' said Adriana, offering Juliet a plate of lavender shortbread. 'Looks like things are going well between the two of you, as well?'

'They are. I think.' Suddenly, the old insecurities came rushing to the surface again. Juliet longed to share her worries and her words came out in a torrent. 'It's just that recently he's been quite withdrawn, and I feel like I keep saying the wrong thing. He either says he's fine or that he's just worried he's not good enough for me, but at one point it even felt like he was encouraging me to go back to my old boyfriend, who was... who was...'

Adriana reached over and squeezed Juliet's hand.

'It's okay, you don't have to explain. Martha told me about Toby. She's usually so discreet, but she really hates him for the way he treated you.'

'Yes. And I let him,' said Juliet miserably.

'It's more complicated than that, I know,' replied Adriana. 'I had a friend who went through something similar. You just have to remember that *none* of it was your fault. People like that are very clever at getting other people to do what they want, and you were *not* to blame.'

Juliet smiled gratefully at Adriana's fierce expression.

'Thank you. I do know that really, but it leaves me feeling so vulnerable. If I fell for it once, maybe I'll fall for it again? I'm clearly not the best judge of these things. Maybe Léo is another master manipulator and he's gaslighting me, making me feel insecure, in order to control me. Or maybe it's something else? Maybe he thinks I'm damaged. Weak and stupid for having stayed with Toby so long. Does he want to push me away but doesn't have the guts to say it himself, so he's waiting for me to?'

'I can't think it could possibly be that. Seeing the two of you together... well, he doesn't look like a man who wants rid of you.'

'It doesn't *feel* like that, but what do I know? Or maybe he's hiding something, and he feels guilty, and *that's* why he's acting so hot and cold. Maybe he's cheating on me – oh Adriana, I hope not.'

'Jools, I'm so sorry that you're this upset. All I can say is that from the little I've seen of him, and of the two of you together, everything seems perfect. I know people can be very adept at hiding their true self, but Léo just seems so genuine. Like he wears his heart on his sleeve.'

Juliet put down her cup.

'Yes, he does. That's a good way of describing him. But something's not quite right, I know it, and I feel so confused. Then I worry that one shouldn't really feel this confused.'

'Why not? Love isn't always straightforward, but that doesn't necessarily mean that something's irreparably wrong. Why don't you just talk to him?'

The two women looked at each other and burst out laughing.

'That does seem like a remarkably sensible suggestion,' said Juliet. 'I suppose I've been too scared of what the answer would be. But it might be better than all this muddle. Oh, I don't know, maybe it would be safer to be single again.'

'I'm sure it would,' replied Adriana, raising an eyebrow, 'but that's not what you want, is it?'

Juliet shook her head and felt tears rising in her eyes.

'No, it's really, really not.'

'Then talk to him, darling, have it out. At least then you'll know.'

Juliet nodded, feeling better for having shared her worries. Yes, she would talk to him, as soon as they got back to Feywood.

But when they arrived home, the first thing they saw was an enormous bouquet of flowers, and a card with Juliet's name on the envelope.

'They're lilies,' said Juliet, her heart sinking. 'They'll be from him.'

'Do you want me to read the card?'

She sighed deeply.

'No, I'll do it. I have to keep confronting it, not hiding behind you or anyone else.' She ripped open the envelope and read the card, then threw it down on the table.

Lettie, stop torturing me and yourself. You know we belong to each other. Toby.

Léo read it, his face pinched.

'What do you want to do?' he asked.

'I'm going to put my bag away, have a cup of tea, then throw the whole lot in the compost,' said Juliet. 'And then we're both going to forget we ever saw them and remember our lovely weekend away. Okay?'

'*Bon.* I will put the kettle on.'

Juliet smiled her thanks, but it was forced. The weekend was soured, no matter how bravely she tried to push past it. Would she ever be free of Toby? she fretted, as she unpacked her bag and slowly put things away. Or would she eventually capitulate, as he seemed so sure she would, whether she wanted to or not?

TWENTY-TWO

'Are you sure there's nothing else I can do? It's so exciting.'

'Honestly, Martha, you've been brilliant already helping to get the rooms ready, and I think Léo and Sylvia have the rest of it under control. I'm surprised you even know who she is.'

'And I'm surprised that you don't! *What's in a Kiss?* is the biggest show on TV. Even if you don't watch it, Pandora James is on every magazine cover and chat show in the country.'

Juliet laughed.

'But why are you watching that rubbish, Martha? I don't get it. It's exploitative, cheap TV. I just think it's funny that someone as romantic as you are falls for all that stuff.'

'You're wrong, it's *so* romantic. Pandora and Hugh made the sweetest couple from the start and now they're getting married. I loved watching them fall in love. Oh, do watch an episode or two on catch up before she gets here. We could kidnap Frankie and make her join us, have a telly night in like we always used to.'

'Oh, all right, I suppose it could be fun. But you mustn't get upset if we take the piss.'

'Deal. I'll speak to Frankie, and we'll find a time before they arrive.'

Juliet watched as her sister floated off, phone in hand. She wondered if Frankie would agree to join them; she was hardly around these days, and her latest piece was sitting forlorn and unfinished in her studio room. But maybe Frankie knew – and cared – who Pandora James was. All Juliet knew was that the woman had won a TV dating show and was now marrying the man she had paired up with on screen. It had all happened very quickly – barely six months between meeting and marrying – and she had her doubts as to how successful the union would be. But Pandora had decided that part of her hen party was to be spent at Feywood, doing cookery classes with her friends and staying over a couple of nights.

'What on earth does she want to come here for?' demanded Frankie the following evening, as they set up the pizzas they had ordered, a couple of bottles of wine and some pouches of chocolate. Martha had somehow miraculously managed to persuade her to join them for the big viewing of *What's in a Kiss?* and Frankie seemed to be on her finest sarcastic form. 'Doesn't strike me as much fun as a hen party, although,' she added, with a sly sideways glance at Martha, 'hen parties of any description don't strike me as much fun.'

'What?' shrieked her eldest sister, taking the bait. 'I love them! The ones I've been to have been brilliant. And anyway, it's a tradition.'

'Not one I'd ever make my friends suffer,' said Frankie. 'They're totally naff. Don't you remember that awful one we went to for Tabitha Merchant?'

Juliet seized a bottle of wine and started opening it.

'God yes, it was horrendous.'

'What are you both talking about?' said Martha. 'It was beautiful – all those cupcakes they'd made in those gorgeous white lacy cases, and the photos of the bride and groom as babies.'

Frankie pretended to stick her fingers down her throat and made a loud retching noise.

'It was ghastly, M, and you know it. So smug – didn't her sister pat you on the shoulder and reassure you it would be "your turn next"? You cried.'

Martha went red.

'Well, yes, that bit wasn't very nice. But the cupcakes *were* pretty.'

'They didn't make up for the lack of booze,' said Juliet, pouring each of them a generous glass of rosé. 'Don't you remember when they asked us what we wanted to drink, and we all said "wine" and they said there wasn't any? You nearly walked out then and there, Frank.'

'Yeah, well, I would have done if I hadn't had my flask. Even you have to admit that saved the day, Martha.'

She smiled.

'Well, I suppose it *was* all a little bit too polite. But I'll defend those cupcakes forever. And I think it's nice that Pandora's coming here for her party; there's something rather touching about learning how to cook before you get married.'

Frankie gave such a loud bark of laughter it made Juliet spill her wine.

'*Touching*? Oh Martha, I do love you, but come on. She's not some little surrendered wife who wants to make a hearty home-cooked meal for her man. All *she* wants is to jump on the inexplicable bandwagon of 1950s nostalgia that seems to be sweeping this country. It'll make her Instagram grid look pretty and *HELLO! Magazine* will be all over it. Very Princess Kate. Give it a few years, and she'll be baking biscuits for the camera with her adorable family as they dab flour on each other's cute little noses. Then it'll be a family cookbook, a TV tie-in and a range of kiddie snacks in Waitrose. The whole thing is just marketing shtick – a savvy selling ploy in a flowery apron.'

And with that, she drained her glass and held it out for a refill. As she poured, Juliet glanced at Martha, who looked stricken. Poor Martha, she so longed for her romantic view of the world to be true, while Frankie refused to entertain it for even a second.

'Come on,' said Juliet, shooting Frankie a warning look. 'Let's find *What's in a Kiss?* and make a start on the pizza before it goes cold.'

They watched several episodes of the programme, including the grand finale, that evening. While Juliet had to admit that it was engrossing, she still couldn't shake off the feeling that the contestants were being exploited and manipulated. But she kept her opinions to herself, not wanting Martha to feel upset again or Frankie to go off on another rant. When the final piece of metallic confetti faded away into the end credits, she switched off the television.

'Well, now we know who's coming to stay,' she said. 'She's certainly not going to be boring.'

'I can't *wait* to meet her,' said Martha dreamily, 'even if neither of you could care less. Maybe if we manage to gel, I'll get an invitation to the wedding. I wish Hugh was coming as well, though, it would be lovely to see them together.'

'She should be the one dying to meet you,' said Frankie. 'She should be in awe of your talent, but I doubt any of them knows who you are.'

'Ooh, that's an idea,' said Martha, her eyes lighting up. 'Maybe I'll ask her if she wants me to paint their portrait. It could be a wedding present. Then I'd be almost certain to get an invitation – and it wouldn't do business any harm if I got a mention in *HELLO!* either.'

'That's more like it,' said Frankie approvingly. 'That's not a bad idea at all, actually. She can hang in your rogues' gallery with Rascally Ralph.'

'Oh, drop it, Frank,' said Juliet, concerned that Martha would feel low all over again about her unrequited feelings for one of her previous subjects. 'I don't see you doing much work recently. What *have* you been up to?'

'Nothing of any interest to you,' said Frankie airily. 'I'm sure I'm very boring. Now, if you do get invited to this wedding, M, who are you going to take as your plus one? You could pluck up the courage to ask Wet Will along?'

'If you're not careful, Frank, I'll take you,' said Martha, squaring her shoulders.

Juliet laughed.

'Now that I would love to see. Game, set and match to Martha, for once. Come on, it's late, I'm going to bed. We've got to welcome this paragon tomorrow, and if she's as gorgeous in real life as she is on screen, I for one would like a decent night's sleep first.'

The next day, there was a palpable buzz at Feywood. Although they had entertained small groups previously, this was the first time they had welcomed in a celebrity, however 'Z list', as Frankie put it. When Juliet woke up, early, the bed next to her was empty, and she could hear Léo and Sylvia downstairs. Looking longingly at the coffee pot and the sofa, she groaned and instead pulled on some clothes and went to see if she could help.

'I think everything's ready,' said Sylvia, 'but if you could be a dear, Juliet, and ask the girls if they've got their pieces ready, that would help.'

'No problem. It all looks lovely; I'm sure Pandora and her friends will have a great time – and the photos will look amazing. Are you looking forward to it, Léo?'

He shrugged.

'I am going to treat it like any other class. I'm not pleased about the magazine photos, but I know it's good for business.'

'Why not?' asked Juliet. 'You're not camera shy at all.'

'Just publicity shy,' he muttered. 'Can you go and ask your sisters? The party will be here soon.'

Feeling rather dismissed, Juliet pushed open the door and stepped into the morning. The autumn sunshine lifted her mood, and she breathed in the chilly air with its sharp yet comforting scent of fallen leaves. Léo was being scratchy yet again, although he had been fine the previous night, and her concern that he was playing some sort of game to keep her on her toes was beginning to harden into certainty. Why did he suddenly have a problem being photographed for a magazine? She shook her head. Surely there *was* no problem. It was just another way to be snippy with her, to squash her. Well, he needed to be careful; she was *not* going to put up with that kind of thing for a second time. As she reached the house, she squared her shoulders; today was no time to be dwelling on such things. For now, he still had the benefit of the doubt, and she smiled as she remembered his gentle touch and loving, sincere words of the night before. Today was an important day for the whole family, and she was going to do her bit.

'Frankie, Martha!' she called, as she went in. There was no response. She jogged up the stairs and opened Frankie's door. The bed was empty and had not been slept in: no chance Frankie would be up already and have made it so neatly. Martha's room was also empty, so she went along to the room she used as her studio and found her sister there.

'Morning.'

Martha jumped and quickly pulled a sheet over the painting she was working on.

'Oh, hello, Juliet, how are you? I was too excited to sleep late so I thought I'd come and get some work done.'

'What is it?'

'Oh nothing, nothing. Not ready to be seen yet.'

'Well, Sylvia asked me to come and get the pieces you and Frank want up in the cookery school. Have you got them? I can't find Frankie.'

'She went out last night. I wish I knew what she was up to. But yes, she left the sculpture, it's gorgeous. And I've got a little painting I did of Sylvia. Here they are.'

She handed the items to Juliet who looked at them in admiration tinged, she had to admit, with a little jealousy.

'You're both so ridiculously talented. I doubt the readers of *HELLO! Magazine* will appreciate these, but you never know. Thanks, I'll take them down. The party's due to arrive at ten, so don't get lost in what you're doing and forget, will you?'

'Not a chance. Not today. I've got my eye on the clock, I promise.'

'Good. See you later then.'

At ten o'clock, even Rousseau was hovering around, pretending to look for a book he'd lost which Juliet had seen on his desk just the day before.

'You're such a fraud, Dad, why don't you just admit that you're dying to see Pandora James in the flesh?'

'Well, if I am, you only have yourselves to blame. I had no idea who this woman was until you all started twittering about her and leaving glamorous photos littering the place. Samuel Johnson said that curiosity is "one of the permanent and certain characteristics of a vigorous intellect", so my being here is rather to my credit, I think.'

Juliet laughed.

'You've got me there. Oh, look, is that them?'

A sleek silver car pulled up in front of the house and started to disgorge glamorous women with improbably long hair and enormous sunglasses. Léo emerged from the front door, and they watched as he greeted them warmly and introduced them to Sylvia. Martha was next out, followed by Will, and Juliet was spurred into action.

'Come on, Dad, you can help with their cases as well. This could be a big thing for Feywood's future. Think of the roof.'

'I only ever think of the roof,' he said morosely, following his daughter outside.

Although she didn't have much involvement, it seemed to Juliet that the weekend went well. Sometimes, perhaps, rather too well. Although she told herself repeatedly that Léo was just doing his hosting duties, and perhaps laying things on extra thick so that Pandora and her friends would gush about the experience once back home, she couldn't help comparing his manner with the moodiness he had been showing towards her recently. She had tried to speak to him once, just to catch up, but had been disappointed.

'Hey, how's it going? From what I can hear when I'm upstairs, they're having a great time.'

'Yes, yes, they seem to be enjoying it. They're pretty demanding, though.'

'Oh, I know. Even I've been changing beds up at the house, and Martha sent me out for a special kind of disgusting sounding coffee substitute for one of them.'

'Thanks for your help. I'm sorry, I can't talk right now. Are you coming to the final dinner party tonight?'

'I'll certainly be there to help things get going...'

'Great, great. See you later then.'

And he was off. Juliet trudged back up to the house to see what help Martha needed now. Doing the extra housework was the worst part of their contribution to Feywood, but she doubted any of them would have been able to concentrate on their work anyway, and she wasn't allowed to take any photos because of the magazine people being there. At least Agnes and the 'girls' were coming at the end of the weekend to help with the final clear-up, but they couldn't afford to have them every day.

'It won't be like this forever,' said Martha, as they changed the sheets on Pandora's bed yet again. 'If things go well, then we'll be able to get people in to help more.'

'It would've helped if Frankie had been here,' grumbled Juliet, balling up a sheet and tossing it into the doorway.

'I wonder,' said Martha. 'She's even sharper than ever at the moment, so I'm not sure she'd make the perfect hostess – unlike us, of course.'

'I'm not sure it's really my *thing*,' said Juliet, wrestling a pillow into its cover. 'But I don't mind helping to get Feywood back on her feet again. Just as long as we don't get many more guests like these ones.'

'They *have* been rather demanding, haven't they? No one's ever asked us to change their bed daily, and some of their dietary requirements are extremely strange.'

'I've got no idea how Léo and Sylvia are handling all that in the school,' said Juliet. 'I'm not sure that almond milk freshly squeezed by the light of the moon is a decent substitute for double cream.'

Martha giggled.

'Sylvia's always so calm, but even she was looking wild-eyed yesterday when one of them said they needed to have "any bread, as long as it was non-processed".'

'I hope she gave her a sheaf of wheat and wished her luck.'

'I think she was on the verge of it. Oh well, maybe a weekend's cooking will teach them a bit about ingredients and what not to be scared of.'

'Maybe. At least they're doing the food for tonight's final dinner party, then there's only one more breakfast to get through. Dad had to drive all the way to Oxford to find organic seaweed powder for one of them to add to their smoothie.'

'Yuck. So, are you still hoping for an invitation to the wedding?'

'Oh Juliet, I'd love it, but only if I don't have to do any of the organisation.'

Everyone gathered in the living room that evening for drinks before dinner. Even Will put in an appearance, at Pandora's insistence. She and her friends had rather taken to him in what Juliet suspected to be something of a Lady Chatterley fantasy. She wasn't going to break it to them that, far from being some hired muscle, Will had a degree in estate management and was currently studying for an accountancy diploma. But she didn't like seeing the pain in Martha's face as the women flitted around him, flirting and pretending to be helpless so that he would come and open a window for them. Mind you, Will seemed completely impervious to their charms and remained his usual stoic, professional self. It wasn't long before Léo tapped his glass with a knife.

'Welcome, everyone, and thank you for coming. Over to our hostess for the evening, Pandora.'

There was a polite round of applause as she stood up.

'Ladies and gentlemen, we hope you have enjoyed the canopies which we have served.'

Juliet didn't dare glance at Martha for fear she would start giggling and sent up a silent thanks that Frankie wasn't there to comment, as she surely would. All the same, she couldn't erase from her mind the image of Pandora and her friends solemnly handing out large canvas awnings, rather than the delicious goat's cheese canapés they had in fact enjoyed.

'Please now be seated in the dining room, where we will start the, er, starter.'

Another flutter of applause, and everyone went through.

TWENTY-THREE

Feywood felt quiet without Pandora and her hens fluttering around the place. Juliet was relieved not to have to change any sheets other than her own for a while, and she was glad for Léo that the weekend had gone as well as it did. They were all excitedly awaiting the publication of *HELLO! Magazine*, and there had already been enquiries from people who had got wind of the visit. However, before the magazine came out, another picture emerged.

Juliet was in her flat one morning, working on some illustrations for the recipe book. She was pleased with how they were evolving: funny and quirky, but not spiteful, and she was sure that Léo and Sylvia would be pleased with them. A timid knock on the door came at just the right moment.

'Oh, hello, Martha, I don't often see you up here. Come in, I was just making a coffee. Would you like one?'

'Yes, thanks. I should come and see you here more often, it's lovely. The light is amazing.'

'Isn't it? I don't need it for my cartoons, but it's brilliant for the watercolour work. Here you go.' She handed her sister a steaming mug and they sat down. 'So, what can I do for you?'

Martha bit her lip.

'There's something I want to show you, although I'm not sure about it...'

She trailed off, looking worried. Juliet frowned.

'Whatever it is, better out than in. Just show me.'

Martha nodded and pulled out her phone. A few taps later she had opened Instagram and held up a photo. It showed Léo and Pandora looking exactly as if they had just broken away from a kiss: their backs were to the camera, their hands on each other's shoulders and their faces wore expressions which Juliet immediately interpreted as guilt. The comments underneath confirmed that she wasn't the only one who thought that. Juliet looked up from studying the phone.

'Was that taken here?'

'Yes, look, you can see the wall in the background, the bit where it's all broken. I'm sure it's nothing. I'm not showing you because I think that anything is – going on. But I wanted you to know about it, in case anything is said.'

'Right. Yeah, I can see why. Thanks, Martha. Can you send it to me?'

'Sure.' She took her phone back and shortly a 'ping' sounded. 'There you go. Don't be cross with Léo, will you? It looks a bit funny, but...'

'Don't worry, I'll sort it. Come on, now you're here, let's change the subject. Tell me how work's going.'

After Martha had left, Juliet tried to settle to her work again, but it was as if her phone had a red-hot laser coming out of it and pointing directly towards her head. She just couldn't ignore it. She snatched up the device and looked again at the photograph.

'Oh, this is bloody ridiculous,' she said out loud, and stormed out to go and find Léo. She didn't have far to go; he was downstairs with Sylvia in the cookery school. They looked up in surprise as she flew down the stairs.

'Is everything all right?' asked her aunt.

'No, not really. It really isn't. Sorry, I've got something to speak to Léo about.'

'All right,' he said slowly. 'It looks like this can't wait. Can you excuse me a moment, Sylvia?'

They went outside, and Juliet led him to a small bench. She took out her phone and showed him the photograph.

'Ah,' he said. 'You know, of course, that this is not how it looks, Juliet?'

'I was hoping not. Because to me it rather looks as if you have been kissing her, and her so-called friend has put it on her Instagram page with a load of sassy little winking faces and comments about how *what happens on a hen should probably stay there.*'

'Do you believe that there is anything here to worry about? Go and ask Sylvia if you must, she was on the other side of the camera at this moment. But don't show me this rubbish and expect to get an explanation. You are better than this, Juliet.'

'Is that all you have to say?'

'Yes, that is all.'

'Fine,' she snapped, and stood up. 'Maybe I *will* go and ask Sylvia, if I'm not going to get a civil answer out of you.'

And she stormed back towards the cookery school door. How *could* he dismiss her like that? Why didn't he just explain? This was Toby all over again.

'Juliet, whatever has happened?'

'Oh, Sylvia!' Juliet burst into tears. 'Léo's being *awful*, he won't speak to me properly. He's making me feel so stupid.'

Sylvia held out her arms, and Juliet sobbed into her shoulder as her aunt patted her back and made soothing noises. As she calmed down, she led her to a chair and gave her a glass of water.

'Try and drink something and then tell me what has happened, lovie.'

Obediently, Juliet took a sip, and then another, until she felt herself calming down.

'It's this photo,' she said shakily, holding up her phone. 'It's horrible, it looks so – compromising. I don't really believe that anything happened, but why wouldn't Léo talk to me about it? He seemed so angry.'

'You know I was there, Juliet, and you're right – nothing happened. Do you think Léo was angry because he thinks you don't trust him?'

'I don't know. We barely even got that far before he just shut me down.'

'That doesn't sound like Léo; he's usually so open. I'm sure he's not really cross with you. There must be more to it than that.'

Juliet was silent for a moment, her heart pounding.

'That's what I'm worried about,' she said quietly. 'It's what Toby did. He was lovely at first, opened his heart to me completely – or so I thought – and encouraged me to do the same. And then when I was well and truly reeled in, that was when all the horrible stuff started: the criticism, telling me that I wasn't thinking straight, denying things I *knew* were true, accusing me of being paranoid. When I asked Léo about that stupid photo, I just thought he'd hug me and reassure me. But he didn't. And now I don't know what to think.'

'Toby pulled the rug out from under you. I hate him for what he's done, for the confusion he left you feeling. I'm not surprised you find it hard to trust Léo, given what you've been through. Darling, you must just do what is right for you, what you believe to be safe and true. But be sure, do be sure, before making any big decisions.'

Juliet hugged her aunt and went upstairs. She knew it was good advice, but what she didn't know yet, was what *was* safe, what *was* true. Maybe it was Léo who would turn out to be dangerous territory. Toby was still trying to contact her, still begging her to speak to him, full of apologies, confessions and promises he had changed. Maybe it was a case of better the devil you know.

*   *   *

As the cookery school door closed behind Juliet, Léo dropped his head into his hands. Didn't she trust him? But *mon dieu*, did he even trust himself? Sure, that photograph looked bad and nothing, *nothing* had happened, but how could he find himself here again, looking as if he was carrying on in some way with another woman who was spoken for, if not yet actually married? He had been very careful that weekend, or so he thought, to manage the image of the cookery school and himself so that they were shown in the best and most professional possible light in a magazine article he had had serious reservations about anyway. And now it was all in ruins. He groaned and dropped his head to his knees, clutching at his hair. What if this compromising photograph reached France? Veronique wouldn't hesitate to push it towards every gossip magazine she could and his reputation, already soiled, would be dragged down further. Even if Juliet believed that the photo was nothing, how could she stay with him when she realised the simple truth: that he was not good enough for her?

After some time, Léo dragged himself to standing and walked heavily back inside, half longing to see Juliet in the kitchen and half dreading it. But there was only Sylvia, dear, kind Sylvia, peering into a bubbling pan with a vexed expression on her face.

'Oh hello, Léo,' she said. 'I wonder if you can work out what might be missing from this *jus*? It's just not working.'

He peered into the pan.

'Have you tried arrowroot? It is not my favourite thing to use but might save this.'

'Oh, thank you, I'll try. And while I'm doing that, you can put the kettle on and start telling me why you look so morose.'

He hmphed.

'I'm sure you have heard from Juliet already. What can I possibly add?'

'Come now, no melodrama. I'm sure the two of you can sort it out.'

'But I am not so sure that we should,' he said flatly, pouring boiling water into two mugs.

'Whyever not? I think you make a lovely couple. I thought you were happy.'

'So did I, but now I see Juliet very *un*happy, and it is I making her feel this way.'

'But Léo, you haven't done anything wrong. She doesn't really think there's anything to that photo, you know, she's smart enough to know how these things can look when there's nothing to see. She was just a bit upset that you hadn't given her a bit more, that's all. Why didn't you?'

She turned casually back to her saucepan, but Léo knew the momentum of the question, even if she apparently didn't.

'Please, Sylvia, sit down and I will explain. The photo, it brought back many difficult memories. Of Veronique, the woman I had been seeing in France who turned out to be married and has made my name dirt throughout the country. I do not deserve any reputation as a marriage wrecker, but if this new photograph goes far, then what is already out there will be compounded. Juliet does not deserve to be dragged along in something like that, however baseless it is. And maybe it *is* partly my fault. Maybe I am a very, very poor judge of these things.' He looked glumly into his tea, and Sylvia patted his arm.

'Oh Léo, you can't really think for a moment that you are to blame for any of it. I was there, remember; you did absolutely nothing – and neither did Pandora. It was just an unlucky shot, and it is her friend who has displayed poor judgement in posting it. Juliet won't care a jot, I'm sure.'

'Perhaps. But I am also concerned that she is not being true to herself anyway. She did not want to come back to Feywood, we know this. Perhaps her heart still lies in London, and with Toby. She was, I think, more angry than necessary over the photo. I wonder if she will take this opportunity to return.'

'You don't honestly believe that. She has been staunch in her refusal to take Toby back, she's seen through him.'

'Maybe, but maybe he really has changed. They have much history together. She refuses to delete his number.'

'If anyone has changed, it's Juliet. But she hasn't become a different person, she's returned to being herself, to being the person she was when she was a little girl, before everything went so wrong with her mother. In going back, she has gone forward, and I believe you can be part of that – if you allow yourself to be.'

Léo drained his tea.

'Thank you, Sylvia. I love Juliet and I want nothing more than to be with her, here at Feywood. But it is not all about what I want. I must bow to her wishes and hope that she is honest enough with me – and with herself – to recognise them.'

He didn't go upstairs then, but back to his room in the house. He went to check the French press and Pandora's friend's social media, but the photograph seemed to have disappeared and not been reproduced anywhere of note. Perhaps, just perhaps, he had been lucky this time, but he was not going to be the architect of Juliet's downfall. He had almost convinced himself that she would be far better off without him.

TWENTY-FOUR

After the evening of 'the photo', Juliet decided against saying anything else to Léo. When they had seen each other the next day, he drew her into a warm hug, and she hugged him back. This felt enough of an apology not to pursue asking him to explain something she truly believed needed no explanation. She trusted him. She would have rather discussed it, but he was trying to keep his moods lighter, she could tell, and she didn't want to spoil things now that they were going better again. She shook off the feeling that things were still not quite as easy between them as they had been, and instead put her energies into worrying about the memorial for her mother, which was fast approaching.

'Jools, have you decided yet if you're going to create a piece in Mum's memory?' asked Martha, on what felt like a daily basis. 'I want to include the details in the programmes for the afternoon if you have and I *must* get them printed up.'

'Yes,' said Juliet slowly. 'I have got something. It's a photographic montage called 'Memories of Feywood'. Probably a bit sentimental, but I know you wanted me to knock something up.'

'It sounds lovely. Can I see it?'

'Sure. It's in my flat, come and see any time.'

Juliet was trying to resist attaching too much emotion to this work, but the truth was it had drained her. She hadn't been sure whether to create a tribute or not, but had decided that to go back in time to the days when her and her mother's relationship had been happy would be the only fitting thing she could do that would honour both Lilith and her. So she had worked hard to produce a photograph of Feywood, taken early one morning recently, and blend in pictures of the family from twenty-five years earlier. It showed them working and playing, enjoying each other's company and the house. It was joyful, yet atmospheric, and gave her goosebumps when she looked at it. She knew it was a strong piece and was already trying to distance herself from it with her apparently casual attitude. She told herself that she would happily sell it to any bidder but knew it would never leave Feywood. Martha's reaction when she came to see it almost overwhelmed her.

'Juliet, oh Juliet.' She stepped closer to the photo and scrutinised every angle, before moving back to take it in in its entirety. Tears poured down her cheeks. 'It's so, so beautiful, I love it. Oh Juliet, this is *wonderful*.'

'I'm glad you like it. Bit soppy, but I suppose it'll do.'

'I *adore* it, and Dad will too. And it's *not* soppy,' she added fiercely. 'It's incredibly powerful. It knocks spots off what Frankie and I have done. Mine's just a boring old portrait, as usual, and Frankie has done a rather... *unusual* sculpture called "Motherhood", with a lot of strange angles and bulging bits. That probably *is* motherhood, not that I'm sure I'll ever know.'

Relieved to move the subject along, Juliet hugged her sister.

'Of course you will. I have every faith. Now, what's left to do for this bloody memorial? It's only two days away.'

. . .

Another morning golden with autumn sunshine welcomed them that Saturday, and Feywood was quickly busy with different people coming and going. Chairs were put out with rugs draped over the backs in case the afternoon grew chilly, awnings set up and caterers rushed about setting up the drinks and dishes that were going to supplement the food provided by Léo and Sylvia. Will had worked hard getting the garden looking immaculate – well, thought Juliet rather uncharitably, the bit of the garden that people were going to see. The other parts, including the formal gardens where she had first met Léo, were still messy and overgrown. Even Ava had had a special wash and brush up for the occasion. Frankie had tied a yellow bow around her neck, but the spirited little dog had soon clawed it off, and it now lay in a streak across the perfectly mown lawn.

'How many people have you got coming?' asked Juliet, as more chairs and tables were set up.

Martha pushed her hair back from her sweaty face.

'No idea,' she replied, looking panicked. 'Responses were still coming in this morning, half of them from people I don't even remember inviting. You know what the art world's like – everyone just passes invitations along and then they all roll up and drink the place dry whether you were expecting them or not. Most of the village is coming, too, so I hope they'll all get along all right. What if we run out of chairs?'

'We've got all those blankets stuffed away somewhere,' said Juliet. 'Why don't we dig those out and people can sit on them if they need to? Thank goodness it's going to be dry today.'

'Good idea.' Martha looked pleadingly at her sister. 'Will you find them? And find Frankie at the same time – she's been no help whatsoever.'

Juliet wandered off, glad for a job. She had woken up that morning with very mixed feelings about the day ahead: far more emotional than she had ever imagined she would be. She had been avoiding her own photograph since she created it, but as well as the artworks in tribute to Lilith, Rousseau had put up a large collage of pictures of her from throughout her life in the hallway, and it had almost floored Juliet when she saw it. Photo after photo of her difficult, arrogant, talented, selfish, hilarious, stylish, cruel, complicated mother confronted her, and she saw herself over and over again in the woman's face and bearing. Were they so similar? Had that been the problem? Had she been unfair, criticising the things in her mother that she recognised and despised in herself? She had been glad when Léo came in and broke the spell, and just as glad when he quickly disappeared to the cookery school, where he would be cloistered away for most of the morning.

At twelve o'clock, people started arriving. At first, it was some people from the village who remembered Lilith with humour and affection; probably, said Frankie spitefully, because they barely knew her. By quarter past, guests were arriving thick and fast. Rousseau was trying to welcome each one personally but was inevitably unable to tear himself away from friends and creating a terrible bottleneck in the hallway as he gathered them into a rapidly growing group.

'You take this one, Frankie,' said Juliet. 'I'm going to go outside and make sure the early arrivals are all still happy. Martha should stay here funnelling people through.'

As she went out into the garden, she could hear her younger sister's piercing tones ordering their father and his entourage into the garden, with the promise of champagne, and she knew they were in good hands.

'Hello, Father Benedict,' she said, spotting the vicar who had so encouraged her bread-making. 'Thank you for coming.'

'Not at all,' he replied, beaming. 'I was fond of your mother, you know, Juliet, even if she only ever wanted to rebuke me for my belief. I'm glad to have the opportunity to remember her in such lovely surroundings. It looks like it's going to be quite the party.'

'I agree. Do let me get you a drink. Champagne?'

'Oh no, no, not for me. Just something soft would be delicious, thank you.'

Juliet went over to the drinks table and poured some of the elderflower and blackberry leaf cordial that her aunt had made. She was reaching for a glass of champagne for herself when a hand swept in, picked one up and handed it to her and a familiar voice said, 'Hello, Lettie.'

Cold tendrils of dread wrapped themselves around her. She turned reluctantly to face him.

'Toby? What are you doing here? Did Martha invite you?'

'No,' he said peevishly. 'Given that I knew your mother well, I was rather hurt that no one in the family got in contact to invite me today.'

Don't apologise, thought Juliet, desperately fighting down the urge to smooth things over whenever Toby started to show displeasure, for fear of how it would escalate. *Don't apologise and don't try to explain.* She kept her voice light.

'But you came anyway.'

'I did. I heard that there was something of an open invitation, and I wanted to come and pay my respects.'

Juliet set her face into a neutral expression.

'Thank you. Now I must go and give the vicar his drink.'

'I'll come with you.'

Juliet shrunk away from him but didn't want to risk a scene by trying to dissuade Toby from following her. Instead, she turned and walked briskly back across the lawn, hoping wildly that he might be swooped up by a passing eagle, or fall into a convenient sinkhole. No such luck. She felt relief wash over her when she reached the vicar.

'Here you are, Father Benedict.' She handed him his drink.

'Ah, thank you. Hello, I don't think we've met?'

'Toby Bartholomew.' The two men shook hands. 'I'm an old friend of Juliet's and I just adored Lilith. So sad.'

'Indeed. She was a very vivacious woman.'

'She was hilarious. Lettie, do you remember that time we went for drinks at the Lawson? It's a very smart bar in Mayfair,' he added, for Father Benedict's benefit. 'Our waiter had only started that evening and was completely hapless – couldn't remember a cocktail order to save his life and kept coming back with the oddest concoctions. Lilith kept veering between wondering in a loud stage whisper about his *suitability* for the job, my darlings, and patting the seat next to her so he could sit down while she talked him through how to make a Cosmopolitan.'

Juliet's shock and repulsion at seeing Toby faded as she was taken back to that night. He had managed to dredge up one of the few happy memories as an adult she had of her mother. She smiled.

'That's right, it *was* funny. Once she'd walked him through the classics, she started moving on to some bizarre combinations, but we drank them up. The headache I had the next day was something else. Didn't she give him a ginormous tip at the end of the evening?'

'That's right, and a glowing endorsement to the manager. She could be so kind, and very generous.'

The champagne was beginning to wind its way through Juliet's body, and she smiled up at Toby, grateful and surprised that the day was taking a more positive turn than she had expected. Then she felt a hand in the small of her back.

'Oh, *bonjour*,' drawled Toby, and she turned to see Léo, giving her a questioning smile. She stepped closer to him, his presence a balm of comfort, even after the awkwardness over the photo. He ignored Toby and spoke directly to Juliet.

'The food is all in hand, so I have a few moments and I

thought I would find you. How are you doing? I did not know that he was going to be here.'

'Neither did I, but I think word spread about today; there are lots of people who weren't actually invited but knew Mum. We were just talking about a funny evening we spent together. Years ago.'

'Ah. I am sorry never to have met her.'

'Yes,' put in Toby. 'Shared history is so special. We were laughing remembering it, weren't we, Lettie?'

'New memories are also special,' said Léo. 'And Juliet and I are happy to be making many of those. I don't think that she wants to rehash the past too much.'

Juliet was suddenly aware that both men were bristling with irritation, and she felt annoyed. Today was meant to be about her mother, but was Léo playing some macho game, coming over and announcing what she wanted, with no reference to her at all? At least Toby had been talking about Lilith, even if she knew better than to trust his motivation.

'Well, actually,' said Toby, looking at Juliet, 'it's the future I would like to talk to you about. I have a friend who owns a flat in Cadogan Square. He's moving to Dubai for a couple of years and wants someone to live in the place. He's keen to get someone reliable, so for a friend of a friend it would be bills only, no rent. I thought immediately of you, Lettie. I can't imagine that you'd want to stay here with all the opportunities opening up to you in London. Why, it was only last week that the editor of *RoundUp* was asking after you. When I told her you'd moved here, she wasn't so interested as she needs someone in London, who is right on the scene of the news and gossip. But if you were thinking of moving back, I'm sure she'd love to meet you.'

'Petra Sharpe is interested in me?' she gasped.

'Very.'

'Who is she?' asked Léo.

'She's the editor of *RoundUp* – it's an online news magazine that moves constantly and has a reputation for being first with major stories and scandals involving politicians – personal and professional. Heaven knows who their sources are, but it's such an exciting site. I can hardly believe she's even heard of me, let alone that she's interested in me working for her.'

'Well, you should believe it, Lettie. You're in the perfect position to drive your career forward: independent, childfree, talented and smart. Don't waste away here at Feywood.'

'I-I don't know,' she stuttered. 'It sounds amazing, but obviously I am happy here...'

She trailed off and looked at Léo, whose face was uncharacteristically blank. *Was* she happy here? She had thought she was with Léo, her photography and painting, her owl-shaped bread, her little dog. But the opportunity that Toby was dangling in front of her, if it was real, couldn't be ignored. The chance to live in London again and to work for such a fresh and exciting company was dizzying. Things with Léo had felt rocky in the past few weeks, and hadn't she sworn to herself that she wouldn't let her decisions revolve around a man again? Her gaze returned to Toby, who looked extremely pleased with himself. She recognised that look and it gave her a chill, reminding her of the many times he had 'sorted things out' for her and she had been swept along, only to find that his promises were castles in the air and had been designed to keep her exactly where he wanted her: under his thumb. Neither man spoke, and before she could, the tinkle of a knife against a glass cut across the garden.

'Lunch is served!' boomed Rousseau, his voice carrying effortlessly through the throng of people.

Relief flooded Juliet.

'Let's go and eat,' she said. 'I can't wait to see what you've made, Léo.'

. . .

The lunch, though informal, was delicious, and Juliet was glad when she remembered that she was expected to sit at a sort of top table, comprised only of family members. Up until now she had been dreading this arrangement, wishing she would have Léo's comforting presence beside her through the lunch and speeches, but now she was glad that her father had insisted on it being only himself, Sylvia, the three girls and Lilith's brother, their Uncle George. It gave her an opportunity to think about what had been said, without either Toby or Léo giving their own opinions on the matter. She half listened to the speeches, only three and mercifully short, as her mind roamed across the years, from the hilarious cocktail evening to her previous life in London to how things were now. She mulled over the concepts of happiness, contentment, fulfilment, but had come no closer to any clarity when Rousseau announced:

'And now, please raise your glasses to Lilith, and enjoy the rest of the afternoon with the kind of gusto she would have appreciated.'

Everyone clapped and cheered and quickly filled their glasses up again just in case the champagne ran out, but it never seemed to at Feywood, no matter how rickety the roof became.

As the golden light of early evening permeated the garden, Juliet saw Léo emerging from the cookery school. Softened by champagne and gladness that the event had been better than bearable, she walked over to him.

'It went well today. Thank you for the lovely food. I think everyone's hoping Dad might pop off soon so that we can do this all over again.'

Léo's smile was tired.

'I do hope not, although it has been a marvellous day.'

'Have you finished now?'

'I think so. I sent Sylvia to sit down as she was looking very tired, but the caterers did most of the cleaning up, so it hasn't been too bad.'

'Would you like to get a drink?'

'*Oui*, that would be good.'

They collected some fresh glasses and went to sit by the side of the pond, where it was deserted. Juliet knew she had to broach the subject.

'I'm sorry for that weirdness with Toby today. I suppose that's why he's been trying to get hold of me recently.'

'What do you make of his offer?'

'I don't know. I don't know if it's even real. And if it is, whether it's what I want.'

'If it's for real, then it's an amazing opportunity, Juliet, very special. I would not be surprised if you went, I would not blame you. In fact, how could I do anything but encourage you?'

She stared at him.

'Are you saying you *want* me to go?'

'Not exactly. What I mean is that I want what is the best for you, and what Toby described... well, maybe you would be happier than stuck here.'

'But I don't feel *stuck* here, not anymore, you know that,' she cried, surprised and hurt by his easy acceptance of the idea of her leaving. 'I'm happy here, you know I am. Happy with my work and...' She faltered, her courage almost failing her. 'Well, happy with you.'

'But is it happiness or acceptance? Your talent, Juliet, it deserves the very best audience.'

'I would stay, just for you alone, Léo. No one...' She drew breath. 'I haven't ever felt about anyone like I do about you. I thought you knew that. But also, I have my book coming out, the cookbook as well, and I'm still working for the paper. And with the other things I'm learning... Do you think I'm squandering myself in some way?'

'*Non*, of course not. And I feel so much for you too, Juliet. I just don't want you to, uh, *a cheval donné, on ne regarde pas les dents*. I don't know how you say this in English – a horse that is a present, don't look at his teeth?'

Juliet laughed, and the mood lifted.

'Don't look a gift horse in the mouth. As long as it isn't a case of *timeo Danaos et dona ferentes* – I fear the Greeks even when they bring gifts. This could be a big old Trojan horse of Toby's.'

'Well, perhaps it is a risk you have to take,' said Léo stubbornly, and the atmosphere grew heavy again. 'I am not going to advise you, Juliet. I cannot do so freely, given my feelings.'

Juliet gave a small smile.

'You have skin in the game.'

'I have *la peau dans le jeu*?' said Léo, looking confused for a moment, before his face cleared, and he grinned. 'Ah, yes, I have an interest in a certain outcome, that is true. But that interest is mine. You must be sure, you and you alone, Juliet. Look, Sylvia is calling me, I must go, but we will speak later, yes?'

He walked away towards the house while Juliet stared into the water, shivering slightly. What was Léo trying to tell her – that he *wanted* her to return to London? That was very much what it felt like. Or was he trying to trick her in some way, manipulate her by refusing to reveal his feelings? Maybe he thought that this 'new' Juliet was boring, provincial, that she should strap herself back into her austere clothes and accept that 'old' Juliet was the truer version. She sighed and stood up. Maybe there would still be a few profiteroles left over; some sugary comfort was just what she needed.

TWENTY-FIVE

'Sylvia, are you all right?' Léo hastened his footsteps as he drew closer to her; she did not look well.

'I'm fine, really I am,' she answered in a slow, small voice. 'I'm so sorry for summoning you like that, especially when you looked like you were having rather an intense conversation with Juliet, but I wanted you because I believe I can trust you. I'm right, aren't I?'

'But of course you are. What can I do?'

'I'm feeling extremely tired, I think I've rather overdone it today. I just need someone – you – to help me upstairs so that I can go to bed. But I don't want you saying anything to anyone, you have to promise me that you won't.'

'I think I should call a doctor,' said Léo, looking in concern at her pale, thin face.

'No,' she said firmly. 'I am not ill – well, no iller than I was this morning, just tired and I don't want to fall down the stairs or something stupid and ruin everyone's evening. Will you help me or won't you?'

'Of course I will.'

'Thank you. Just put out your arm so that I can lean on you, that's all I need.'

Léo offered her his arm, and she drew herself up to standing. As they turned to go into the house, he glanced across the lawn and saw Juliet deep in conversation with Toby.

'What is it?' asked Sylvia, as he paused and stiffened momentarily. She followed his gaze towards the talking pair. 'What are he and Juliet talking about? I was surprised when I saw him here.'

Léo started moving slowly towards the house.

'He said he had come to commemorate Lilith, but he also had an offer for Juliet – an affordable flat in London and the possibility of a very special job.'

'Ah. That sort of too good to be true package sounds just like Toby. What did she say?'

They stepped onto the bottom stair, and Léo braced himself as Sylvia laid all her weight on him. He had not realised how weak she was.

'She has not given him an answer. Yet.'

'And what do you think?' She sounded breathless.

'I think maybe we should concentrate on the stairs, and not on talking.'

'No, no, it's good. Takes my mind off the fact I can't climb the bloody stairs on my own. Tell me what you think of this offer.'

'I think that perhaps it is for the best.'

'*What?*' Sylvia grasped the banister and turned to face him. 'The best? How on earth would that be for the best? She seems so happy back here at Feywood, with you. I haven't seen Juliet like this in years.'

'But I cannot be the reason she stays, if there is a better life for her in London, a life she understands, a life that fulfils her. *Non*, it is better if I stand aside. I do not want her to resent me. You do not know all, Sylvia, but believe me when I tell you that

I am not good enough to be her reason to turn these things down.'

'What utter nonsense. For a start, you wouldn't be the only reason she stayed – any fool can see that her art is flourishing, as is her general... well-being, I suppose you'd call it. For goodness' sake, don't let her back into Toby's tender embrace, although I can hardly believe she'd go back to him, or back to London at all. She's so happy here.'

They had reached the door of Sylvia's room and Léo opened it.

'Juliet is a wonderful woman who can make her own mind up. It's not a case of me 'letting' her do anything, or not. I must accept that this has just been a pleasant diversion for her in a glittering life.'

He helped Sylvia sit on the bed, and she handed him her shawl.

'Well, I think you're being melodramatic and very stubborn for some reason. Whatever it is that you think you've done or haven't done that makes you unworthy – well, don't you think Juliet can decide for herself about that as well? The point is that you have always treated her well, simply loved her and been loved back, and that is more than enough.'

Léo shrugged.

'I am not so sure. Now please, let me help you. What can I do?'

'Nothing. I'll be fine now, I promise. Go and tell Juliet to stay, that's the best thing you can do.'

He smiled sadly.

'*Bon nuit.* Until tomorrow.'

When he had left Sylvia, Léo headed back towards the cookery school, hoping not to see anyone else; this was not to be the case. As he crossed the lawn, he saw a figure making its way rapidly towards him, and although he quickened his steps, he was not able to avoid Toby.

'A word, if I may, Brodeur?'

Léo stopped, sighing.

'I do not think we have much more to say to one another.'

'Well, I have something to say to you, and you'll bloody well listen.'

Léo shrugged.

'Speak quickly, please, my work is not yet over for the day.'

'I hope you're not going to stop Lettie going back to London. You must realise that she can't achieve her potential stuck here.' He waved his arm around dismissively. 'With you. The opportunities I mentioned will soon make her forget all of this.'

'And help her, perhaps, to remember you?'

'Lettie and I are just good friends now, that's all,' said Toby pompously. 'And as a friend, who has known her and her family for many, many years, I am both well placed to make such an offer and to understand what it means to her. Do you want to hold her back in some way?'

'No, no, of course I do not want this,' said Léo, taken by surprise. 'I may not know Juliet as well as you do, but I also want the very best for her.'

'And do you think you know what that is?'

'I do not pretend to, no,' replied Léo.

Toby gave a contemptuous laugh.

'You don't even believe that you are the best for her. And if you don't believe that, then there's not much else you can do than say au revoir.'

Léo bowed his head slightly.

'I allow Juliet to decide for herself,' he said. 'Good night.'

He walked the short distance to the cookery school quickly, feeling somehow as if he had admitted to something he didn't agree with, but he wasn't sure how Toby had managed to do that. He pushed the door open. Work was what he needed now; he was not ready for bed.

He had been sitting at his laptop for nearly an hour, when the door opened slowly, and Juliet slipped through.

'Oh, you're here,' she said. 'I thought you'd gone to bed.'

'*Non*, I wanted to work. I find it a comfort.'

'Right. Well, I'm going to bed.'

'Are we not going to discuss what happened today?'

'Is there anything *to* discuss? From what I remember, you pretty much gave me my marching orders back to London.'

'I did not say that. I do not want to stand in your way, I want you to make the best decision for *you*, aside from me.'

'Well, if you thought our relationship was serious and had any kind of future, then you would think that wouldn't be possible. Any decision I made about where to live and work would of course include you. But I think you *do* think that, and this is some weird way of forcing me into some gesture that isn't actually about me at all.'

His head spun. What was happening? Why was she so angry when he was trying to do the noble thing? Once again, it seemed that he was causing problems, even though that was not his intention. He did not want to confuse or manipulate her, but this was what had happened with Veronique: when he tried to behave well, he was accused of being nefarious. It seemed these women saw through to some truth that he had not dared to acknowledge about himself. He opened his mouth to speak, but her torrent continued.

'Well, I *shall* do what I want then, regardless of you. I won't be tricked into thinking differently. I shall go back to London, and I shall be glad to, away from this boring, poisonous house and back to where I know what's what. There, are you happy now?'

He didn't have an opportunity to speak before she had turned on her heel, stamped up the stairs and slammed the door firmly behind her. A tear ran down Léo's cheek and he brushed it away with his work-roughened hand. So that was that. He had done it, saved her, and she had seemed only too willing to go. It was not what he wanted, no, in fact so far from his dreams of being with her forever that he would laugh if he didn't feel so devastated. But maybe, he thought, as he packed up his computer and started to trudge back towards the house, when he had got used to the misery and grief of her absence, he would also be able to feel glad that she was able to live the right life for her.

* * *

After Juliet slammed the door behind her, she ran to her bed, threw herself down and buried her head in the pillow, desperate that Léo should not hear her sobs. He had to believe that her decision was strong, not realise how devastated she felt and come up to continue disorientating her with his words. As the tears subsided, she sat up shakily and went over to the window to peer out. No lights shone out of the downstairs windows – he had gone. Juliet went over to the little kitchen area and put on the kettle. Thank goodness, she thought, that Martha had left some camomile teabags there one day; they were just what she needed. She took her drink over to the sofa and pulled a blanket across her tucked-up knees.

She turned on the TV and tried to quiet her mind with a rerun of an old show about people looking around lovely houses in the country, keen to move from the suburbs or the city and find some sort of rural nirvana. But all the programme did was to add to the questions swirling around in her mind. Was living at Feywood truly making her happy, helping her self-actualisation, or had she merely been lulled into some kind of grass-scented torpor which would ultimately stultify, rather than stimulate her? Were the opportunities Toby had offered in London real and, if so, would she be a fool not to grab them with both hands? And what about Léo? She gazed sadly at the screen, watching the mouths of the people move but not hearing the words they were saying. Had she really been so much of a gullible drip to have fallen for the same controlling shtick a second time? It still didn't fit, somehow, she just *couldn't* believe it of Léo, who had always been so kind, so encouraging... so safe. When she was in his arms, she felt strong, not weak, empowered rather than overprotected. But she had believed Toby so many times, been taken in. She clearly wasn't the right person to make good judgements about others.

A thought suddenly came to mind which caused such a chill to trickle through her that she hugged the blanket tighter. What if he had been lying about that married woman, that it really was him who had caused all the problems and no matter how loudly Veronique shouted about it, he was determined to keep denying her truth? Maybe he had left France and hidden in the depths of the English countryside because he was, in fact, guilty as all hell and had no hope of redeeming himself at home? Now that this had occurred to Juliet, it attained the ring of truth, and she felt sure that she had him all figured out.

Hot with confusion, she threw off the blanket and went to open her laptop, where she clicked through to the *RoundUp* website. It was exciting, no doubt about it, and now she looked at the scrolling news ticker and exclusive stories, she felt her heart speed up. She had just gone to the section where sharp and funny sketches and cartoons, so like her own work, were gathered, when she heard a gentle knock on the door. A spurt of adrenaline shot through her: Léo?

'Yes!' she barked, uncertain of whether or not she wanted to see him, but when the door pushed open, it revealed Martha, in pyjamas and wellies.

'Hi,' she said, as she stepped into the flat. 'I couldn't sleep after everything today and I saw your light was on. Sorry, are you working?'

Juliet glanced at the screen.

'Sort of. Come and have some of this tea and I'll tell you.'

Soon the sisters were sitting side by side on the sofa, their feet tucked underneath them and each clutching a fresh mug of camomile tea.

'Did you see Toby today?' asked Juliet, and Martha nodded.

'Yes. I didn't invite him.'

'No, I know. He said he believed it was an "open invitation". Anyway, he said that the woman who runs that website' – she gestured towards the laptop – 'is interested in hiring me. It would be a big deal, Martha, but I'd have to move back to London.'

'But you can't!' exclaimed Martha, sitting up and nearly spilling her tea. 'What about Feywood, and Léo and, well, *you*. Oh, please don't go away again, it's been so lovely having you back.'

Juliet took a deep breath.

'And I have loved being here, Martha, if I'm honest. But it's not going so well. Things with Léo are – difficult. I think I may have misjudged him, or our relationship, or both. And the opportunities that Toby is offering... They would mean I could still give Dad money for Feywood, but I could be back in London, not just with my old life but maybe with an amazing new job. I don't think I can pass it up. Coming back here – it was never meant to be permanent.'

'I know,' replied Martha, wiping away tears. 'But we all so hoped it was, and then when you and Léo got together, every-thing seemed so perfect.'

'Well, life isn't some perfect fairytale,' said Juliet, more harshly than she had intended. 'Especially not mine. But I *can* rely on work. The job at *RoundUp* would be a dream come true, if it happens, but there's my book as well, and I've had some other people interested. I'm sorry, Martha, but my mind's made up.'

'When will you go?'

'Tomorrow.'

Martha gasped.

'So soon?'

'I've already contacted my old landlord, and I got lucky: the flat's vacant at the moment for a short let while I work things out. I have to. If I doubt myself, or let other people try to talk me out of it, I'll lose my strength. I can't let that happen. I'm sorry.'

And she was sorry, sorry to have upset her sweet sister, sorry that things had soured at Feywood, sorry that she was, for now at least, turning to Toby for help. When Martha had gone, Juliet stepped into the shower, trying to picture this new, glittering future and resolutely pushing away the creeping feeling that the shine she imagined might tarnish very rapidly.

TWENTY-SIX

The next morning, Juliet woke early. She packed up a couple of bags and then went to find her father, who was preparing breakfast.

'Morning, Dad.'

'Ah, good morning. Thank you so much for yesterday, what a wonderful day it was. I feel that your mother's spirit can now be quite free, and so can ours.'

'Mmm. It was a good day. And Dad...'

Her father looked up from the pomegranate he was bashing and smiled at her.

'Yes? Oh, what are those bags? Are you and Léo going somewhere?'

'Just me, Dad. I'm going back to London, for a while at least. I'll still send the money I promised. And – will you look after Ava?' Her voice was threatening to break; she would miss the friendly little dog more than she could express.

'Of course I will. But darling, why this sudden up and leaving?'

'Do you mind if I don't go into it now? I just need to go, think about some stuff.'

Rousseau nodded.

'I understand, even if I haven't got the faintest idea what's going on. Will you have some breakfast first?'

'No, I just want to go. I'll catch one of the early trains.'

'Well, at least let me give you a lift to the station. No, I insist. It's a cold breakfast and ready anyway. Anyone who wants it will doubtless find it, they always do. Come on, my darling, you look like you're itching to dash off.'

Feeling intensely grateful for her father's unquestioning support, Juliet waved him off and went to wait for the train, feeling only tired as she climbed on board for the journey to London. She pulled out her phone and sent a businesslike – she hoped – message to Toby, letting him know she had decided to come back to the capital and asking if he could put her in touch with his contacts. As she typed, she could almost feel her fingers resistant to forming the words; it felt wrong to be approaching him, but what else could she do now that she had made the leap to come back to London? One thing she did know: she wasn't going back to him. That was one opportunity she definitely didn't want to take up. But maybe they could reach a place of some civility; after all, they had known one another for several years. She arrived at the flat just before ten o'clock, put in the correct combination on the key safe and pushed open the door to find it immaculately tidy, far tidier than it had ever been when she lived there. It was musty, though, and she threw open the windows to let in some fresh autumn air. The next thing she did was to open up her laptop, take a deep breath and turn to the only thing that ever gave her comfort: work. Not knowing now what would happen with the cookery book, she decided to focus on her own project, the children's book she had been contracted to write. She had done some of the preliminary work, but looking through it agitated her. It was to be a funny and charming story about fairies in the forest at Feywood, complete with her signature line drawings, softened for a younger audience, but every sketch reminded her of home – was it still home? – and of Léo. As a double-decker bus thundered past under her window, she pictured the dappled sunlight coming through the trees, the morning dew on the lawn, Léo's arms around her...

'Oh, for heaven's sake,' she muttered, and grabbed her phone. There were plenty of people who would claim to be delighted to see her back in London, and she would start with Dex, who was always up for a party. She checked the time: ten thirty. Hopefully, he would be awake. The phone didn't go straight to voicemail, which was a start.

'Hello?'

'Dex, hi, it's Juliet.'

'Darling. It's been years, how are you?'

'I am fine – and back in London.'

'How long for?'

Good question.

'Forever.'

'We must celebrate! Look, your timing's bloody impeccable, as ever. It's Loulou's thirty-first tonight, she's devastated to be so comprehensively out of her twenties, so it's bound to be the most terrific car crash. It's at a new place called Nostrum just off Park Lane, do say you'll come.'

'Loulou won't mind me turning up, will she?'

'Loulou will be blotto by seven thirty and she won't mind anyway. Just make sure you bring her a present that makes her feel young.'

Juliet laughed.

'I'll do my best. All right, thanks Dex, I'll see you there later.'

'Mwah mwah, see you later, so glad you're back, it's been boring without you.'

Juliet felt better for the conversation, not to mention the invitation. Maybe a return to London life *was* just what she needed. Pushing aside an unbidden image of sitting in the untidy kitchen at Feywood, socked feet up on a chair while she gossiped with Martha over a cup of tea, she picked up her phone again.

'Santos Hair, Jenna speaking?'

'Jenna, it's Juliet Carlisle. Is there the tiniest chance I could be squeezed in today? I know it's horribly lastminute.com, but I'd be so grateful.'

As she walked down the street on her way to the hairdresser, she passed a small cemetery she had never noticed before. She had a few minutes, so slipped through the crooked iron gate and ventured between the gravestones. Most were illegible, faded and worn by time, and many had collapsed altogether, but on one or two she could make out names and dates – beloved William, 1812-1873; Hetty, wife of James, taken by our Lord in 1902. As Juliet reached for her phone, she thought she would take some preliminary photos before coming back with her proper camera: the ivy creeping over every surface was irresistible and the pathos of the crumbling stone cried out to be captured. Then she remembered with a jolt that she had left her camera at Feywood, determined to take back with her only the things she would need to further her career. The cemetery pictures wouldn't have been of much commercial interest, it was true, but oh! How she would have loved to capture the atmosphere in that place. She squared her shoulders. Too bad. She had moved back in order to move forward, so she had better get on with it.

· · ·

The bar she was going to that night, Nostrum, was – according to its website – 'the place you've been waiting for. Why drown your sorrows, when we can make them float away on a sea of the best cocktails and longest wine list London has to offer?' When she skimmed the drinks menu, she certainly hoped it was worth it. Had she really forgotten in such a short time how expensive the city was? Another memory popped up, and she smacked it down like a whack-a-mole. Thinking about swigging cheapish wine with her sisters in the village pub wasn't going to help. No, she would raid her savings and enjoy herself tonight, even if cocktails were – gulp – seventeen quid a pop. As the Tube drew into Green Park station, she felt an uncharacteristic jerk of nerves. After all, she hadn't seen the London crowd for what felt like an age, and none of them, herself included, had bothered much with keeping in touch. At least she knew she looked good, even if she was horribly uncomfortable in the tight-fitting grey dress and high heels. She kept touching her hair, which hadn't gone for so long without a cut in years. It felt smooth, blunt, familiar, but she also kind of missed the wispy tendrils that had started to drift out of it, softening her look. As she strode through the door of the bar, held open for her by a uniformed doorman, she almost turned on her heel and strode right out again, but a voice shrieked 'Juliet!' and was joined by another, and another and she was surrounded by familiar faces, all of which looked delighted to see her back in town. Somebody pushed a drink into her hand – 'it's called a Devil May Care, *fearfully* strong, but we're all guzzling them to help Loulou forget how ancient she is' – and she, in turn, thrust her gift at the birthday girl.

'Oh, Jools, I *adore* it,' she trilled, showing everyone the white leather lipstick case. 'So chic, so very you and also so very me. You *are* clever! Come on, let's have another drink to celebrate.'

Juliet was mildly surprised to see that she had nearly finished her cocktail.

'Good idea. Or shall we do shots this time?'

'So good to have you back!' screamed Loulou. 'You haven't changed a jot. We all knew you'd be bored silly in the country, or is the place simply littered with gruff but handsome game-keepers to keep you occupied?'

Images of first Will and then Léo flitted through Juliet's mind.

'Oh *God*, no!' she replied, before downing the tequila she had been handed. 'It's all ancient vicars and Labradors. But I intend to make up for lost time.'

A cheer went up and someone handed her another Devil May Care.

'You are what you drink!' she yelled, toasting the group who all whooped and followed suit.

The evening continued on repeat as everyone drank and gossiped until Juliet glanced at her watch and realised it was nearly one in the morning.

'I think I'd better go home,' she slurred to Dex, who was leaning on her shoulder, nearly asleep.

'Mmm, home,' he agreed amiably, and snuggled down further.

'Come on.' She hoisted him up. 'Wake up, I think you'd better go home too.'

He awoke suddenly and grinned at her.

'Home, Jools, no way. I've had my little power nap – thanks for propping me up, by the way – and I'm ready to go on now. Hey, Loulou!' Juliet followed his gaze to where the birthday girl sat, cross-eyed with alcohol and tiredness. 'Time to move on? Glisten should be open now, and Nathan can get us in.'

Loulou raised her glass, spilling half the contents over the girl sitting next to her, who didn't notice.

'Yeah, Glisten, love it, less go,' she croaked.

Juliet didn't know what Glisten was, but she knew one thing categorically: she didn't want to go there. The cocktails had left a sour taste in her mouth, her stomach was heaving, and the room appeared to be jolting about in front of her eyes. The people who had seemed so witty and fascinating only an hour ago now looked as booze-sodden and dissipated as she imagined she did. Designer clothes were rumpled, make-up smeared and hair beginning to escape from its bondage of clips, ties, gel and spray. All she wanted to do was go home. As this thought came, so with it appeared an image of her cosy little flat at Feywood, the windows open to the summer night air. Home. Tears sprang to her eyes, and she snatched a little mirror from her handbag to dab at them with a napkin. None of these people would notice if she cried them a river, but she couldn't bear the idea of looking pitiful all the same. When she had composed herself, she stood up shakily.

'I'm heading home,' she announced. 'Loulou, are you sure you don't want to get a cab with me? You're on my way.'

'I don't wanna get cab!' shouted Loulou, flailing her hands about furiously. 'Whaddo I wanna get cab for? You not get cab either, Jools, have more drinkies! Come dancing at Glisten! And find lovely, lovely man to take home, hooray!'

The group echoed her cheer and Juliet smiled.

'Enjoy yourself, guys, I'm done, I'm afraid. Happy birthday!'

She had swiftly exited enough events to have become an expert at it, and she was up and weaving her way to the door before anyone could protest further. The night air was cold, but it felt refreshing, and Juliet decided to walk a little way before trying to get a cab. She had to try and stop everything swirling around her head and her body before she dared get into a moving vehicle, and it was about fifteen minutes later that she felt confident of keeping the contents of her stomach where they were. Her taxi app informed her coldly that there was nothing available for another thirty-five minutes, so she gritted her teeth and hailed a black cab. At the rate she was spending money, having been back in London for less than twenty-four hours, she could replace Feywood's roof within a fortnight, but there was no way she was getting a night bus or the Tube: she just needed to be home.

Fifteen grateful minutes later, she opened the front door and kicked off her punishing shoes, stripping off her dress as she walked through to the kitchen to put the kettle on for a large cup of tea and a bowl of pasta. She hadn't felt hungry until now – she supposed that all the drinks had kept her blood sugar going – but she was starving. As the pasta cooked, she stepped into the shower and washed the evening away, then pulled on the soft pyjamas she was pathetically grateful she had brought with her, one of the few 'new Juliet' items that had made the cut. She sank onto the sofa and turned on the TV, scrolling through the channels until she found something anodyne enough to give her some background comfort while she ate and her mind roamed over the events of the evening. It had been fun, in some ways, but utterly exhausting holding her own amongst all the bitchy repartee. She knew she had redeemed herself, burst back into flames as the Juliet they had all known, but there was no satisfaction in it. They had probably forgotten she had even been there once they moved on to the club, their affections shallow and existing only in the moment. Tears rolled rapidly down her cheeks, and she had to stop eating as the sobs rose in her throat. What had she done, cutting herself off from everyone at Feywood? Maybe they would never trust her again, and she would be out in the world alone, left with the likes of Dex and Loulou. Would that be so bad? Maybe she could find a way to live in London that was more substantial; it must be possible, thousands of people did it after all. She had to know. She would throw herself into work, avoid drinking buckets of cocktails again and speak to Toby about the flat and job. What she mustn't do was simply return to the life she had walked away from previously, just because it was familiar. She couldn't let her old friends define her any more than her family. Thus resolved, the tears subsided, and she started eating again, only wobbling when she thought of dear, sweet Ava, her silky ears probably now being stroked by Léo's workworn hands... This was hopeless. She switched off the TV. The only thing to do now was to go to bed, pray the hangover wouldn't be too bad and make tomorrow her own.

TWENTY-SEVEN

Léo put away the last of the pans and sat down heavily at the island in the cookery school. It had been a week since Juliet had left for London, without even saying goodbye, and he felt no better now than he had that morning when he had come up to the house and Rousseau had gently broken it to him that she had gone.

'Try not to give it too much thought,' said the older man. 'She's trying to sort out her feelings. She'll be in touch.'

'No,' said Léo firmly. 'I am giving it no thought whatsoever. Juliet has done the right thing for her, and I am so happy for her. I am going to think only of my work; that will give me solace.'

Frankie, back on one of her flying visits which now took her to London, looked thinner and paler than ever, but her tongue was just as sharp.

'If you're so sure she's done the right thing, you need to drop the Cistercian monk act and get back out there. Honestly, between you and Juliet, you could start your own soap opera, her flouncing off to London, you nobly bearing your pain in silent labour. The pair of you need to stop looking for problems and just get on with it.'

Martha, although she wouldn't have put it quite like that, privately agreed with her sister. When Frankie had left again, Martha had tried to get hold of Juliet, but the phone just went to voicemail and her texts were responded to hours later with brief, dashed-off messages about being horribly busy. She hated seeing Léo so sad, but she thought the solution was simple.

'Just go and find her and tell her how you feel.'

'She knows how I feel,' he replied stubbornly. 'I will not push myself onto her; she can make her own decisions and her answer is clear.'

Martha might have tried harder, but instead she told him how seriously worried she was about Frankie, who was still seeing her new boyfriend and still refusing to tell anyone who he was, on the basis that they would all disapprove of him, and she couldn't be bothered arguing about it.

'Let her do love her own way,' was Léo's response. 'We must all find our paths ourselves in the end.'

He had been sorry when even the patient Martha had rolled her eyes at him and gone to take her feelings out on an innocent canvas, but he remained stoic. At least this way he knew that he wasn't bringing any more calumny on Juliet's head, that she could not hold him responsible as Veronique had done. If any sin was to be his, it would be of omission, not commission. With this comforting thought, he scooped Ava up onto his knees and picked up his phone. He and Sylvia had been working on building up a social media platform for the cookery school, mostly for promotional reasons but also because he felt that he could better control his own image if he were in the lair of the beast, so to speak. He tapped through to upload a photo of the incredible prawn curry he had made earlier, smirking as he added the hashtags #prawnpanic and #crustaceanfrustration in reference to the number of queries he always got about how long to cook the shellfish for, and how to know when they were ready. Pleased with his efforts, he started idly scrolling through the people their account followed, admiring various kitchens and dishes. But he sat up when a picture of Juliet appeared. He hadn't even known she had an Instagram account, or that Sylvia had followed it, for he certainly hadn't. As the initial shock of seeing her ebbed away, he looked again at the photo. She looked incredible: she had cut her hair and was wearing a tight grey dress which showed off her slim shoulders. Her arm was slung around a rather cross-eyed blonde woman with smudged mascara, who was beaming and holding up a drink. Juliet was also smiling, but her face was more reserved. *You are the Juliet I first met*, thought Léo, staring at the little screen. *I hope you are happy, chèrie, I hope you have found what you want.* He stood up, cuddling Ava close to his chest.

'Come on, little one, it is time you and I turned in for the night, we are so tired, aren't we?'

It was only nine o'clock, but despite his assertion of exhaustion, he was going to bed earlier and earlier, as waking hours only brought constant thoughts of running to Juliet, which he couldn't – or wouldn't – do.

TWENTY-EIGHT

Juliet's hangover had been absolutely punishing, but once it had passed, she began to feel more positive again. She returned Dex's and Loulou's texts and agreed to another night out the following week, although she was determined to drink far, far less. She had put up a single photo on Instagram in which she looked reasonably sober, although Loulou was a bit worse for wear, and had been flattered by how many people had commented to say they were thrilled she was back in town. After her message to Toby, all the help he had offered came with a proviso: come out for dinner with me so that we can discuss it. Not confident of putting herself in that position, and fearful of what might be the next thing he insisted on, she had sent a polite holding email back to him and ignored his subsequent attempts to get in touch. The idea of the flat and the job introduction had been tempting, but she didn't want him to feel she owed him anything; no, she would work this out without anyone else's help. Work was going well on her children's book, and she had had another meeting with the publisher, who was pleased with her progress. She had tried to arrange a meeting with Petra Sharpe at *RoundUp*, but – surprise, surprise – no one there had ever heard of her. When she followed up with an email, she was sent a standard response, saying that she could submit examples of her work and not to expect a reply in less than three months' time, if at all. She had put together some pieces but didn't hold out much hope. Time was ticking away on the flat, and she knew she had to dedicate some energy into looking for something she could afford. One morning she was searching through the adverts and realising she had to be significantly less picky if she wanted to stay anywhere inside the M25, let alone central London, when her mobile rang: Martha.

'Hi there, what's up?'

'Oh, Juliet, I'm so glad you picked up.'

'What's wrong? Is everyone okay?' Juliet could hear her sister's worry vibrating down the line. 'It's not Dad, is it, or Sylvia... or Léo?' She was washed with panic herself. Surely nothing had happened to them while she dealt with her pathetic existential crisis in London? She would never forgive herself. But she didn't have time to dwell on the thought.

'No, it's none of them, it's Frankie.'

'Frankie? What's wrong with her?'

'Well, I don't actually *know* that there's anything wrong, but Juliet, I'm so worried. You know she's had this boyfriend for ages, and she won't tell any of us who he is?'

'Yes...'

'Well, I think I found out and it's not good news, and now I can't get hold of her at all, and she hasn't been home for ages.'

'Well, who is he?'

'He's another artist, she knew him at art school, I think, and they must have caught up again – his parents only live a mile or so from Feywood. His name's Dylan Madison.'

'Oh jeez, I've heard of Dylan Madison, he's a complete wreck, isn't he? Always off his face on something. Wasn't he arrested last year?'

'Yes, that's him. You can see why I'm so worried.'

'I don't blame you. What on earth is Frankie doing with him?'

'I don't know, but now I can understand why she wouldn't tell us who he was. What are we going to do, Jools? We've got to make sure she's all right.'

Juliet took a breath. She could hear the rising panic in Martha's voice and didn't want to be infected by it.

'Look, Frankie's not stupid. She might be with Dylan, but she wouldn't take drugs.' Privately, she wasn't so sure. Frankie had a reckless streak and was liable to get carried away, but she didn't want Martha any more worried than she already was. 'The chances are that she's with him, so I'll ask around and see if I can track them down. Try not to worry too much, M, I'll let you know as soon as I can that she's all right.'

'Thank you. I'd come down to London myself, but I wouldn't know where to start.'

'You stay put at Feywood. I'll let you know if I need anything, okay?'

'Okay. Speak soon, Jools.'

As soon as her sister rang off, Juliet dialled another number. She hadn't spoken to Germaine Halliford for years, a dissipated old crony of her mother, who was always hanging around with the much younger art crowd, despite only having a very dubious talent herself. She was the most obvious choice of someone who would be able to give her the lowdown on Dylan Madison.

'Hello,' croaked a voice down the line. 'Who is this?'

'Germaine? Hi, it's Juliet Carlisle, Lilith's daughter?'

'Oh yes, what can I do for you? Oh, sorry I didn't make the memorial, by the way. I raised a glass to your mum and remembered her in my own way.' Her voice was suddenly replaced by a hacking cough, and Juliet held the phone away from her ear until it stopped.

'I'm trying to get hold of an artist called Dylan Madison. I know you know all the young crowd, and I wondered if you knew where I could find him?'

A gravelly laugh came down the line.

'Trying to find Frankie, are you? I heard those two were an item. Yes, I know where he lives when he's in town, hang on a moment...' A loud clunk was followed by some rustling before Germaine's voice came on the line again. 'Here it is.' She rattled off an address of what she called a 'Warehouse Community' in Tottenham, North London. 'They're a nice lot of kids living there, but it's a far cry from the family seat.' She laughed her rattling laugh again, then had another coughing fit.

'Thanks very much,' said Juliet, once the hacking had stopped. 'I'm really grateful.'

'My pleasure, darling. I might go and have another drink to your mum now.'

Germaine ended the call, much to Juliet's relief. She quickly opened the maps app on her phone and looked up the address she had been given. It was only half an hour on the Underground, not bad at all. She tapped out a quick text to Martha and set off.

Stepping out of Seven Sisters station she gazed around, not sure what she had been expecting but pleasantly surprised, nonetheless. It wasn't a part of London she knew at all and, if she was being honest, was one she had – until now – had no interest in visiting. But as she walked along the main street, she enjoyed the lively vibe and although the bookies and mobile phone shops weren't of interest, she liked peering into the Turkish barber and Latinx supermarket she passed. Her burgeoning concern about Frankie faded as she imagined her sister settling nicely into a multicultural, artistic community, and she could hardly blame her for abandoning Feywood for London when she had done the same thing herself. She walked past some warehouses that had been converted into smart-looking flats, some of them also advertising artists' studios, and her hopes were raised higher. Checking her phone, she took a left and then double-checked as the right turn she was then instructed to take seemed to lead down a track between two buildings, rather than a road. No, that was definitely what it said, and as she hesitated, two men wearing paint spattered T-shirts and tracksuit trousers emerged from it, deep in conversation, and disappeared in the direction of the Tube. Shrugging, she put her phone in her pocket and walked down, hoping that it would suddenly open up into some kind of funky urban space. No such luck. Instead, she found herself in what looked like a piece of wasteland, lined on three sides by what must be old garages or storehouses, brick-built, painted white with corrugated roofs and small, barred windows. Most were grubby and several daubed with graffiti. She had a sinking feeling in her stomach that she had found the right place then. As she glanced around with the forlorn hope of being proved wrong in some way, she saw a hand-painted sign that read: 'Airframe Lane'. This was the one. She picked her way across the rubble-strewn grass towards number twenty-three, then knocked gingerly on the door.

'Come in!' shouted a voice, and she pushed it open to reveal the scene she had feared. There was one space, clearly used as a studio as well as living quarters. Huge canvases daubed with thick black paint and goodness knows what else were propped up against the walls, and an emergent sculpture, which she recognised as Frankie's work, stood on an upturned plastic milk crate. There was a metal sink and draining board in one corner, smeared with paint but with mugs and plates piled up in it. Across the room, on the floor, was a double mattress adorned with a dirty, crumpled sheet, and it was here that she found Frankie and Dylan. Bleary-eyed and unkempt, they looked up as she entered.

'Juliet!' shouted Frankie, waving the cigarette she was

smoking in greeting, but not getting up. 'Dylan, this is my first big sister, come to find out what's happened to me.'

'Welcome, welcome,' said Dylan in grandiose tones, giving a mock bow from his reclined position and spilling his red wine on the mattress, adding to the stains.

For a moment, Juliet froze, her eyes roaming over the scene before her, trying not to wrinkle her nose at the stale, musty odour of the room, or to look too appalled. It wouldn't do to be seen as disapproving, that would only egg Frankie on. She forced a smile to flicker across her face.

'Hi, Dylan. Good to see you, Frank, I can report back to Martha that you're alive at least.'

'Alive and kicking,' said Frankie, waving a foot in the air and giggling. 'Tell Martha to do something else with her time other than worrying about me, such as getting Wimpy Will between the sheets.'

'Right. You could have sent her a text or something, just to reassure her.'

'Hey, man,' chimed in Dylan. 'Chill out. We don't bother with all that tech here, we're creatives, we need to be able to focus on our art.'

Juliet ignored him and looked at Frankie.

'*Are* you getting any work done?'

With a laboured sigh, Frankie struggled up to standing and tugged her clothes straight. She was wearing a silk camisole that Juliet recognised as one of their mother's, and a pair of boxer shorts with garden gnomes on them.

'Actually, I am, look.' She went over to the half-finished sculpture. 'I'm really pleased with it, it's called 'Crazy in Love' – what do you think? Obviously, it's not finished yet.'

'Frankie, it's really, really good. Another level.'

Frankie smiled, and Juliet saw the sister she knew through the matted hair, wandering eyes and defensive stature. Frankie was working, working well, and had pride in what she had done:

surely that was evidence that, whatever their dwelling looked like, something was going right. She didn't feel in a position to judge, given that she herself had needed to move away, but she couldn't say nothing either. She turned her sister away and spoke quietly.

'Look, Frank, I'm glad the sculpture's going well, but is he – Dylan – all right? He's got a name for... well, for doing drugs and stuff, you know?'

Frankie snorted.

'Of course I know, and I tell him he's stupid to muck around with the stronger stuff, but he says it helps him work.'

'What's he taking?'

Frankie shrugged.

'Oh, you know...'

'No, I don't know, I haven't got the faintest idea. Enlighten me, please.'

Her voice had become louder, and now Dylan heaved himself up from the mattress and stumbled over. Juliet instinctively took a step backwards, but Frankie leant into him as he slung an arm around her shoulders.

'I don't think you're being very friendly,' he slurred, swigging his wine. 'Coming here and asking nosy questions. You can see that Frankie is fine – better than fine. She's got me now, she doesn't need big sister fussing around. Time you left.'

Juliet opened her mouth to reply, but as she did, she caught Frankie giving her a tiny shake of the head, a look of fear flashing across her face.

'Really, Jools, it's all good. Look, why don't I go to Feywood at the weekend, see Martha and let her know myself that it's all okay? Yeah?'

The hint of a pleading tone in her voice, so unusual for her sister, shocked Juliet almost more than anything else she had seen that day, and she nodded.

'All right, that sounds like a good idea. Please do, Frank, I'll try and get down too, maybe.'

Not wanting to get too close to Dylan, she gave her sister a little wave rather than a hug. When Dylan offered a mock salute in return, his sleeve slipped down, and she saw what she had dreaded – telltale marks on the inside of his arm.

'Time to go,' said Frankie quietly, and Juliet knew that unhappy though she was, it was the best thing she could do. For now.

TWENTY-NINE

When Juliet got back to the flat, she stood under a long, hot shower and tried to wash the afternoon away. Although she was glad that Frankie's work seemed to be going well, that was the best that could be said for what she had witnessed that afternoon. But what could she do? Frankie was an adult and had to be left to make her own decisions, and after all, what would she, Juliet, think if someone turned up unannounced at her door, judged her lifestyle and announced that it didn't pass muster? She'd be furious and flatly refuse any offer of help or attempts at persuading her to do things differently. She sighed as she dried herself and put on a cosy fleece robe. She and Frankie were cut from the same cloth in that respect, and as she had promised that she wasn't touching hard drugs, there was nothing to do but stay in touch and hope for the best. She tapped out a quick message to Martha, assuring her that Frankie was fine and planning to visit Feywood that weekend, then having no appetite to resume the house hunt – maybe she would end up as Frankie and Dylan's next-door neighbour, it was probably all she could afford – she once again opened the invitation she had been sent for that evening. It was for an art exhibition and cocktail party being held in a very smart office space in Spitalfields. She had no idea how she had got on their list, as it wasn't being organised by anyone she knew and wasn't her usual stamping ground. The art looked awful, and she suspected that the evening was, more than anything, an excuse for the bankers and hedge fund managers who used the offices to pretend they knew something about culture, tick a few 'we support the arts' boxes and pour cocktails down their throats before moving on to their private members clubs to talk about their next skiing holiday. She had initially deleted the invitation after a cursory glance but had pulled it back up more than once. Wasn't she trying to embed herself more firmly in London? Wasn't this what she had come back for? She didn't have any other plans that evening and, execrable though it looked, maybe there would be – she shuddered at the thought – *networking* opportunities. If she was going to do this, she had to commit to it, and after the encounter with Frankie and Dylan, she could certainly do with a drink.

Juliet stepped out of the Tube at Liverpool Street, already regretting her choice of shoes. She didn't even know why she had kept them, let alone brought them back from Feywood with her; they had a history of shredding her feet and had been an expensive present from Toby. But they were extremely glamorous with the barely-there straps studded with crystals and thin, silver stiletto heels and she thought they might fit the bill on the cool edge of the Square Mile. Of course, there was always the possibility that everyone else would be in board shorts and flip flops; that was the problem with London, styles changed dizzyingly fast. But she would always rather run the risk of being overdressed. She pushed through a huge glass door into a brightly lit foyer, stuffed with chattering people. She was secretly relieved to see that her outfit wasn't out of place as the men were mostly in suits and the women in cocktail attire like herself, or smart work clothes. She made a confident beeline for the bar, as she had learnt to do in situations when she didn't know anyone, and picked up a drinks menu. All the cocktails had been given rather tortured 'artistic' names, but eventually she decided to ask for a 'Vodka Van Gogh' and hope it didn't come with extra ear. She leant on the bar as she scanned the room for a familiar face, eventually spotting a woman she knew in passing from the newspaper. She had decided to go over and join her, even though they had barely ever spoken, when she felt a warm hand on her shoulder and a familiar voice said, 'Lettie. So glad you could make it.'

Toby. Of course, that must have been how she had got the invitation, *why* hadn't she realised? She summoned up a weak smile.

'Oh, hello.'

'You realised, of course, that I had you invited? This isn't your usual scene, I know, but I was sure you would come. And wearing my shoes as well, how sweet of you. I must say, I was rather disappointed that you didn't seem to want to discuss the flat and the job any further. I went to a lot of trouble to sort out those introductions for you and you left me looking foolish.'

Juliet automatically opened her mouth to apologise, then snapped it shut again. *No, no, no.* She was *not* going down this path again, taking his reprimands like a good girl, admitting she had been naughty, begging for forgiveness. And besides, he had clearly lied to her about the opportunity at *RoundUp*.

'I did email, Toby,' she said in as mild a tone as possible. 'I said I needed more time to think about it. If you promised your contacts more than that, it isn't my doing.'

'I just thought you'd be rather grateful for my help, especially considering everything you put me through.'

Don't rise to it. Deep breath.

'It was a kind thought, but I'm still figuring out my next

steps.' She decided to change the subject. 'Do you know lots of people here?'

Toby waved a gracious hand in a sweeping arc.

'Everyone. Would you like me to introduce you to some of them? And it looks like you need another drink.'

'I will have another drink, then maybe look at some of the art. Most people seem to be ignoring it.'

He flicked an eyebrow at her and grinned.

'Well, you know this lot, more interested in yakking and drinking than culture, but at least they can now tell their friends they've been to an art exhibition. Come on then, let's go and look at some of it.'

This was the Toby she liked, the one that emerged every so often and had kept her working at their relationship for so long. When he was on good form, he was funny and observant, not to mention genuinely interested in art, unlike any of his friends. He handed her a fresh drink, then they slid through the crowd until they reached the far wall, where a familiar-looking canvas hung.

'Not really my thing,' said Toby, screwing his face up and staring at the thick swirls of black paint with unidentifiable lumps in places. 'What do you think?'

Juliet pointed to the label.

'I think I've seen one of these in progress this afternoon,' she said. 'Dylan Madison. He's Frankie's new squeeze.'

Recognition dawned on Toby's face.

'Lettie, you do know he's an addict, don't you?' He sucked air in through his teeth. 'Not really who you want your baby sister to be hanging out with.'

'I know, I've been to see them. Martha's worried sick, and I'm not much happier, even if Frankie does seem to be working well. She's *promised* she's not taking anything.'

Toby frowned.

'Look, if you want any help, I'll come back with you.

Frankie's a pain and she's always hated me, but I don't want to see her in trouble.'

'Thanks. I think she's all right for now, but I will ask if I need backup.'

Toby's apparently genuine concern for her sister allowed Juliet to lower her defences further, and as the evening progressed, she found she was enjoying herself. After looking at some of the other pieces on display, they got talking to a few of Toby's colleagues, and although the artworks were forgotten, the conversation went along at a fast clip so that when Juliet glanced at the time, she was horrified to find that it was nearly midnight. At least she'd slowed down on her cocktail consumption this time, despite the constant stream of full glasses that appeared.

'Toby, I really have to head off now. It's been a fun evening, thank you.'

To her surprise, rather than trying to persuade her to have another drink, or go on somewhere else, he said, 'It's later than I realised. I'll come too.'

They strolled towards the station, the streets still busy with cars and pedestrians. Juliet was just thinking how unexpectedly successful the evening had been when Toby grasped her hand and pulled her to the side of the pavement.

'What are you doing?'

'I've been wanting to do this all night,' he said huskily, and slipped his arm around her shoulder, lowering his face to hers.

'No!' she shouted, pushing him away. He stumbled, then righted himself. 'I'm sorry, but what are you *doing*?'

'Only what's been clear you wanted me to do,' he said, his tone snide. 'You've been flirting with me all evening, Lettie, don't try to back out now.'

She felt tears come to her eyes at the injustice.

'I *haven't* been flirting, you're wrong. I thought – bloody stupid me – I thought we were actually having a pleasant time together – as *friends*. We've been through this a hundred times, Toby.'

'I don't think you know *what* you want. Come on, let's go and get another drink, and we can talk about it.'

'*No!*' She was practically shouting now. How could she make him listen to her? 'I'm going home, alone. I'm sorry, Toby, but I'm not going to see you again, ever.'

His lip curled and his face took on the disgusted expression she knew so well, all trace of the pleasant, charming man she had spent most of the evening with gone.

'How dare you raise your voice to me?' he hissed. 'You should be *grateful* that I still considered taking you back after the way you've behaved.'

There it was again, the demand for gratitude. Juliet realised now what it was she should have been grateful for, and it didn't lie here.

'Good night, Toby,' she said quietly, and turned to walk down into the station hoping, despite everything, that she was not hobbling too badly in the ill-fitting shoes and ruining her attempt at a graceful exit. At the flat, the shoes went straight in the bin – she wasn't going to pass them on and let someone else suffer – and she headed to bed.

THIRTY

Another successful weekend had drawn to a close in the cookery school, and Léo and Sylvia were having a debrief in the sitting room at Feywood.

'Do you think that the plum tart was too easy?' asked Sylvia, her brow creasing. 'It's hard to gauge how difficult people will find things, and I want to make sure they learn something new.'

'I think it was perfect,' replied Léo, pouring them both more tea. 'They learnt the best ways to pick and pit the fruit, about sugar balance and that amazing pastry you do so well. I think we should keep it on the list.'

'Agreed. That's it then, we've got a few days off now. Any plans?'

'Well, I will keep working on the cookbook – there are some recipes I want to perfect. How about you?'

'I'm feeling much better, so I think I'll get some gardening done. Those poor roses are looking dreadfully bedraggled.'

They fell silent, which was unusual for them when they usually chattered easily about food and planting. Then Sylvia spoke again.

'Léo, I hope you don't mind, but I want to speak to you about Juliet.'

He looked up at her but said nothing. She continued.

'If it's not too rude, I think you've been a complete idiot. You're obviously absolutely miserable without her, and I'm quite sure she feels exactly the same. You two were so happy together, you just *fit* so well. I know one can't ever know properly what goes on inside other people's relationships, and I'm not usually one for interfering, but *really*, I'm finding it quite exasperating you moping about and doing nothing to put it right. There, I've said my piece, I'll shut up now.'

The silence stretched between them again until Léo finally spoke.

'You are right, I am moping, but there is nothing I can do. I will try to pick up, as you say.'

'It's not about picking up, Léo, it's about sorting out. Won't you tell me what's happened?'

'It's all my fault.'

'Well, that's never the case, but tell me more.'

He went on to explain in full what had happened with Veronique, how guilty he felt and how he had sworn to himself never to risk bringing such sorrow on someone else again.

'I came very close with Juliet, to making her miserable, so it was best to let her go.'

'And by "let her go" you mean "push her into leaving", I suppose?' said Sylvia tartly. 'Why on earth didn't you tell her how you feel? There's no way she would have left if she had felt wanted here.'

'Because it had to be her decision, I did not want ever to feel that I had stopped her doing what she wanted.'

Sylvia snorted.

'I can't believe you've lived this long with the Carlisles and still believe for a second that any one of us would ever not do exactly what we want. It's a family trait – even Martha, in her own quiet way. But we won't hang around if we're *not* wanted, or push ourselves on people, which is why, incidentally, bloody Martha won't get her act together around Will.'

'But Juliet *must* know I love her.'

'Why? You practically put her on a train to London and, from what you've told me, made her feel rather unsure about that whole stupid Instagram picture. You must know that she needs someone who will be straight with her, after all that business with horrible Toby? She's incredibly wary of being controlled or manipulated, so she's gone off to London in order to take charge of her life, which is admirable in many ways, but I'm sure not what she really wants. She can't make an informed decision, can she, if you won't just tell her what's what? By heaping all this guilt on yourself and taking a tonne of responsibility that isn't even yours, you've actually done her a disservice. She's a big girl, she can take this stuff on and would probably rather do so. She can sense you're shielding her from things, and that can be infantilising, you know.'

'Do you mean,' said Léo slowly, 'that she is worried I'm controlling her while I am trying incredibly hard not to do exactly that?'

'Right,' said Sylvia in exasperation. 'You are a pair of ninnies. You're both tying yourselves in knots over something that isn't happening. Dear me, darling Léo, you are something of a drama queen. How do you say that in French?'

Léo grinned.

'Sometimes, we use the same expression, or maybe "diva", but I think you imply that I am *hystérique*.'

He pulled a suitably tragic face and they both laughed.

'You know I adore you. I just want to see you both happy, and I think that means together,' said Sylvia firmly.

'And I think you are right. So, then, how is this for drama? I am going to go to London and see her, today.'

'That's the spirit! Although the trains on a Sunday afternoon are hopeless – I'd leave it till the morning if I were you.'

He laughed.

'Pragmatism trumps romance. Tomorrow then. Wish me luck.'

Maybe it was luck he would need, maybe a miracle, but he knew he had to try.

THIRTY-ONE

When she awoke the next morning, the hangover was familiar but not incapacitating, and she supposed that was something. But the conversation with Toby played over and over again in her head as she searched for evidence first that he was right, that she *had* been flirting and then, furiously, that it was *she* who was the injured party. To distract herself, she scrolled through her phone, and although she found it full of invitations, she wasn't tempted by a single one. Instead, she let an image fill her head, of the kitchen at Feywood. She was sitting on the wicker basket chair in the corner, her feet tucked up, Ava snuggled in her lap. She held a cup of tea and was chatting to Léo as he cooked, and laughed, and fed the little dog scraps, which she devoured before promptly falling asleep again. Members of the family wandered in and out of the scene: Rousseau, his hands grey with clay, looking for a sculpting tool he'd left in the cutlery drawer; Sylvia, tasting the bubbling sauce and telling Juliet how pretty she looked; Martha, drifting in to make coffee, getting distracted by the light on the apple tree outside the window, then wondering aloud why she had come to the kitchen, at which point Léo handed her the drink he'd made for her, knowing the routine; Frankie, perching on the table and bitching about an old school friend she'd bumped into in the village, then disappearing to answer a phone call. Juliet had been pushing away these memories for days, but now she allowed herself to disappear inside them, to see and feel exactly how it had been. She thought about Toby, then, about how he had made her feel for all those years, and how the fear and horror of finding herself controlled again had pushed her into an uncomfortable kind of independence, which was no better than being indentured to him. It was just another kind of paralysis, not the freedom that she sought, and it had denied her the ability to meld with another person, something that had revolted her in the past but, when it came to Léo, had felt more like relief as if she had found a resting place. Had Léo really been trying to control her, she wondered, or had he in fact only ever been working in her best interests, something she never anticipated from others? Maybe it was time to be truly brave and find out.

Once she had had the thought, Juliet had a surge of energy, despite the remnants of her hangover. It suddenly felt urgent that she should get back to Feywood and, hopefully, Léo as soon as she possibly could. What had she been thinking? It was as if the clouds had parted, and sunlight was streaming into her life again. She showered and dressed quickly and threw down some coffee and the last of the muesli, then set about packing, glad now that she had taken so little with her when she left. As she folded her clothes and grabbed her toiletries, she ignored the regular pinging of her phone, knowing that it was not likely to be the only person she wanted to hear from. Next, she set to cleaning the flat, a job she hated but did with some relief, knowing that she would have had to do it soon anyway, but at least this way she knew exactly where she was going and was glad to be going there. She stuffed some house share details from an estate agent into the recycling, remembering the inspiring peace of Feywood – of *home*. Her next thought caused her to freeze. What if Léo didn't want her back? What if he really *had* wanted her to move to London, not for her own good but to be free of her? Surely not Léo, surely he would have had the courage to break up with her? She felt the familiar panic rising in her chest and took some deep, steady breaths.

'What you need,' she said out loud, 'is to be back at Feywood. That's *you*, even if you have screwed everything up with Léo. Now come on, get moving.'

The pep talk helped, and she finished the cleaning quickly, then finally picked up her phone, lighting up the screen to see message after message from Toby, who had apparently used every method possible to bombard her with pleading, abuse, adoration and accusations. She ran her hand through her hair and sat down heavily on the sofa. It was time to end this, once and for all, and she would take the responsibility for doing that. No more favours on the table, no more suggestions of friendship, no more ambiguity. She had told him last night that she was done with him forever, and she meant it. Without reading his vitriol in full, she deleted emails, texts and WhatsApp threads and then blocked him on every single platform she had. Short of turning up at Feywood, which she wouldn't put past him, especially since his appearance at her mother's memorial – he could not contact her. She was no longer afraid of him using a different phone number to speak to her; her confidence was such now that hanging up would not seem the impossible task it once had. Job done, she switched the phone off altogether and shoved it to the bottom of her handbag. No more noise; it was time to go home.

She turned everything off and left the flat as she had found it: ready for someone else's life. She stashed the key in the little safe outside the door and made her way down the stairs into the low sunshine, then she started walking to the station. The throb in the balls of her feet, now comfortably shod in suede ballet shoes, was the only remnant of her old-new life. The area around the station was busy with late commuters and tourists, and she paused for a moment to find her Oyster card and make sure her luggage was firmly strapped together before descending into the Underground. As she zipped her handbag firmly shut and started towards the steps, she heard a voice that sounded thrillingly familiar.

'Juliet?'

She glanced around hopefully but didn't see anyone so, shrugging, stepped forward again.

'*Juliet!*'

It couldn't be, it couldn't be, but it was.

'Léo?' she gasped, as he patiently waited for an elderly couple to shuffle aside with their huge paper map. 'What are you doing here?'

He grasped her shoulders.

'Oh Juliet, I've been so stupid, such a fool, forgive me.'

'Why, what do I have to forgive you for, what have you done?'

Oh no, was he going to confess to an affair with Pandora? Was he returning to France, to Veronique? What had he done?

'For being such an *imbécile* as to urge you to leave Feywood and come to London. If that is truly what you want, then I will step aside gracefully, but it is not what I want and I should have said that.'

His dear face looked so worried, Juliet could do nothing other than put her hands to his cheeks and kiss him. She meant it only to be brief, but once she started, she found she couldn't stop, and it was obvious that he didn't want her to either. Eventually, they stepped back and gazed at one another. She spoke first.

'Léo, I was coming back to you, to Feywood.' She indicated her luggage. 'But you found me first.'

'*Oui*, and now I do not want you to leave again. Do you mind?'

'Mind? It's what I want as well. Come on, let's go home, unless you have anything else to do in London?'

'*Non*, I have come only for you.' His eyes followed hers to the oddly shaped bag he had slung over his shoulder. 'Ah, this? Ha! Now, this *is* something very important, but it is also coming back with us.'

He pulled the bag round to the front, and Juliet could see that most of it was made of mesh. Then he unzipped it and out popped little Ava's head. She barked with delight to see Juliet, who immediately scooped her out and cuddled her, while the dog licked her chin frantically.

'You brought Ava!' she said in delight. 'I missed her so much.'

'Well, I thought that if I could not persuade you to come back with me, then maybe this would clinch it.' Léo grinned.

'You would have been spot on,' said Juliet, beaming back at him, 'but, lucky me, I get both of you.'

As they drove up to the house Juliet felt that she was quenching a long-held thirst with a cool glass of pure water. The roof still looked terrible, the lawn needed mowing and her phone, now switched back on, was struggling to find any reception, but she was home. They walked around the side of the house to the cookery school and upstairs, where her little rooms waited, as light-bathed and serene as ever.

'Shall I put the kettle on?' she asked, putting down her bags and filling a bowl of water for Ava.

'Maybe in a little while,' replied Léo, reaching for her, and she gladly fell into his arms.

THIRTY-TWO

The August morning was hazy and golden as Juliet swished open the heavy curtains from the large bedroom window. She used her little flat above the cookery school exclusively as a studio now and had moved into the house permanently, sharing Léo's large suite in the new wing.

'Today's the day,' she said, scooping up Ava, who had jumped off the big bed where Léo was now sitting up, and bustled over to Juliet, ready for her breakfast. 'It feels kind of unreal that we're finally sending that cookery book out into the world.'

'Indeed. I think it will all go very well; the book is so beautiful, thanks to your photos and drawings. Are you looking forward to it?'

'I am. There'll be a few London faces I haven't seen for a while, but that's cool. How about you? Are you feeling okay about the publicity?'

'Finally, yes. At least this is work, and I've got used to my face being out there a bit more thanks to that Instagram page of Sylvia's.'

Juliet laughed.

'It really took off, didn't it? She seems to have some innate knack for social media that none of the rest of us do. Did I tell you she was helping me set up my own page for my flower art?'

'She's amazing. I just hope today isn't too taxing for her.'

'She'll let us know if it is, but I think she's doing really well, isn't she?'

A note of worry crept into Juliet's voice. Although her aunt had been coping well through the treatment and now beyond, she knew she wasn't yet out of the woods. She was beginning to understand why her mother had jeopardised Feywood's future for her own treatment; when it came to it, you felt as if you'd pay for anything that promised results.

Léo got out of bed and put his arm around Juliet.

'She's doing great,' he said, kissing her and then Ava, so she didn't feel left out. 'Come on, we'd better get some breakfast before the circus begins.'

It wasn't long before everything started arriving, reminding Juliet vividly of the day of her mother's memorial, which had been very similar with chairs, tables and awnings being traipsed through the house, although this time she hoped that Toby wouldn't be joining them. His final communication to her had been an actual letter a couple of months after she left London, detailing all her faults and breaking the news that he never wanted to see her again, so please could she leave him alone from now on?

'Gladly,' she had said, and threw the missive onto the fire.

'Are you *sure* they're bringing champagne glasses?' asked Martha for the third time, as she passed Juliet making a neat display of the lovely books.

'They definitely are,' said Juliet, grimly hoping that she had, in fact, remembered to ask the catering company to include them.

'And thank goodness for this beautiful weather,' continued her sister. 'It would have been a shame to have had this indoors.'

'Yes, especially given the state of the place. Do you know when Dad's going to get going on the roof?'

'Soon, he says. I think now that he's regularly putting away enough money the bank has backed off. But you know Dad, he gets distracted.'

Juliet laughed.

'Seems to run in the family!'

'Do you mind? Oh dear, maybe I should have spoken to him, got him to get going on it more quickly...'

Her sweet sister's face crumpled with worry.

'Not at all,' replied Juliet, hugging Martha. 'Don't worry about it, it'll all be fine.'

'I know, I know, I just want it all to be flawless for the three of you, you've worked so hard, and the book is so utterly gorgeous, it deserves a perfect introduction to the world.'

She picked up one of the books and leafed through it. Juliet stopped work for a moment to look over her shoulder; she didn't think she would ever tire of seeing what they had produced. Its title was *Feywood: Simple, delicious food from an English country garden*, and the matt cover in palest sage green had a photograph she had taken of the kitchen garden at its best last summer, with Léo and Sylvia picking berries and chatting. The book was filled with recipes for Léo's exquisite quiches, Sylvia's flower-strewn cakes and Rousseau's breakfasts. Martha had contributed some simple pesto combinations that she enjoyed making, and even Agnes had given them a recipe for a traditional Oxfordshire Hollygog Pudding: pastry and golden syrup rolled up, cooked in milk and served with custard. When Sylvia had tested the recipe, the family agreed that it tasted surprisingly good but was probably best kept for special occasions. No one could manage more than about three spoonfuls without feeling full, other than Rousseau of course, who finished his up and declared the rest of them lightweights. Juliet had declined to contribute more than a couple of cocktail recipes.

'Unless you want a method for making inedible scrambled eggs, I don't think it's really my *milieu*. I'll stick to the illustrations.'

They had asked Frankie several times to send something, but after her last visit to Feywood a few months ago, they had barely heard from her. Sometimes, they picked up bits of information from the internet, and they knew that Dylan's work was, inexplicably, garnering huge success, but that was all they had to go on to assume she was alive and well.

'Maybe she'll come today,' said the ever-hopeful Martha, placing the book carefully back on the arrangement, where Juliet instantly twitched it into perfect line with the others. 'You did invite her?'

'You know I did, but I haven't heard back. I wouldn't hold your breath. Look, maybe once all this is over, we can go down to London and see her, assuming they're still living in the same place.'

Martha smiled.

'I'd like that. Oh, look, these must be the TV people.'

Juliet looked over to see two women carrying a couple of large cameras and some sound equipment, followed by a man with a clipboard and a third woman who looked as if she were going to Ascot, in a long dress patterned in different shades of pink, with a small, veiled hat clinging for dear life to her lacquered hair. Her heels were sinking into the lawn as she followed the crew over to the small awning they had requested. Comfortable in her light sneakers, Juliet jogged over to them and introduced herself.

'Ah, hello,' said the done-up woman graciously. 'So pleased to meet you. All ready, are we? Good. Philippa here is going to be roaming and chatting to your guests, soaking up the atmosphere, do you see? And I'll be in here much of the time with Tara, filming little vignettes we can include in the broadcast.' Finally, she waved at the man. 'This is Jamie, he'll make sure everything stays on track.'

Jamie already looked harassed but shook Juliet's hand.

'Do you think that Léo and Sylvia would be able to give us a moment? I'm afraid we're running late already.'

Glad to be out of a similarly pressurised environment, Juliet went to fetch them. Guests were arriving already, exclaiming at the beautiful gardens and keen to meet the authors. Luckily, she managed to find them first, putting the final touches to some of the food that would be set out for people to sample.

'Can you both come to the TV tent?' she said. 'They're keen to get you interviewed and people are arriving already. Good luck!'

She followed them out and went to mingle, feeling proud of her contribution to the book. She might struggle to boil an egg, but she knew one end of a camera from the other, and she was pleased with the gentle sketches she had done, so different from the waspish newspaper cartoons she was still putting out. Maybe, she thought, her book launch would be next. *Fairies of Feywood* was finally finished, sent to the publisher just a week ago. She was about to approach some of the guests, when a loudly chattering group led by Pandora James swept through the door, looking around them in amazement as if they had come to Mars, rather than a country house. She recognised a couple of them as London-based 'foodfluencers' that Sylvia had heard of and insisted would be smart to invite, and went over to greet them. They all clashed cheekbones with her and said the journey down had been appalling, which she took as her cue to lead them over to the refreshments table where, thankfully, there were now neat rows of champagne glasses. As they walked across, one of the men said:

'I'm sure I know you from somewhere, you look very familiar. For a moment, I thought you were a friend of Dex Caurruthers, but... it doesn't seem very likely.'

Juliet laughed.

'No, I have to say that wasn't really me.'

And leaving him to his champagne and confusion, she crossed the lawn to find Léo.

A LETTER FROM THE AUTHOR

Dear reader,

Huge thanks for reading *Escape to the Country Kitchen*. I do hope you enjoyed following Juliet and Léo's journey, and getting to know Frankie and Martha, who will have their own moments as heroines in subsequent books! If you want to join other readers in hearing all about my new releases and bonus content, you can sign up here:

www.stormpublishing.co/hannah-langdon

If you enjoyed this book and could spare a few moments to leave a review that would be hugely appreciated. Even a short review can make all the difference in encouraging a reader to discover my books for the first time (and I love reading your reviews too!). Thank you so much!

I started writing *Escape to the Country Kitchen* several years ago. I had the idea to write three books about three sisters, all different and all finding love in their own way. But apart from the family and the love interests, there was to be another character in these books: the house, Feywood. It was not originally based on a real place, although over time it began to morph with the stunning Athelhampton House in Dorset. But real or not, I see every inch of its crumbling beauty in my mind's eye, and I hope that you feel you, too, have visited. I wonder what your favourite room is. That dated kitchen maybe, where you can kick off your shoes and have a coffee with Martha; or perhaps you prefer to wander into the old stable block and see Sylvia and Léo at work? Wherever you are most comfortable, Feywood welcomes you, and I hope that you return for the next instalment in the lives of the Carlisle family.

Thanks again for being part of this amazing journey with me, and I hope you'll stay in touch – I have so many more stories and ideas to share with you!

HANNAH LANGDON

facebook.com/hannahlangdonwrites

x.com/hmvlangdon

instagram.com/hannahlangdonwrites

ACKNOWLEDGMENTS

Once again, I would like to start with thanking everyone at Storm for their incredible help and support. I truly appreciate the friendliness, care and professionalism from all of you. Kathryn Taussig has been incredible, steering me through the edits of this novel with kindness and sensitivity, totally understanding what I was trying to do and helping me make it into the book I always wanted it to be. Thank you. Thank you also to Naomi Knox for her input with the editing and to Amanda Rutter for her thorough copy edit.

Rose Cooper has done the most ravishing cover design, and I can't stop looking at it! Thank you.

Huge thanks to my early readers. Emily always manages to fit a read of my early drafts into her hectic schedule, and it is so appreciated, as is her friendship, always. Kathy offered me a very special sort of encouragement, somehow managing always to say exactly what I needed to hear and repeatedly restoring my confidence in this book when it was flagging. And Sarah gave a great deal of her time to read and comment thoroughly on the manuscript, helping me iron out inconsistencies and making sure I don't change people's names halfway through!

Mum, I have dedicated this one to you: thank goodness you are nothing like poor Juliet's mother! Rather, you have always championed me and shown me that 'the only way is up'.

Rose, you have been taken to visit many old houses, and I hope that, when you are old enough to read this book, you will enjoy wandering through Feywood as much as you have the others. Or maybe I should add a tearoom and children's trail? And finally, always, John. Time for some Blanc de Noirs?

9 781805 083597